Linda Mangram was born, and lives in Opelika, Alabama, with her husband, Craig, and dog, Roscoe. She is retired from AT&T, and now enjoys a slower pace of life. As a child, her mother took her to the local public library once a week where she was allowed to search the children's section for the latest Nancy Drew mysteries. Her love of reading stems from those wonderful Saturday mornings. Her love of writing also started at a very young age although she never had time to actually write a book until she retired. She published two books of poetry before she found her true love in writing—mysteries. This current book is the second in a series that she hopes to continue.

Following are the books that are in The Marshals of Richmond series:

Scammed: The Marshals of Richmond

Revenge: The Marshals of Richmond

As with the first book in this series, I would like to dedicate this book to the brave men of the United States Marshals Service. They do a wonderful job looking out for us. And as with the first book, *SCAMMED: The Marshals of Richmond*, my husband listened to each chapter as it unfolded. When I had his complete attention I knew I was on the right track.

Linda Mangram

REVENGE: THE MARSHALS OF RICHMOND

AUSTIN MACAULEY PUBLISHERS™

LONDON * CAMBRIDGE * NEW YORK * SHARJAH

Ordering Information
Quantity sales: Special discounts are available on quantity purchases by corporations, associations, and others. For details, contact the publisher at the address below.

Publisher's Cataloging-in-Publication data
Mangram, Linda
Revenge: The Marshals of Richmond

ISBN 9781685623784 (Paperback)
ISBN 9781685623791 (ePub e-book)

Library of Congress Control Number: 2022923786

www.austinmacauley.com/us

First Published 2023
Austin Macauley Publishers LLC
40 Wall Street, 33rd Floor, Suite 3302
New York, NY 10005
USA

mail-usa@austinmacauley.com
+1 (646) 5125767

Thank you to all my dear friends who encouraged me along the way.

Cast of Characters

Deputy United States Marshal Hershel Bing: Supervisor of Criminal Investigations in Richmond. Head of investigations into drug cartel operating out of Mexico. Hershel got involved with this investigation when a couple came to his office to report a telephone scam. He and his men were able to shut down a criminal empire in the U.S. Can he do the same with the drug cartel located in Mexico? If so, at what personal cost?

Rebecca Bing: Hershel's wife. Small in stature but larger than life in her fight for children's rights. As a social worker, she is faced with removing children from abusive situations. She faces down parents, judges, and defense attorneys in her fight to keep these children safe. But is she up to facing a ruthless drug lord bent on revenge?

Deputy United States Marshal Bill Everett: This Marshal has served with Hershel the longest and has the most experience of any of Hershel's men. But will his experience be enough when Rebecca's life is on the line?

Deputy United States Marshal Andrew Long: IT specialist in the Richmond office and one of Hershel's most trusted men. This time he has been left at the Richmond office to handle the logistics of this operation. Will he be forced to leave his post in order to help his boss find Rebecca before it's too late?

Deputy United States Marshal Cliff Harrington: The youngest Marshal serving under Hershel's command. Stood with Hershel to take down the drug smuggling ring in the U.S. He now has one major operation under his belt. But is he up to what he will be facing in Mexico?

Deputy United States Marshal Jeff Bloom: Newest addition to Hershel's office but with loads of experience. Transferred from the New Orleans Marshal's office after an undercover operation gone bad. Taking down Diego Garcia is a personal matter. But can he do it on Garcia's home turf?

Victoria Stone: A young widow with 18-month-old twins. She runs a Bed and Breakfast in Hadbury. Is she strong enough for this?

Diego Garcia: Head of one of the largest drug cartels in Mexico. This outlaw is totally ruthless and has Hershel and Rebecca in his sights. Can he be stopped in time or will Rebecca pay for Garcia's hatred of her husband?

Manuel Perez: Head of the Mexican Police for this remote area. Is he as upstanding as he had seemed? Or does his allegiance lie elsewhere?

General Morales: Perez's boss and liaison between Mexico and the United States. Will he be a help or hindrance?

Chapter 1

Hershel couldn't believe the carnage that was unfolding in front of him. How could this have happened? This operation had been carefully coordinated with the Mexican Federal Police. Their informant had been adamant that Garcia and his men would be in the camp. They had even had men posted to watch the camp. And yet, all he saw from his vantage point were women and children and a few unarmed men.

Bill, Hershel's second in command, said, "Hershel, we have to stop this! Those people aren't even armed. Why are the Mexican Police still firing?"

Hershel didn't wait to hear the rest of Bill's outrage. He stormed down the hill, shooting in the air as he went.

He grabbed the first Mexican soldier he came to. "What the hell are you doing? These people aren't armed! It's obvious Garcia and his men aren't here!"

The soldier lowered his weapon. "El Capitan Perez ordered us to shoot, Senor Bing. We are just following orders."

Hershel didn't wait to hear anymore. He forged ahead until he spotted Perez.

"Tell your men to stand down, you imbecile! Can't you see there's no one here but women and children? What the hell are you thinking?"

Perez yanked his arm away from Hershel's grasp. "You are in Mexico, my friend. You are only here as a courtesy from our government. As such, you are not in charge of this operation, I am." And with this he turned and fired one more time into the confusion of fleeing peasants.

Hershel knew this would cost him dearly with the Mexican government but at this point, he was past caring. He grabbed the rifle out of Perez's hands and pulled the man up so that their faces were only inches apart.

As Hershel was six-foot four-inches tall and Perez only five-foot four-inches tall, if he was standing on the tips of his toes, that meant Perez's feet were no longer on the ground.

Hershel gave one fierce shake and ground out the words, "Tell your men to stand down!" He let the man go and watched as he hit the ground, bounced once and slowly got to his feet.

Perez raised his rifle and shot in the air as he yelled a command for his men to halt their fire. All was quiet as the men turned to face their leader. Perez turned to Hershel. "Well marshal, what now? Do you intend to take over my command? Are you going to issue orders to my men?"

Slowly, Hershel's two marshals, who had accompanied him to Mexico, flanked their boss. Bill on his right and Cliff to his left. They weren't sure where their boss was going with this but they were ready to follow his lead.

Bill had served with Hershel for most of his career and never knew a man he trusted and admired more. If Hershel wanted to take on the whole Mexican army, he would stand shoulder to shoulder with him.

Cliff was the youngest marshal in the Richmond office. What he lacked in experience, he made up for with his dedication to his job. He had a strong sense of right and wrong and what had happened here today was just wrong.

If Perez thought Hershel was going to back down just because he was outnumbered, he was fixing to find out just how wrong he was.

"No Captain Perez, I have no intentions of issuing orders to your men. You, however, are a different matter. I am well aware that I am in your country. But if you think you outrank me, you would be wrong. And if you think your superiors will see this massacre as justified, you would be wrong again. Now tell your men to tend to the wounded and issue a burial detail for those you had cut down in cold blood."

Perez looked around at his men. He didn't want them to see him back down but he knew the marshal was right. His superiors would not see his actions as justified. Their intelligence had been flawed. Garcia and his lieutenants weren't here. He had been so intent on proving he was in charge he had rushed in without checking the camp first. When everyone had started to run, he had given the order to fire.

"Alright men, you heard the marshal. Divide up. Half of you start digging graves and the rest see what can be done for the wounded."

Perez walked away to supervise his men. He wasn't finished with Marshal Hershel Bing but it would have to wait. This needed to be taken care of so he could figure out how to save face with his men and come up with a good story for his superiors. There had to be a way to shift the blame back onto the marshal. After all his entire career had been built on shifting the blame for his incompetence to other people.

Cliff turned to his boss. "Wow Hershel, that was close. I thought for a minute there we were going to have to take on Perez and all his men. I mean, I know we could. We were pretty outnumbered but hey, there are three of us and maybe fifteen of them. But we are United States Marshals and we could have done it."

Hershel just let his youngest marshal talk until he had wound down. When Cliff began to blush, Hershel knew he was about done. Cliff had never been able to control that blush. Hershel figured a few more operations like this might do the trick. But Cliff had been shot on their last mission and that hadn't made any difference.

Hershel reached out and put his hand on Cliff's shoulder. He knew his young marshal would have held in the face of twice the odds.

"Let's see if we can help any of these people. We need to get the wounded back for medical care as fast as possible."

As Cliff walked off to see where he could help with the wounded, Bill returned from doing a quick reconnaissance of the camp.

"Hershel, I don't think we are going to have any to take back for medical care. I counted seven dead. If there were others in the camp, they made it out through the woods. Perez's men are digging the graves now."

Hershel looked around, taking stock of the activity around him. "What was that idiot Perez thinking? He didn't even check to see if Garcia or any of his men were here. He just rushed in firing."

Before he could get worked up again about Perez's incompetence, Cliff was back. One look at his face told Hershel he was about to hear something he wasn't going to like. The blush Cliff had left with was gone and in its place was no color at all. The blank look made Hershel think of someone who had suffered a severe shock. Cliff opened his mouth but no sound came out. He cleared his throat and tried again.

"I think we may have one alive. But not for long. I found her not far from the tree line. Looks like she almost made it into the woods. Hershel, she's hardly more than a child. She couldn't be more than fourteen."

Hershel didn't touch Cliff. He could tell he was barely holding it together.

"Bill, take Cliff and see what you can do to help Perez's men with the graves. I'll see what I can do for this young girl."

With this, Hershel started off for the tree line on the far side of the camp.

He saw her tattered body seconds before he got to her. No wonder Cliff had been in a state of shock. She really was little more than a child. Cliff had been right about that. He knelt down and took her hand, wiping the blood from her face with his other hand.

"Hold on, we're going to get you some help." He knew she was beyond help but he had to give her hope if he could.

She was going in and out of consciousness and mumbling words Hershel couldn't make out. All he could do was gather her in his arms and hold on.

Maria knew she was hurt bad but there was no pain. She didn't know the man who held her but was glad he was there. Where was her brother? He was supposed to be here. Tomorrow was her fourteenth birthday. Where was Diego? Her mother was going to be so mad when she found out she had left to find him. All she wanted for her birthday was to see him. He had been gone for three weeks.

She knew he was a busy man with many responsibilities. Her mother told her she couldn't depend on him. That he was just like his father. Well, her grandfather had been an important man too. He had been rich and so was her brother.

Her mother didn't think she knew about the bank account. But she had found the little bank book one day while she was searching for a hair ribbon. She knew her brother put money in there so she and her mother could have a better life. She didn't understand why her mother wouldn't use some of it. Instead, her mother cooked and tended house for others. She never touched the money.

She had to find Diego then get home and tell her mother she was sorry for running off.

But she was so weak. Maybe she could rest just a little first. Maybe Diego would come and take her home. He could talk to mama so she wouldn't be so mad. He had always been able to make things right for her.

Yes, that's what she would do. Just rest for a few minutes.

Hershel knew when she was gone. She had been mumbling but Hershel couldn't understand any of what she had been saying. Now, she was completely still. No breath left in her.

Not much got to Hershel but the senseless killing of this child was just too much. He continued to hold her for a few more minutes. Like if he held on to her, she might come back.

Bill and Cliff found him there still holding her.

Cliff reached for her. "Here, Hershel. Let me take her. I was the one to find her. I'll see that she gets back and we'll find her family. She'll have a proper funeral and her family can lay her to rest and maybe find some closure as well."

With this said, Cliff reached and took the child out of Hershel's arms.

Diego Garcia watched from the top of the mountainous terrain. He held his binoculars to his eyes and watch his precious baby sister being cut down as she tried to make it to the trees and safety. His men held him back knowing there was nothing they could do.

He lowered the binoculars. He couldn't see anyway for the tears streaming down his face. He wiped them away and looked again. He wanted to see who was holding his sweet Maria's body. He wanted to see who had taken the life of the most important person in his world. He wanted to see the face of the man he would hunt down and make pay for what he had done.

He watched until the man lifted his head and handed Maria's body to another man. They were Americans. He looked closer at the one still on his knees covered with Maria's blood. He knew this man. United States Marshal Hershel Bing. He had a huge reputation for being tough. Well, he wouldn't be so tough when he was finished.

The one thing this man loved more than life itself was his wife. He took Garcia's baby sister, now Garcia would take his wife. He would take her and kill her on the very spot his precious Maria had died. And then this Marshal Hershel Bing would die too.

Garcia lowered his binoculars and faced his men. "You will go to Richmond and bring me this man's wife. She shouldn't be hard to find. He is United States Marshal Hershel Bing and her name is Rebecca. I will have my revenge."

After giving this order, Garcia turned his back and walked away from his men. He stood on the edge of the cliff and shouted, "I will have my revenge!"

Chapter 2

Rebecca sat in stunned silence as she listened to the judge. She couldn't believe he was leaning toward remanding that poor child back to his abusive father. She had seen the bruises and raw marks on this child's back and legs. Some were scars left from older beatings. Some bruises were more recent and darker blue. Burns were scattered up and down his small arms. The abuse was horrendous. The child was five.

She had to stop this now before the judge made his ruling and it was too late. Rebecca dropped her eyes and said a quick prayer.

Lord, please help me turn this situation around. Give me the words to convince this judge to allow me to place this child in a home where he will be loved and allowed to develop into the potential I know you have for him. And Lord, give me the strength to say them.

Rebecca lifted her eyes and stood.

The judge stopped midsentence and eyed Rebecca. "Yes, Mrs. Bing? I gather you have a good reason for interrupting these proceedings at this late date."

"Yes, your honor. Permission to approach the bench."

The judge sighed. He obviously just wanted this hearing to be over. "Granted. Mr. Scott, will you join us as well?"

Mr. Scott, the attorney for the slimeball father, stood and followed Rebecca to the bench to stand before the judge.

"Alright, Mrs. Bing, let's make this quick. It's been a long day and it's getting late. We need to conclude these proceedings."

"Yes, your honor. I'd like a few minutes of your time." She paused and added, "In your chambers where we can speak in private."

The frown on his face said it all. "Is this really necessary?"

"Yes sir, I believe it is."

The judge banged his gavel, probably a little harder than necessary and addressed the courtroom. "We'll take a 15-minute recess. Mrs. Bing, Attorney Scott, in my chambers."

Rebecca followed the two men from the courtroom. They both entered the judge's chambers ahead of her. *Well,* she thought, *so much for gentlemanly behavior.* She shook her head. It was what she had expected anyway.

As she was the last to enter, she turned and softly closed the door. She took a deep breath and turned to face the men. As she did so the image of that poor defenseless child's bruised and battered body flashed across her mind.

Rebecca drew up to her full five-foot two-inch height and straightened her shoulders. Gone was the mild and gentle lady. Gone was the timid social worker. Gone was the child advocate willing to let her charge be sent back to his father for more abuse.

She marched across the room and got right in the judge's face. The attorney she ignored completely. As far as she was concerned, he wasn't worthy of her attention. He should be more selective when choosing his clientele.

She stopped just short of poking the judge in the chest with her finger. Hershel would be proud of her restraint. His chest had been the recipient of her finger on more than one occasion.

"What are you thinking? Your honor," she added as an afterthought. "How can you even consider sending that child back into that horrendous situation? What if that was your child? Would you want him to live that way?"

The judge drew in a deep breath as if to speak but Rebecca didn't let him get a word out.

"Come back to the holding room with me where that little boy is waiting to hear his fate. Look at the scars and bruises. The bloodred marks and the burns on his little body. Watch him shake with fear when his father walks into the room. Then you be the one to tell him he has to go back home with that monster that calls himself a father."

The judge took another breath but Rebecca wasn't finished.

"Then go home to your own children and tell them what a wonderful thing you did today. How you reunited a five-year-old defenseless little boy with his abusive father."

The judge managed another half breath but Rebecca continued, "I've got an even better idea. Why don't you pack their jammies and let them go over for a spend the night party? The more the merrier. At least I'll bet that's what that pervert that calls himself a father would think. I'll bet he would love some more children to abuse. Surely what's fine for this little boy would be ok for your children as well."

This time the judge managed a full breath. But when Rebecca moved a little closer, he choked on it.

"If you even think of turning that child back over to his father, I will bring the full force of the Richmond Child Protective Services Department down on you. I will personally represent every child in a custody case that comes before you. I will be in your face for each and every hearing. You will see me in your sleep at night."

Having said her piece to the judge, she turned on the attorney. "You should be ashamed of yourself. You should have to walk one day in that child's shoes. You call yourself a man. You're as bad as his father."

Without another word, she turned and left the judge's chambers. She had done her best.

Lord, I know that's not exactly what you had in mind for me to say. But that judge wasn't going to let me have too much of his time. I admit I was flying by the seat of my pants but I couldn't wait. I had to get it all said while I could. A lot of those words weren't yours. They were my very own. But I could feel your presence.

And with this silent prayer, she returned to her seat in the courtroom. And waited.

Ten minutes later, the defense attorney returned to his seat. She watched out of the corner of her eyes as he and his client carried on a whispered conversation. She wasn't close enough to hear what they were saying nor could she tell anything by their expressions.

Ten more minutes passed before the judge entered and took the bench.

He banged the gavel, and Rebecca held her breath.

"In the matter before us as to the welfare of this minor child. It is my ruling that said child be removed from his present home and the custody of his natural father and be placed in the care of Mrs. Bing and the Richmond Child Welfare Services." And with one more bang of the gavel, he said, "Court is adjourned. Mrs. Bing, would you approach the bench please?"

Rebecca figured she was in deep trouble. She didn't care. The child was safe. Her job was done and no matter what came next, she could sleep tonight.

As she reached the judge, he bent down and for her ears only said, "The next time you feel a need to give me a severe dressing-down, would you be sure an attorney isn't present. I do have a reputation to uphold after all."

Rebecca left the courthouse feeling like a heavy burden had been lifted from her shoulders. Now she could turn her thoughts to a more personal concern.

Hershel had been gone for ten days. As a United States Marshal, he often had assignments that took him outside the country. Often, he was not allowed to communicate with her. That was for his safety as well as hers. But this time he was out of communication with everyone. Even the other marshals in his office.

She knew Bill and Cliff and Jeff were with him. That made her feel a little better. She knew they had been working on a drug smuggling case and that took that 'little better' right off the table. She hated drugs. She had witnessed their effects on too many families and as a result the children that got caught in the middle.

She knew Andrew had stayed behind for this mission. Andrew was the IT specialist for Hershel's office. She wondered if Andrew had been tracking Hershel and the others from this end. That made sense. If anybody had heard from Hershel, it would be Andrew.

Rebecca looked at her watch. It was getting late but she was only a few blocks from the Federal Building. Andrew was single and often worked late. She'd take a chance and stop by.

She wished she had something to bribe Andrew with. He loved her cooking. Especially her chocolate chip cookies. Unfortunately, she didn't have any with her. Maybe she could scare some information out of him.

She used different methods to get information out of Hershel's men. They loved her. They were afraid of her. They definitely wanted to stay on her good side. Hershel knew all of this but turned a blind eye. After all, where Rebecca was concerned, it was every man for himself.

As she pulled into the parking lot, she spotted Andrew's car. Just as she'd expected, he was working late.

The guard let her in. Like most of the others, he had a soft spot for Rebecca. Besides, Hershel would have his hide if he made her stand outside.

Rebecca took the stairs to Andrew's office. She needed time to plot her strategy. She decided the direct approach would work best. After all, she had the surprise element on her side. He didn't know she was coming. He wouldn't have time to hide. Rebecca tapped on his door and then went in without waiting for an invitation.

Andrew looked up. He was sitting at a bank of computers. Little dots of light blinked off and on. They would pause, travel a little way across the computer and then stop again. He reached to turn the computer off when he saw Rebecca standing in the door.

"What are you doing, Andrew?" She positioned herself right in front of him and smiled.

No way could he turn the computer off now without raising her suspicions. He knew this woman. She was going to try to get him to give her information about her husband. Hershel and three other marshals were on a mission in Mexico. Anonymity was of the utmost necessity. There could be real danger associated with this cartel. It was led by one of the most ruthless drug lords in Mexico.

But the danger wasn't just confined to south of the border. Diego Garcia was the supplier for a large network of drug pushers here in the United States. Since he supplied them with the contraband that was making them rich, they would jump to do his bidding. Besides being greedy, they were also afraid of him.

"Now Rebecca, I know what you're going to ask me. And you know I can't give you information about Hershel. Not his location nor when he might be coming home. You know it's a security deal. Besides that, there are laws that prevent communications when we're on assignment in other countries. Sometimes we have to play by their rules to secure their cooperation."

Andrew knew he was babbling. He just couldn't help it. Rebecca made him nervous when she was on a mission. And she was definitely on a mission. She was worried about Hershel. He knew she wasn't going to leave without some assurance he was ok.

Andrew took a deep breath. Damn! He was a highly trained United States Marshal. He had been trained in interrogation and espionage. He had been trained to deal with hostile forces. Not that Rebecca was a hostile force. She was just a force and it didn't look like she was going away anytime soon.

Rebecca hadn't spoken again since entering the room. She knew Andrew so she would just wait him out.

"Listen, Rebecca. I know you wouldn't want to get me in trouble or anything. Wait! What am I saying? It's been less than six months since the last time you came in here trying to get me to spill my guts about Hershel. Remember what happened that time? I ended up on some Godforsaken island in the middle of nowhere standing on a cliff facing a firing squad. Don't you remember, Rebecca? You were there. We were dealing with cartels and drug lords and all kinds of scary dudes then too."

Rebecca didn't move a muscle but her intake of breath and the fact that all the color had drained out of her face, made Andrew aware of his mistake. While trying to talk his way around Rebecca, he had told her exactly what she wanted to know. Well, not everything she wanted to know. She was going to want assurance that Hershel was safe. And he couldn't give her that.

Right now, his boss and very good friend was only a blip on his computer screen. The Mexican government was very tight with their security. Hershel and the other marshals had been forced to turn over their cell phones when they reached the office of the Mexican Police for the remote area, they needed to access to find Garcia's camp and hopefully capture him. They had been assured extradition would be no problem. The Mexican government would be glad to be rid of him.

It was only due to Andrew's ingenuity that Hershel and the other marshals were even a blip on his computer screen. He had devised a tiny transmitter that would allow him to track them. But that's all it did. He couldn't communicate with them or they with him.

Rebecca was just standing there watching him. "They've gone after Garcia. I knew they would eventually. I just didn't think it would be this soon. Oh Andrew, he's a ruthless killer and he has a whole band of cutthroats just as bad as he is. Please tell me they're safe. Andrew? Please tell me they're ok."

Rebecca had reason to know just how bad Garcia was. He was the drug lord supplying the thugs that had nearly killed Hershel and the other marshals just six months ago. They all would have been killed had it not been for Jeff Bloom. He was a United States Marshal out of the New Orleans office who had gone under cover to infiltrate a drug gang led by Clint Montgomery. Diego Garcia had been his supplier. He had been on the island to negotiate a larger drug shipment with Clint and had left just before all hell broke loose and Jeff had to blow his cover to keep them all from being killed.

Andrew pulled a chair around so Rebecca could sit down and see his computer screen. The cat was out of the bag now. Might as well share what he knew. Not that he knew much.

"OK Rebecca, you see these little blips on my computer screen? See how they are moving around? That's Hershel and Bill and Cliff. We know they're ok 'cause they're moving."

Rebecca leaned forward for a better look. "Which one's Hershel?"

Andrew wasn't ready for that question. He should have been. After all, this was Rebecca.

"Well, it doesn't work that way, Rebecca. But see, I put these tiny transmitters on three guys, Hershel and Bill and Cliff, and there are three little blips so they're all fine."

"But if one of the little blips goes away, how do you know who's missing?" Rebecca looked at Andrew for an answer.

"Well, we don't. But Rebecca, they're all there so everyone is fine. You have to have faith that these guys know what they're doing and will take care of each other."

Rebecca digested that, but then had another thought. "What about Jeff? This was his mission before our guys got involved. No way he didn't go with the others. Where's his blip?"

"Jeff was the only one Garcia would recognize. He was introduced to Garcia as Clint's first lieutenant when he was undercover. He had to stay at the Mexican Police headquarters and monitor things from there. He has a blip. I just haven't activated it yet because he's staying in one place and there's no reason to think he's in any trouble."

"Rebecca, they're all fine. If they, weren't I promise I'd tell you. It wouldn't do any good to try to hide it from you. You'd get it out of me anyway."

Rebecca slowly got out of the chair. Andrew was right. She had to trust that Hershel and his guys could handle whatever came their way. And that God would take care of the rest.

She made it to the door and then turned to look at Andrew. "Hershel is way bigger than all the others. Next time make his blip bigger so we can tell which one he is." And with those parting instructions, she turned and left.

By the time Rebecca reached home, it was completely dark. The hearing at the courthouse had taken longer than anticipated and then her little side trip to see Andrew had taken up even more time.

Rebecca wasn't afraid of the dark but she was feeling a little uneasy. It was probably just the side effects of her visit with Andrew and thinking about Hershel and the others being in danger.

She parked and fumbled in her purse for her house keys. She didn't keep them on the same keyring with her car keys. Her thinking was that if she lost her car keys, she would still be able to get in the house.

She smiled when she thought about Hershel's reaction to her reasoning. He had said, "Honey, if you lose your car keys, how are you even going to get to the house?"

Alright, enough woolgathering. Time to get inside and get things ready for tomorrow. She could hear her pajamas and her bed calling.

As soon as Rebecca entered the house, she could tell something was off. Just a feeling but she knew her home and something wasn't right. She stood for a moment without turning on the lights. She moved slowly through the living room. Nothing looked out of place. She started toward the kitchen and there it was. A shadow. Now she wished she had listened to Hershel and kept her small pistol in her purse. Hershel had bought it for her after their experience with the drug smugglers six months ago. She had even taken lessons but none of that was going to do her any good now. The pistol was upstairs in the draw of her bedside table. And the shadow was between her and the stairs.

Hershel always said if you can't get away and you have no weapon—hide. So that's what she did.

Rebecca slipped inside the closet just off the living room. She felt in her purse for her phone and being as quiet as possible called Andrew. As soon as he answered, she said, "I need some help, someone is in the house. I'm hiding in the closet off the living room. How quick can you get here?"

Andrew's entire body went cold. "Rebecca, don't move; I'm on the way. I can be there in less than ten minutes. Just stay quiet. I'm on the way," he repeated. "Rebecca, do you hear me? I'm coming."

But Rebecca didn't answer. She was already gone.

Chapter 3

Hershel, Bill, and Cliff started back to the Police Headquarters. Perez and his men had gone on ahead. Since Hershel had held that young girl in his arms and watch her take her last breath, it probably was a good thing. He didn't know if Perez's bullets had been the ones to take her life but as far as Hershel was concerned the fault lay squarely at his feet. Perez was in charge of the Mexican Police. He gave the order to open fire.

As they drove along the back roads, Hershel thought how beautiful this country was. The extremes of mountains and canyons, deserts and rain forest were breathtaking. He wished he was here under different circumstances and that Rebecca was with him. She would love it.

Maybe when this mission was finished, he could bring her here. But as long as Garcia and his cutthroats were free to kill and plunder, he didn't want Rebecca anywhere nearby.

She had barely missed crossing paths with him on their last mission. He still had nightmares about what could have happened.

The police department was on the edge of town. A two-story building made of weathered stone. It looked as if it had been there for centuries. Maybe it had. Time had a way of slowing down in this part of the world.

Bill stopped the car in the back parking lot. Turning to the others, he said, "Does it look like more than the average amount of activity taking place in there? This is the first time we've had to park in the back."

They got out and Hershel said, "Well, we won't know if we keep standing out here." He had a bad feeling. Something was definitely going on.

As they entered the building, a police officer flanked them on each side and two more brought up the rear.

Hershel looked around for Jeff. He had stayed behind to handle things here. He couldn't go on the raid. He had been introduced to Garcia as Clint Montgomery's second in command. Jeff had been undercover. Clint was in prison and there was no reason to believe Jeff's cover had been compromised. They had planned to use that to their advantage if this raid had not produced the desired result. It hadn't. They hadn't even seen Garcia and his men.

As they made their way into the main room, Hershel could see Jeff sitting in Manuel Perez's office. He definitely looked uncomfortable. There was also three other men Hershel had never seen before.

Since their escort didn't stop, they had no choice but to continue on to Perez's office. Hershel would have welcomed an opportunity to clean up a little first. All three marshals were covered in dust and sweat. Hershel and Cliff were covered in a fair amount of blood as well.

As they entered, Jeff started to rise but one of the men Hershel didn't recognize, put his hand on Jeff's shoulder to keep him in place.

"Come in, marshal." Perez stood and closed the door behind them. He motioned to one of the men who stepped forward. "This is General Morales. He is the equivalent of your internal affairs and also is the liaison between our two countries. He has some questions about your recent raid."

Hershel took stock of these new men but most of his attention was focusing on Perez. "You mean our raid, don't you, captain? Or don't you remember being there and opening fire on a bunch of unarmed civilians?"

General Morales turned his attention from Hershel to his captain. This was certainly a different version from what he'd been told when Perez had called his office. According to Perez, this America marshal has gone rogue and fired on a camp of innocent peasants. Since there were no survivors, he had to decide who was telling the truth. He waited.

Perez walked around the other men and stood behind his desk. He felt better with something solid between him and Hershel.

The smirk on his face told Hershel all he needed to know. Perez was covering his ass and his men would be too afraid to contradict him.

Perez took a seat. "You're the one covered in blood, marshal. My men will testify to your actions. I have requested appropriate steps be taken and a severe reprimand issued. You are in our country and must abide by our laws. You can't come down here and take over and expect there will be no consequences."

Perez paused and stole a glance at his General. He had to make this believable. This gringo had a stellar reputation in law enforcement.

Hershel waited. He figured Perez would talk himself into a hole if he gave him time. Bill and Cliff followed their boss's lead. They had complete confidence in Hershel's ability to handle this situation.

The only one to react was Jeff. He had only been under Hershel's command for six months but it didn't take even that long to find out what kind of man Hershel Bing was. No way would he kill innocent people.

Jeff shook off the restraining hand that had been holding him in place. "That's a bunch of damn lies! No way would Hershel open fire on innocent civilians."

Hershel turned to his marshal and held his hand palm out in a sign for Jeff to stop. He wanted to let Perez finish.

Jeff slowly lowered back into his chair but stayed just on the edge. If things got ugly, he was ready to take out his share. His loyalty to these other marshals he served with never wavered.

Hershel turned back to Perez and waited.

Perez didn't disappoint. He was on a roll. "You see, my general, these Americans are a bunch of hotheads. They think they can take over. This one, and he motioned toward Jeff, wasn't even there. It was the same in the village. They just rushed in and started firing. They didn't care how many innocent people they killed. They were just a bunch of Mexican peasants. I'm just surprised they didn't go in with a rebel yell, waving their damn flag as they went!"

Hershel had heard enough. "Stop!" He slapped both hands down on the table in front of Perez. "My family and I have served under that flag for generations." And to punctuate his next words, he brought his hands down again hard for each one. "And served proudly with integrity."

Hershel didn't step back. Instead, he learned over the desk, getting in Perez's face. One of Perez's men took a step forward. All three of Hershel's marshals did the same.

General Morales did nothing to interfere. He wanted to see how this would play out.

Hershel paid no attention to the commotion going on behind him. He never took his eyes or his attention off Perez.

"I had two men under my command, Captain Perez. How many did you have?" Before Perez could answer, Hershel continued, "If I, and my two men, were out of control, why didn't you stop us? You had guns and certainly had us outnumbered. And this blood you see on me is not from anyone I shot. It was from holding a child in my arms as she took her last breath. She was riddled with bullet holes alright but not from our guns. We took her body back to her mother for a proper funeral."

Hershel turned and looked at Morales. "If you want to know who did the shooting, check the bullets in that child's body. They haven't had time to bury her yet. You'll see whose gun they match and I guarantee it won't be mine or either of my men's. Now if you'll excuse us, my men and I are tired and in need of a bath. We'll be in the barracks we've been assigned. I'd also like our phones back. This mission is over. I'd like to call my wife and let her know I'll be heading home in the morning."

Morales moved to block the door. He wasn't as big as Hershel but he wasn't afraid of him either. All his men were armed and unlike the marshals their guns were already out.

"I'm afraid that won't be possible. In fact, I'll have to hold on to your weapons as well as your phones until this matter is resolved. As far as going to your barracks, that will be fine. I'll have a couple of my men escort you there and stand guard until we get to the bottom of this." And with this, he stood back so his men could relieve Hershel and the other marshals of their guns.

All went well until they got to Jeff. He had been undercover for a long time before he had joined Hershel's office. He had become a little rough around the edges. Posing as a thug tended to do that to a person. The phrase "kill or be killed" had taken on a very real meaning to him. He had moved up to second in command to Clint Montgomery himself. He hadn't attained that position by playing nice. In fact, he had killed the man who had that title before him. In actuality if he hadn't the man would have shot an innocent woman just because he didn't need her anymore. But still, he had killed him and left his body floating in the water.

When General Morales reached for Jeff's weapon, Jeff put his hand on the butt of his gun and backed up. "I don't think so," Jeff said, backing up.

He backed all the way out of Perez's office. He would have kept going except he came in contact with an unmovable object. Hershel.

"Give him your weapon, Jeff," Hershel said. "We'll work this out. We came down here to arrest Garcia and take him back to stand trial. We haven't done that yet. We need to regroup and come up with a new plan. Let's use this time to do that."

Jeff hesitated. It went against all his training to give up his weapon. It was the old 'live or die' mentality that had enabled him to stay alive while he was undercover. But he wasn't undercover any longer and this was Hershel doing the asking.

Jeff slowly pulled out his gun and handed it to Hershel. He'd give it up but he'd be damned if he'd hand it over to Morales. Hershel took the gun and handed it to the General. He knew what that action had cost his marshal.

The four marshals left the police station and headed to their assigned barracks. They needed a bath, some food and a plan, in that order. After a bath and something to eat, they settled around the small table to try to come up with a plan. Hershel leaned back in his chair with a cup of coffee in his hand. A coffee maker had been provided for their use. It had been assumed all Americans liked their coffee. It had been assumed right.

Bill and Jeff poured theirs and settled in at the table with Hershel. All three took their coffee black. They watched as Cliff added some water to cool it down a little. Then milk and lots of sugar.

Bill turned to Hershel. "Is it still coffee after all that?"

Cliff brought his cup to the table and said, "Is it still a marshal if his front teeth are missing?" Then his face turned bright red.

The other three men doubled over laughing. It was hard to take a man seriously when he was blushing.

"All right, guys, we needed that but let's get down to business. I've been thinking. We know what didn't work. We are going to have to do this on our own. Even if Morales accepts our version of how our mission went down, we can't work with Perez."

The others nodded. They were all on the same page.

Hershel continued, "Morales seems like a smart guy. I'm counting on him seeing through Perez's version of events. After all it wouldn't make sense for us to go in guns blazing and kill a bunch of civilians. We are here by the good graces of the Mexican government. We have always worked well with them in the past. Why would we all of a sudden go rogue? This mission is important to us. We want Garcia."

"And besides that," Cliff said, "You have to figure this is not the first time Perez has pulled a stunt like this. He likes to be in charge and when things go south, he looks for someone to take the blame."

If Cliff had left it at that, it would have been fine. But then he added, "You know I learned about his type personality at the academy. Some people aren't smart enough to be in charge and when things go bad, they look around for a scapegoat. They come across as inept but they are really dangerous." Cliff realized no one else was talking and he felt the blush starting up again.

"Alright, Sigmund Freud," Bill said. "We all went to the same academy and took the same classes. We don't need a refresher course on the different kinds of personalities. We know what class Perez falls into. Asshole."

This started a heated argument between Hershel's three marshals. He set back and watched. They all needed this to destress. He let the good-natured banter go on for a few minutes longer.

"OK guys," he said. "I think we all agree that Morales is a pretty smart guy and Perez an idiot. So, when Morales figures out his captain is a moron, we need to have a plan. We're not going back home without Garcia and for that we need Morales's help. When he calls us back to his office, we need to have a solid plan. One that doesn't include Perez and one we can sell Morales. After all, there are only the four of us and we can't depend on the Mexican government for backup."

Hershel took a deep breath and continued, "I have several things in mind and the one I like the least is the one that keeps circling back to the front of my brain."

He paused and looked at each of his men. They waited. He knew they would follow his lead under any circumstances. That was what made this so hard. He wanted to take Garcia back to stand trial. But he wanted them all to go home alive. His plan was risky and very dangerous.

He took a breath and looked at Jeff. "How would you feel about going back undercover?"

Chapter 4

Rebecca slowly regained consciousness. She lay very still trying to remember what had happened. Everything in her brain seemed to be fuzzy and unfocused. She was afraid to open her eyes. One step at a time. Something bad had happened to her and until she could remember what, she felt it would be better not to call attention to the fact she was awake.

Her head didn't hurt so that ruled out any kind of head trauma. She concentrated on remembering. Slowly, events started to come back in bits and pieces.

She remembered the trial and the confrontation with the judge. She immediately dismissed any danger from that. Judges had confrontations all the time. If they retaliated every time they had a confrontation, they would all end up in jail. Then all the felons would run free because no one would be left to sentence them.

Rebecca gave herself a mental shake. The effects of whatever she had been given was making her mind wander. She had to concentrate. She remembered leaving the courthouse and something about Andrew. Oh yes, she remembered stopping by his office. But why would she do that? Hershel wasn't there. That wasn't something she would be likely to forget.

It became very important that she remember what had happened with Andrew. If she could remember that, she had a feeling the rest would come back as well.

Rebecca felt herself drifting away. She didn't fight it. Maybe if she let her brain rest, the memories would come back and she could figure a way out of this. Whatever this was.

Rebecca slowly started to emerge again into consciousness. This time she didn't move or open her eyes because she was paralyzed from sheer terror. The memories came back in a flood this time.

She had entered her house with an uneasy feeling. She remembered seeing the shadow and hiding in the closet. She remembered calling Andrew for help. That was why it had been so important to remember Andrew. He was the only one who knew she was in trouble.

Now she remembered pushing to the very back of the closet and watching as the door slowly opened. That was when the true terror had set in. She was trapped. At first all she could see was a hand pushing the clothes aside. And then she was being yanked from the closet and a foul-smelling rag forced over her nose and mouth. Chloroform. That was probably why she was having such a hard time waking up. It would also account for the nausea.

She had never been up close and personal with the drug but she had studied the effects it had on the body. She had been involved in a child custody case where chloroform had been used to subdue a ten-year-old child. The little girl was big enough to struggle but she was no match for a rag soaked in chloroform. Rebecca's research had helped put the abusive uncle away for twenty years. It should have been life but sometimes justice wasn't perfect.

Now that Rebecca's memory had returned and the nausea had subsided somewhat, she couldn't put off the inevitable. She opened her eyes and tried to roll over.

The fact that she wasn't blindfolded had her concerned. Her abductors evidently weren't worried about her identifying them. So, she could rule out being held for ransom. Not that she and Hershel had enough money to make that worth risking jail time for.

Revenge was her next thought. She made a lot of enemies working in the child care division of the Social Services Department. She had been threatened many times but no one had ever followed through with any of them. Besides if that were the case, they could have killed her there in the closet.

No, whoever had taken her wanted her alive at least for a while. This thought spurred her to action. She had no way of knowing how long she had.

She needed to turn over so she could check out her surroundings. Her arms and legs weren't bound together, so what was holding her? She held both hands up in front of her face. No problem there. She tried to pull her legs up so she could turn her body. That's when she realized something was holding one of her feet. She was chained to the wall by one foot. The chain was just long enough to allow her foot to remain on the floor and was anchored about two feet up the stone wall.

Ok. She could work with this. Rebecca rolled herself as close to the wall as possible so she could use it for balance. Next, she pulled on the chain to help her set up and then to stand. Finally, she was able to turn and place her back against the wall. She would never again complain about those Pilates lessons her friends had talked her into.

Now that she was standing, she could check out her surroundings. There wasn't much to see. She was in a small room with stone walls and a concrete floor. The only window was way up high. Much too high for her to reach. At least there were no bars on it. Not that she had a way to reach it. However, any information was more than she had before so she filed it away. Even useless information was better than no information at all.

Rebecca slowly slid back down to the floor. She was still weak from being unconscious. Just how long had she been unconscious anyway she wondered? Surely someone would come check on her eventually. The thought that she might be left here to die was unthinkable. It almost made her panic.

She closed her eyes and thought of Hershel and what he would do to these people if they hurt her. She was so tired. She felt herself drifting off. She didn't fight it. She needed to recover some strength if she was going to get out of this alive.

Rebecca came awake slowly and watched as the door across from her opened. She didn't try to stand up. Until she could assess this new threat, she was staying put.

A man entered carrying a tray of food and a bottle of water. She didn't realize how thirsty she was until she saw that bottle.

For a minute, the man just towered over her without saying a word. It was as if he knew how badly she wanted that water and wanted to make her beg for it.

Rebecca gritted her teeth together to keep from doing just that. She instinctively knew it would be a mistake to show weakness.

The man finally bent over and placed the tray and water beside her. "Eat up. We still have a long way to go and we may not stop again," he said.

He stood up and headed for the door before Rebecca spoke. She didn't want to give him a reason to stay but she needed information.

"Wait! What do you want with me? Where are we?" She waited but the man left without saying another word.

Rebecca couldn't stand it another minute. She grabbed up the bottle of water and twisted off the cap. She downed half of it before she stopped. She could easily have finished it off but the thought that the man might not give her any more stopped her. She better conserve what she had just in case.

She picked up the tray to see what was on it. Her stomach turned over. A pile of beans and a stale piece of bread. She picked up the fork and began to eat. She was eating for strength, definitely not for taste. She didn't think she would ever be able to eat beans again.

She had only taken a few bites when she put her fork down and bowed her head.

Lord forgive my lack of appreciation. Thank you for these beans and the strength I know they will give my body.

And with that prayer, she picked her fork back up and started to eat with renewed determination. Rebecca finished off the last bite of beans and bread. The food sat like a rock in her stomach. As bad as the food had been, she felt stronger.

She checked out what was left on the tray. She needed a weapon. A tray, a plate and a fork. Not much to work with. She picked up the fork, wiped it off and stuffed it deep in her pocket. She hoped her abductor wouldn't notice it was missing.

The tray and plate were too big to be any use. She had no way to hide them for a surprise attack. The only other item was the half empty bottle of water. Would he let her keep it or take it? She wasn't going to take a chance. She unbuttoned the front of her blouse and stuffed it inside. She maneuvered it to fit just under her arm where it would be less noticeable.

As weapons, they weren't much but they were all she had. Now she needed a plan. She thought about what her abductor had said. They were going somewhere else. That meant he would have to free her from the chain that had her tethered to the wall. He would also have to take her outside this building. That was going to be her best opportunity to get free. She wasn't going to waste it.

Rebecca leaned back against the wall. She would rest and let the food make her stronger. She didn't exactly sleep but she let her mind wonder. She thought about Andrew. She knew he would have gone to her house to help her. She wasn't sure what he would find. Did they trash her house? Had they been looking for something? Did they leave evidence that would help Andrew find her?

She didn't even know how many there were. She had only seen the one.

At some point she must have dosed off. She jerked awake. Her abductor was towering over her. He kicked her foot. "Get up; we go now!"

Rebecca looked at her feet. He had unchained her and she hadn't even known it. Rebecca slowly tried to stand but she couldn't seem to get her feet under her. The one that had been chained had lost all feeling.

The thug reached down and yanked her to her feet. "We go now," he repeated. He grabbed Rebecca by the arm and pushed her toward the door.

As they left the room, she realized they were in a tiny house. She could see a small bathroom off to her left.

"Please," she begged. "I need to go to the bathroom before we go." Until now she hadn't known just how true that was. Something about being on her feet brought on the urgency.

He just grunted and pushed her in that direction. "Hurry. We have a long way to go before daybreak."

Rebecca entered the small bathroom and pushed the door shut. She waited a minute, half expecting him to throw open the door and allow her no privacy.

He must really be in a hurry to miss an opportunity to torment her.

Rebecca hurried to take care of business and then checked out her surroundings. She could see nothing that might help her escape.

A half-used bar of soap and a small amount of toilet paper. She had no idea what she could do with these but she stuck them in her pocket anyway. Then she retrieved her water bottle from inside her blouse and finished filling it up before replacing it back in its hiding place.

She looked around but there just wasn't anything else. There were even bars on the small window. She looked out but it was too dark to see much. They were in a small clearing in what looked to be a dense forest. She rested her hand against the bars and was shocked when they moved.

She tugged and couldn't believe it when they swung inward. She pushed on the window and it moved up just a little.

Her abductor banged once on the door. "Don't make me drag you out of there. We need to leave now!"

Rebecca needed no other encouragement. She pushed hard on the window and as soon as it was opened enough, she wiggled through. She hit the ground with a thud and was up and running by the time the bathroom door burst open.

She reached the edge of the forest at the same time he came barreling out the front door. Rebecca crouched down behind the trunk of a huge oak. She had no idea if he had seen which way she went. She wanted to go deeper into the forest but was afraid if she moved, she would give away her hiding place.

She held her breath and moved just enough to see around the tree. What she saw made her heart almost stop.

The thug had retrieved a spotlight from the car and was slowly and methodically shining it along the edge of the woods.

Rebecca had no choice now. She couldn't wait any longer. In a few seconds, the light would be on her. She eased back away from the tree and took off. Maybe she could outrun him. She was pretty fast but having to pick her way through the dense underbrush was slowing her down.

For the first time, Rebecca felt she might make it. She could no longer hear him thrashing through the bushes. She dared a glance behind her and when she did, she tripped. She was at the edge of a dry riverbed and tumbled down the incline.

When she stopped rolling, she couldn't do anything but lay there. The breath had been knocked out of her. Maybe he hadn't been close enough to see what had happened and he would pass her by.

She closed her eyes when she saw the light and heard him making his way down the ravine. She had given it her best. She remembered one of Hershel's favorite sayings. When everything seemed to be going wrong, he would say, "Let it go and live to fight another day."

And so, she opened her eyes and waited.

She didn't have to wait long.

The thug towered over her. He reached out and yanked her to her feet.

"If my orders weren't to bring you back alive, I would shoot you right here. If you try anything like that again, I just might forget those orders."

He lifted her off her feet and threw her over his shoulder and started back the way they had come.

When they got back to the clearing, he dropped her to the ground. Opening the trunk of the car, he said, "I was going to let you ride in the backseat but now this is what you get for taking off like that."

Without another word, he picked her up, threw her in, and slammed the trunk shut.

Chapter 5

Hershel, Bill, Cliff, and Jeff made their way into Perez's office. They had been summoned about an hour ago. Told to have some breakfast then report to the police headquarters.

It had been two days since they had been relieved of their weapons and instructed to remain in their assigned barracks.

The first thing Hershel noticed was the absence of Perez and General Morales sitting at his desk.

"Please come in and be seated," he said as the marshals filed in. Everyone except Jeff compiled. He leaned against the wall, by the door, and crossed his arms over his chest.

This small act of defiance didn't go unnoticed. "Please join us, Marshal Bloom," Morales indicated a chair closer to his desk where the other marshals already set.

Jeff glanced at Hershel and when he got a subtle nod complied.

Morales leaned back and cleared his throat. "I believe our little misunderstanding has been resolved."

Hershel leaned forward. "It wasn't a little misunderstanding, General. What you accused my men and I of doing was pretty serious. Since Perez was the person doing most of the accusing, don't you think he should be here for this meeting?"

Morales waited a moment before shaking his head. "I don't think that will be necessary. In fact, it wouldn't be possible. You see, Captain Perez has been transferred to another precinct where he will serve, shall we say, in a lesser capacity."

The Marshals looked at each other. It appeared Morales was ready to accept their version of what went down during the brief and one-sided battle at the small encampment where Garcia was reported to have been holed up.

Morales continued, "I went to the site to see for myself and was able to talk to one of the peasants who made it to safety by hiding in the woods. He confirmed your version of events. He even witnessed your little confrontation with Perez. I also checked the bullet taken from the young girl before they had a chance to bury her. It matched the type of weapons used by our men. It didn't, however, match Perez's rifle. That's the only reason he was demoted and reassigned elsewhere instead of court martialed."

Morales reached into the desk drawer and took out the weapons he had taken from the marshals two days before. As he handed them back, he said, "I apologize for any inconvenience this may have caused. Our countries have always worked well together but these matters have to be resolved. I am sure if we had been in your country, you would have done the same."

He reached out his hand to each marshal in turn. They all shook his hand, even Jeff.

Morales took a deep breath. "We do however have a problem. The young girl that was killed was Garcia's little sister. There was a strong bond between the two. He is not going to let this go. He is vicious and well known for his particular brand of retaliation. I fear his anger will be directed toward you men. He has spies everywhere and by now he knows his sister has been killed. I think it's time you returned to your own country. With you gone I may be able to keep a lid on things here."

Hershel glanced at his men. They had worked out a plan but they had to sell it to Morales. Without his buy-in their hands were tied. They would have to go home without completing their mission. They wanted to take Garcia back to the United States to stand trial. His drug cartel supplied a wide array of distributors that spread all across the country. With him out of commission they could start taking down these distributors one by one. It wouldn't stop all the drugs but it would slow them down.

"We know everything there is to know above Garcia," Hershel said. "We still want to apprehend him and take him back to our country for trial. That would be a win for both our countries. We could deal with Garcia while you clean up the rest of his gang."

Hershel paused to give Morales a few minutes to think about what he was proposing and respond. He had to tread lightly. They were here by the graces of the Mexican government. He could try to go over Morales's head but that would make things so much harder. Besides, it would give Garcia too much time to react. A lot of innocent people could get hurt.

"To have a chance at capturing Garcia, you would first have to infiltrate his camp. We don't even know where that is now," Morales speculated.

At least they had his attention, Hershel thought. He continued by saying, "We can put out the word Jeff is looking for him. Let him find us. He was introduced to Garcia as Clint Montgomery's second in command. He had left the island before we took Montgomery and his band down. We have no reason to believe Jeff's cover has been compromised. We can use that to get Jeff into his camp. When Jeff gives us the signal that the time is right, we can move in and take him."

Morales sat back and studied the U.S. Marshals sitting in front of him. Especially Jeff. Jeff seemed like a hothead to him. But he had worked with men who had done undercover work. He knew it took a special breed to pull that off. He could see that in Jeff. The bad-boy persona came through loud and clear.

"And if I agree to your plan, what role will my men play? You will need our help or you will be vastly outnumbered."

"Yeah, about that," Hershel said. "That didn't work so well last time." At this point Hershel had to choose his words carefully. He couldn't afford to offend General Morales.

"We would need and appreciate your help with the take-down, General. But until that point, it would work best if you left this mission to my men and I. We would keep you informed, of course. In a mission like this, the fewer men involved, the less chance someone can leak our plan to Garcia. I am sending one of my men in with virtually no backup. His life could depend on the utmost secrecy."

Hershel waited for Morales' reaction. He didn't have long to wait. "So, you are asking me to allow you to conduct this operation on your own? America Marshals on Mexican soil with no coordination with us? I'm sorry, marshal, I can't do that."

Hershel started to speak but Morales put up his hand to stop him.

"You must understand, I have superiors too. Others that I must answer to. Would your government allow us to send our men to conduct a clandestine mission on American soil with no coordination with your government? I think not, Marshal Bing."

This time it was Jeff who spoke up. "General, it would be my life on the line if my cover is blown. I can't be worried about the politics when I am worried about staying alive. The more people who know our plans the bigger the chance I won't live through this mission. It is my sworn duty as a United States Marshal to fight these drug cartels in both our countries. I hate the drugs and would gladly give my life to get them off the streets. But I would appreciate the chance to live."

He sat back and waited. Hershel waited too. He had never been prouder of his marshal. He couldn't have said that better himself.

Morales seemed to be taking in Hershel's request and Jeff's reasoning. "Let me make this plain," he said. "I cannot sanction an American mission on Mexico soil with no involvement from our government."

He held up his hand to stop anyone from speaking. "However, I understand your concerns. That is why I will personally represent our government. I will be an active member of your team. That, gentleman, is the best I can do."

"Then we'll accept your offer, General. And thank you." Hershel stood and offered his hand.

The rest of the afternoon was spent planning the best way for Jeff to infiltrate Garcia's camp. Morales said he could provide earbuds that were small enough not to be seen. With them they could maintain communications with Jeff. They came up with the code world "rocket" to be used if Jeff got in trouble and needed them to move in immediately.

They decided Morales would put out the word an American drug dealer had moved into the area. They would let Garcia find Jeff instead of the other way around.

Jeff would move out of the barracks he was sharing with the other marshals. Morales would help relocate him into a less desirable part of town. They would make it easy for Garcia to find him.

It would be Jeff's job to separate Garcia from his men so he could be taken with the least amount of danger possible for all involved. They didn't want this to turn into a blood bath. If they tried to take him in his own camp that's exactly what would happen. Garcia's men were fiercely loyal. Probably because they were so afraid of him.

After Garcia was in the custody of the marshals, Morales would lead a contingent of Mexican Police to mop up the rest of them. Without their leader that would be much easier to accomplish.

It sounded like a good plan. But like all plans a dozen things could go wrong. Jeff knew how quickly things could go south. He learned that the hard way the last time he went undercover. He had buried two of his fellow marshals. They weren't just fellow marshals. They had been his friends.

Two days later Jeff left the others behind. He rode off on an old second-hand Harley. He looked every bit the outlaw he was pretending to be. He was a little dismayed how easy he had slipped back into this role.

When this was over some serious counseling might be in order.

Jeff roared up on his bike and parking behind an old rundown cantina. He chained his bike to a concrete post. He was sure it wouldn't be there when he came out otherwise. Even chained, he wouldn't be surprised to find it stripped. It was that type neighborhood.

Jeff entered the cantina and let his eyes adjust to the dim light. Ordinarily, in a place like this, he would have kept his back to the wall but this time he wanted to be noticed. He wanted to be approached by someone in Garcia's band of thugs.

General Morales had put out the word a gringo was in town. That he was involved in the drug trade and had fled the United States to avoid prosecution. He even put Jeff's name out there. Garcia would be sure to connect him with Clint Montgomery's organization. It didn't matter if Garcia knew Montgomery had been taken down. In fact, it would help. It would make sense that Jeff was looking to hook up with another drug organization.

Jeff eased up to the bar. He ordered tequila. He hated the stuff but figured beer was too American. He turned around and surveyed the room. He wasn't sure he would recognize any of Garcia's men. He had only brought a few with him to the island.

No one in the bar made eye contact. It just wasn't that kind of place. Jeff turned back to the bar and motioned to the bartender. When the guy put down the dirty rag he had been wiping down the bar with and approached Jeff, he didn't speak. He winked.

Jeff almost stepped back but stopped himself just in time. He looked closer. He couldn't believe what he was seeing. "Bill?" he whispered. Bill gave a slight nod.

"Stage makeup," he whispered back. "Thought you might need some backup. But this is as far as I go. When you leave here, you really are on your own. The only communication will be the earbuds. Don't lose them. Oh yeah, that's not tequila. I know you hate the stuff. It's water."

Jeff didn't want to press his luck so he didn't answer. He couldn't take the chance someone was watching them. He gave a slight nod and turned his back on Bill.

A few more patrons had entered while his back had been turned to the door. Any of them could be Garcia's men. They were a rough looking bunch. Just the kind he'd hoped to find here. Just the kind of place Garcia and his men might frequent.

A large tough-looking guy separated from the other newcomers. He eased up beside Jeff and ordered a beer. Well, so much for looking too American. He took his beer and walked away.

An hour passed but no one else approached Jeff. He was just about to give up and call it a night, when the door slowly opened and a woman entered the bar. All the men turned to stare but then quickly turned away as if they were afraid to look at her. Her head was covered with a shawl and it was impossible to see her features.

She quickly crossed over to stand beside Jeff at the bar. She never looked at him but whispered, "I was sent to ask you to step outside. Someone is there that wishes to speak to you."

"And who might that be?" Jeff asked as he made eye contact with Bill.

Bill turned his back to pour some tequila for a guy at the other end of the bar. The message was plain. "You're on your own from here."

The woman didn't speak again. She just turned and walked out. Jeff put some money down on the bar and followed her. When Jeff reached the door, no one turned to look. It was as if they wanted no part of what was fixing to happen.

Jeff shrugged it off but felt icy fingers up and down his spine. He pushed on through the door and that was the last thing he remembered.

Chapter 6

Rebecca didn't move. She just couldn't. It wasn't the confined space. She was small. She could have stretched out some. It was the fear. She didn't know where she was being taken. Heck, she didn't even know where she'd been. She had been unconscious part of the time. How long had it been since this nightmare had begun? She just had no way of knowing. She just hoped Andrew had found something that would give him a clue how to find her. He was her only hope. Hershel didn't even know she was missing.

Rebecca was tired. She wished she knew what time it was. She didn't wear a watch. She used her phone to keep up with the time. She supposed her phone was still in the closet at home. She remembered dropping it when she was yanked out of the closet. Andrew would find it. Not that it would help him figure out what happened. It wasn't like she had time to leave him a message or anything.

Rebecca closed her eyes and tried to relax.

Lord. The Bible says you will never leave us. That wherever we are that you are there too. I guess that means you're in this trunk with me. I really don't want to be here. If you can get us out of here, I would appreciate it.

Rebecca knew she had no control at this moment. Even if she could get the trunk open, they were going too fast for her to jump out. All she could do was check her surroundings for anything useful. She had been doing that a lot lately. But it, at least, gave her some sense of control. She was doing something.

The trunk was dark and since it was night, there was no glimmer of light coming from around the trunk lid. All she had was her sense of touch.

It took all her nerve to reach out into that darkness. She wasn't exactly sure what she was afraid of. Maybe it was all the CSI crime shows she had watched on television. The criminals always put the bodies in the trunk.

All right, Rebecca, she thought to herself. *Your body is the only one in here. Get a grip.*

First, she ran one hand along the left side of the trunk. She found the spare tire pushed way over to the side. Not much she could do with that. She located the jack, but couldn't see how that would help her. Rebecca pushed it to the side with the spare tire. She fumbled around until she located the long piece of iron that went with the jack. She thought she remembered Hershel calling it a tire tool. Anyway, it went with the jack.

Rebecca hesitated for just a minute but just as quickly dismissed it. If she were stronger, she could use it like a club. It would certainly cause some damage. But from her prone position, she doubted she could do much damage with it.

Rebecca pushed it to the side with the other tire stuff. However, she made a mental note of its location.

That was all she could reach on that side.

She was able to reposition herself so she could check the other side. Her hand came in contact with a paper bag. She opened it but couldn't see well enough to tell what was inside. A can of something. Whatever it was, she was going to hold on to it.

Rebecca unbuttoned her blouse and put bag and all under the arm opposite of where she had the water bottle. She was running out of spaces to hide stuff.

She felt all the way to the back on that side but the only other thing she found was a pencil. Stuffing it in her pocket, she wasn't sure what use it would be. If all else failed, maybe she could use it to jab her abductor in the eye. Since the thought of that made her a little nauseous, she quickly moved on.

Nothing else on that side. Now for the very back. This was harder to do because it was a deep trunk and meant she had to work her way further back into the darkness. If there was going to be a body, that's where it would be. More space.

Ok. Enough with that thought. She would file dead bodies in the same place with jabbing someone in the eye with a pencil.

When Rebecca maneuvered far enough so she could reach the back wall of the trunk, she had found nothing else. She ran her hand from one side to the other to make sure she hadn't missed anything. Rebecca was nothing if not thorough, so she started back in the opposite direction just to check one more time.

When she got back to the middle, her hand sunk way into the material. She pushed hard. Her hand broke through into what she assumed was the backseat.

She had found a possible way out of the trunk. But how to make that work for her? She couldn't just push through. He would see her.

That thought brought on another. She could see light and it wasn't coming from her new found escape hatch. It was coming from behind her. It was coming from the back where the trunk closed. It was daylight.

Rebecca remembered her abductor saying they had to travel at night. On the heels of that thought, she felt the car turn. It felt like they were now traveling on a rutted dirt road.

She held her breath when the car started to slow down. By the time it came to a complete stop, Rebecca had wiggled back into her original position.

She waited. She figured they were stopping to wait for dark before traveling any further. She wondered how far they had come and what direction they were headed. If she knew that, she might be able to figure out where he was taking her. She strained to hear any sounds from outside the car. Nothing. No traffic. No sounds of civilization at all.

Finally, she felt the car move a little as if he had shifted in the seat. Then she heard the driver's side door open and close. She waited again but nothing.

What seemed like an hour passed but could have been less. It was hard to tell.

She tried not to jump when the trunk suddenly opened.

"Get out," he said. "We would have made better time if you hadn't tried to escape from that bathroom window. Stupid. Where did you think you would go? Try that again and I won't chase you down. I'll just shoot you and face Garcia's wrath."

He kept talking but Rebecca didn't hear another word after Garcia. He was taking her to Garcia? Why? She had hoped never to hear that name again.

Then she had another thought. That's where Hershel had gone. Was he still there? Was Garcia going to use her as bait to lure her husband into a trap?

She couldn't let that happen. At the next opportunity, she would try again to escape. If he shot her, so be it. She would not be used to cause Hershel harm. She would rather die.

When she didn't move fast enough, the thug grabbed her by the arm and pulled her out. She was unsteady but managed to stand. She didn't want to give him any reason to put his hands on her.

She looked around. They had left the dirt road and the car was between two large bushes. It would be virtually impossible to see from the road.

He took her to the far side of one of the bushes and let her go. "I am going to let you take care of business. I don't want you messing up my car. I'll be on the other side of the bush. If you try to run, I will shoot you. There's nowhere for you to go anyway."

As soon as she had a little privacy, she took care of business.

Rebecca had to think. She needed a plan. But before she could come up with anything, the thug was back. He seemed disappointed she had finished her business and was apparently waiting for his return.

Actually, she was lost in thought. Trying to come up with an escape plan.

"Why are you taking me to Garcia?" she said the first thing that came to mind. "He doesn't even know me."

"Let's just say he knows who you are and has a special date planned for the two of you."

Without another word, he pushed her back to the car. But instead of opening the trunk, he pushed her to the ground. He reached into the backseat and retrieved a pair of handcuffs.

As he bent over and snapped them around her wrist, he said, "These will keep you out of my hair until the sun goes down and we can get back on the road. If you stay quiet and let me get some sleep, I may even feed you before we start again."

Rebecca thought of the beans he had given her before. Her stomach turned over at the thought. But even as it did so, she knew she would eat them. She would need the additional strength they would give her to get away. And she would get away, tomorrow, because she had no way of knowing how close they were to their destination. She could not allow him to take her to Garcia. Hershel's life might depend on it.

With this thought she settled back and got as comfortable as was possible for a person chained to the back of a car. There was no chance of escape until he took the handcuffs off.

She let her mind wander. That was better than obsessing over her present predicament. She thought of the new friends she had made six months ago from Hadbury. They had been in a tough place then too.

Nancy and Mary Alice had been kidnapped by a drug smuggler. They had been taken to an isolated island and held there. Nancy's husband Joe, Mary

Alice's future husband Albert, their close friend Beth, a nurse at a local hospital and Hershel had tracked them to the island. She had to smile when she thought of how she had bullied Hershel's marshals into letting her go along to try to rescue them. Bill, Cliff and Andrew were fiercely loyal to Hershel and were afraid to take her into danger. She had threatened to follow them, if they left her behind. They finally figured they could keep her safe and out of trouble if they took her with them. If it hadn't been for an undercover marshal that was already on the island, they would have all been killed. Jeff Bloom had become one of her husband's marshals shortly afterwards.

Rebecca must have fallen asleep. She woke with a start when something landed in her lap. It was a small bag of candy and beside her was another bottle of water.

"That's all you get till we reach our destination. Make it last. We'll be leaving as soon as it gets just a little darker."

Rebecca looked up at her abductor. "What happens when we reach your camp?"

"Not my problem. You'll be turned over to Garcia. I'll be off to find a bottle of tequila and a willing senorita. I doubt you'll be there when I get back."

She wanted to ask about Hershel but something stopped her. Until she had more information, she felt she shouldn't assume anything.

Hershel had three of his marshals with him. They wouldn't be easy to take down. And what about the Mexican government? Surely there had been some coordination with them.

No. Until she knew more, she would assume Hershel and the other marshals were safe. And she had no intention of letting them use her as bate.

Rebecca ate a few pieces of candy and put the rest in her pocket. She unscrewed the water bottle and took a big swallow. She'd have to hold on to this bottle and hope her captor would let her keep it. She was out of hiding places.

Rebecca leaned back and tried to relax. There was nothing she could do but wait for an opportunity and be ready.

Night came suddenly. It seemed like one minute it was light and the next dark. She realized she had no idea where she was. She knew their final destination was Mexico. But how close were they? And what route had they taken?

She looked around. They were in another forest but this one was different. It wasn't as dense and the ground was more sand than rich earth. She was sure he would put her back in the trunk. She wouldn't be able to see her surroundings until she made her move. She'd be ready.

It wasn't long until her abductor was back to remove the cuffs. He allowed her to visit the bushes on the far side of the car again. She didn't resist when he pushed her back into the trunk. She had to be patient. One more chance would probably be all she would have. If she wasn't successful, she would either be shot or delivered to Garcia. She wanted to avoid both.

Rebecca tried to get comfortable. She wanted to rest. She would need her energy.

She took an inventory of her resources. A roll of toilet paper, a partially used bar of soap, a fork, a bottle of water, a paper bag with a can of fix-a-flat and a pencil. He also had allowed her to keep the last bottle of water. He had told her they were close to their destination. It didn't matter to him if she had the bottle of water or not.

Rebecca closed her eyes and prayed:

Lord, you fed the multitudes with five loaves of bread and two fish. If I remember from our Bible classes, you did that twice. If you can do that, you can take my meager resources and help me use them to escape this horrible situation.

After her prayer, she felt better. She relaxed and even dosed off and on until she felt the car slow.

She didn't know what was happening but she felt this might be her best chance. She wiggled closer to the back of the trunk and tried to push part of the seat out of her way. It was harder than she thought it would be.

It just wouldn't budge. She waited till he came to a complete stop and got out. It was now or never. She grabbed the tire tool and started working on the back of the seat as quietly as she could. She didn't know how close to the car he was or what he was doing.

She finally made an opening big enough for her to wiggle through.

When she was all the way into the back seat, she waited a minute listening. When she didn't hear anything, she raised just enough to see out the window.

He had parked at a pump in the rear of a gas station. He was walking toward the building probably to pay for the gas. Since his back was turned to her, she took a chance to check out her surroundings.

There was literally nothing else in sight other than the station. They were in the middle of a dessert. Sand and a few large cactuses were all she could see. She could work with that. She didn't have an option.

She started to slip out the door opposite of the station. Her hand hit something hard that fell to the floorboard. She looked down. It was the handcuffs.

She quickly changed to plan B. It was riskier but if she could pull it off, it would buy her some time. Rebecca picked up the handcuffs and slipped as far down into the floorboard as possible.

She waited for him to get back in the car. He put one hand on the steering wheel and reached the other out to close the door.

It was time for her to act. With a quick prayer, she leaned over the seat and slapped the handcuffs on his right wrist and then to the steering wheel of the car.

And then she ran.

Chapter 7

Andrew felt cold fear. Rebecca was in trouble. He had to get to her fast. He hoped she would stay hidden in that closet. He hoped he could get to her before she was found.

This had to be a random burglary. No one who knew that Hershel Bing, United States Marshal, lived there would dare break in. They would move on to easier pickings. Hershel had quite a reputation.

Andrew opened his desk drawer and removed his pistol. He was a crack shot but seldom had to use his weapon. He worked in the IT department, for heaven sakes. For a moment he thought of checking to see if any of the other marshals were in the building. But quickly dismissed that idea. It was late. He was the only one who ever stayed this late.

Most of the other marshals had families to go home to. When the work day was over, they were out the door in a flash. It wasn't that Andrew liked being single. He just hadn't met anyone he thought he could spend the rest of his life with.

Well...there was this one lady he had met about six months ago. Victoria. Victoria Stone. He had met her in the middle of their last mission. She ran a bed and breakfast in Hadbury. Victoria was widowed with twins.

The first thing he had noticed was how pretty she was. The second was her cooking. It had only been breakfast. But, man, what a breakfast. But the thing he just couldn't get out of his mind was her courage.

She and her husband had dreamed of opening a bed and breakfast. Tragically, he passed away before they could make it a reality. Victoria had been left with two small children, a dream and a whole lot of grief.

She could have given up but instead had pulled her life together and opened the B & B on her own. She had made friends there in Hadbury and found someone was always willing to lend a hand when she needed it.

Andrew had found reasons to visit her several times in the last six months. He had gotten to know her kids. They weren't even two years old yet but what rascals those two little guys were. She would have her hands full when they got older.

It was early in their relationship. He wasn't sure he was ready to take on a readymade family. He wasn't sure he wasn't.

All these thoughts ran through his mind as he stuffed his gun in its holster and ran out of the building.

He passed the night guard and called out to him, never breaking stride. "Call the Richmond PD and tell them there's been a break-in at Hershel's house. I'll meet them there."

Andrew crossed the parking lot at a sprint. He had the door open and the car started way before he got to it. As soon as he had the door closed, he slammed the gear into reverse. He stomped the gas and had the car in drive almost in one motion. Not waiting to get to the entrance, he jumped the curb instead.

The cars that were issued to the marshals were high-power sedans equipped with emergency lights and sirens. He used them both. He reached Rebecca's house in under ten minutes. Two police cruisers pulled into the driveway behind him. Not waiting, he was out of the car and halfway down the walk when the officers caught up with him.

One of them grabbed him by the arm and tried to pull him to the side of the house. Andrew just shook him off and kept going. It finally took all four officers to bring him to a stop.

"Hold on, man," one of the officers told Andrew. "You can't go rushing in there not knowing what we're facing. We could be cut down as soon as we walk in the door. Let us go in and clear the house first and then you can come in."

Andrew tried to shake them off but they held on tight and maneuvered him to the side of the house. At least they were no longer in the direct line of fire if the perpetrator was still inside.

"You don't understand. Rebecca is in there alone. She could be hurt by now." He couldn't even let his mind go to anything worse.

One of the officers let Andrew go and just rested his hand on his shoulder. "Alright then. Let's get this done. But we're going in with the proper protocol."

"Ken, you and Frank take the back. Henry and I will go in through the front. We go in on my signal."

The other three officers had followed suit and released their hold on Andrew. They looked to see if Andrew understood what they were fixing to do, but he was gone.

Andrew had noticed an open window and while the police officers were coming up with their plan, he was already inside.

He knew where Rebecca was supposed to be. He removed his gun from its holster and cautiously approached the closet just off the living room. The door was standing open. He used the barrel of his gun to open it the rest of the way.

The closet was empty. Rebecca was gone.

He let the four officers search the rest of the house. When they had finished, they found Andrew sitting at the kitchen table. He was holding Rebecca's phone. He looked up. "Someone took her."

The four officers looked at each other. The one who had taken charge outside, did so again. "You need to come down to the station and give us a full report. We'll send in a forensic team to process the house. If there are any clues, they'll find them."

Andrew agreed. He didn't think they would find anything but there wasn't anything else for him to do. The police had a job to do. He wouldn't stand in their way.

As soon as Andrew gave his statement, he headed back to his office. He didn't know what he would do there, but he couldn't just go home. When he walked in, he unsnapped his holster and placed his gun back in the draw.

Hershel had said on many occasions, Andrew was the calmest marshal he had. The man never got ruffled. If Hershel were here now, he might change that assessment.

Andrew slammed the drawer shut. Rebecca had needed him and he had failed her. He wanted to slam his fist into something. Anything would do.

Instead, he sat down and picked up the phone. It rang three times before a sleepy voice said, "hello."

Andrew looked at the time. It was after midnight. "Victoria, I'm sorry. I didn't check the time before I called. Did I wake you or the twins?"

Even though it was after midnight, that wasn't as stupid a question as it might have been. At their age, the twins often had Victoria up at all hours.

She ignored the question entirely. "Andrew, what's wrong? You sound awful."

"Rebecca's gone," was all he could get out. The sob that came after those words had Victoria sitting on the side of the bed, reaching for the light.

"What do you mean, she's gone?" When there was no response from the other end of the line, she said, "Andrew, what do you mean she's gone?"

Andrew had to clear his throat several times before he could speak. The words finally came tumbling out. She didn't interrupt. When he finished, she simply said, "I'm on the way."

"Victoria, no. I just needed to talk to you. That's all, just talk to you. I didn't know who else to call. Rebecca has gotten so close to you and all the others in Hadbury, I knew you would understand."

Victoria listened but all she said was, "I'm on the way."

Andrew was shaking his head. "You can't just up and leave. What about the twins? What about the Bed and Breakfast? What about your guests?"

Victoria was already up, pulling clean clothes out of the closet. "I'm on the way," she said and hung up.

As soon as she was dressed, she picked up the phone and called Nancy Murphy. Her husband, Joe, answered the phone.

When she explained what she needed, Joe interrupted. "Victoria, you can tell us the rest when we get there. We're on the way." He hung up the phone and then called Albert and Mary Alice.

When he explained as much as he knew to Albert, all Albert said was, "We're on the way."

Joe would have called Beth but knew she was on call at the hospital. Regardless, Joe knew if they needed her, she would be on the way too.

They all arrived at the bed and breakfast at the same time. It was a small town and it didn't take long to get to anywhere from anywhere.

Victoria met them at the door. "Thanks for coming. I have coffee ready in the kitchen. Let's fix a cup and I'll tell you everything I know."

They followed her to the kitchen where she had laid out blueberry muffins, orange juice and a fresh pot of coffee. They had just fixed their plates and poured coffee, when someone knocked on the door. They looked at each other. No one knocked. They used the doorbell.

They all filed out of the kitchen to see who it was. By now, it was two in the morning.

Victoria opened the door.

Beth stepped in. "What's going on?" she said. She looked at each of them as if they had planned something and was going to leave her out. Well, that wasn't going to happen.

"How did you know they were here?" Victoria stammered.

"I got up to get a drink of water and saw Albert and Mary Alice drive by and I followed them."

Joe said, "I would have called you but I knew you were on call at the hospital."

"And what's that got to do with anything?" Beth responded as she stepped through the door. As Victoria closed the door, she said, "Is my doorbell broken?"

"No. I didn't want to wake the kids. I know firsthand how hard it is to get them back to sleep."

Beth followed the others back to the kitchen. When they were once again seated at the table, Victoria related everything Andrew had told her.

These were Rebecca's friends. They would do anything they could to help her. They had only known her for six months but time meant nothing. They had all been involved in a kidnapping that had ended up with them on a supposed deserted island being held captive by a band of drug smugglers. That kind of experience tended to bind friends for life.

"So, you see," Victoria said. "I have to go to Andrew. He's by himself and needs me."

As usual, Beth took charge. It just came naturally. "Victoria, go upstairs and finish getting ready. You're not making that drive this time of night by yourself. I'm going with you. Joe, you and Nancy take care of the kids. They are used to that. Nancy keeps them once a week anyway. Albert, you and Mary Alice take care of the B and B. We'll all keep in touch by phone."

And with that, they all went off to do as Beth directed.

Chapter 8

Hershel watched as two men eased up behind Jeff. He winced as one hit him in the back of the head with the butt of his pistol. Through the earbuds, he heard Jeff grunt as he went down.

General Morales placed his hand on Hershel's shoulder to keep him from moving. He knew what it took to watch one of his men being attacked and be forced to stand down. "Wait," the general told Hershel. "We can't afford to move too soon and be spotted. If they meant to kill him, he would be dead already."

Hershel gritted his teeth. "And maybe they're taking him back for some of Garcia's sick brand of torture."

Bill had joined them, he knew what Hershel was feeling. He felt the same. "Listen," he told the others, "Jeff understood what he was getting into when he agreed to this mission. As hard as it is, we've got to let him do his job."

Cliff eased forward to get a better look at what was happening at the front of the cantina. The two men were dragging Jeff toward an older model station wagon. He appeared to be unconscious.

"Listen," Cliff said. "We can help him more by keeping up with where they're taking him. These little earbuds only allow for communication up to a mile. And no GPS, so if we lose them, Jeff is going to have more to worry about than a knot on the back of his head. I sure wish Andrew were here with some of his little gizmos."

Genera Morales glanced at Cliff. "I have heard of this guy. He has quite the reputation in the tech world."

Hershel only nodded. He had worried some company would lure Andrew away with the promise of more money. According to his information, some had even tried. So far Andrew seemed content being a marshal. If Andrew ever married and had a family, he might look at things differently. Kids were expensive. Hershel knew, he had four.

Bill had been watching as Jeff was stuffed in the backseat of the car. One of the men got in back with him and the other took the driver's seat. "We need to get to our cars. They're fixing to leave."

They made it to the other side of the building just as the two guys pulled off with Jeff.

Hershel and General Morales got in an old pickup and waited a few minutes before falling behind them. Bill and Cliff made it to a new model Hummer just as they pulled off. They waited for a few cars to pull in behind the others before pulling out. They would leapfrog back and forth with Hershel and the General to keep Jeff's abductors from suspecting they were being followed.

Traffic was fairly heavy this time of day. That would play in their favor. They wouldn't be as easy to spot. As they left town, Hershel and the General fell back and let Bill and Cliff take the lead. They could communicate by cell but so far there had been no need. About five miles out of town, they made a left turn onto a lesser traveled road. Three more miles they made another left. This time the road was dirt and heavily rutted. The dust billowed up behind the lead car. The others fell further back. It would be easier to be spotted on this less traveled road. Besides all the dust being kicked up made it virtually impossible to lose them.

Hershel and General Morales slowed and pulled to the side of the road. When Bill and Cliff caught up, they pulled in behind them. General Morales pulled the pickup into the underbrush way off the road then he and Hershel covered it with a few tree limbs. He left the keys in the glove box. They made their way back to the road and got in the Hummer with Bill and Cliff.

Bill turned back in his seat and said, "They made a right turn just ahead where the road dips and curves a little to the left. With all the dust they're kicking up it won't be hard to pick up their trail."

"Ok," Hershel said. "Let's go. We'll leave the truck here in case we need backup transportation."

They made the next turn and then slowed down. There was no sign of Jeff and his abductors. They traveled on for another mile, looking for roads that turned off in either direction. Nothing.

Bill pulled to the side of the road and let the hummer idle. He looked at the others. "Now what?"

Cliff had both hands over his ears. "Listen," he said. "I hear something through the earbuds. Cut the ignition."

Bill cut the car off and they sat in complete silence, trying to hear what Cliff heard.

General Morales dropped his head and closed his eyes. "I don't hear anything," he said.

They all listened in silence for a few moments longer.

"There," Cliff said. "Did you hear that. Voices, very faint but I can hear them. What did you say the radius on these things is?" He turned and looked at General Morales.

"A mile at best," the General answered. "Let's pull the car off the road and walk. We've got to be within a mile of their camp."

After hiding the hummer, Hershel said, "Let's walk back the way we came. They must have turned off somewhere. It's a good thing we passed on by their turnoff. We would have driven straight into their camp. If Cliff can hear them, they have to be within a mile."

The others nodded. They started walking, keeping well to the tree line. No one wanted to admit they hadn't been able to hear anything. If Cliff had, that was good enough for them. Hershel and Bill didn't want to get Cliff started on having better hearing because he was younger. General Morales just seemed content to follow their lead.

When they had gone about a quarter of a mile, they came across an old logging road. So many weeds had grown up in the roadbed, it was almost impossible to see the road at all. So many leaves had fallen over the years, the dirt was completely covered. No wonder they haven't seen any dust.

Hershel held his hand up for the others to stop. Now he heard what Cliff had. He looked at the others. They were listening as well.

General Morales took the lead. As they moved deeper into the woods, the sounds coming through their earbuds became more distinct. They were hearing through Jeff's earbuds so the voices were impossible to understand. At least they were still in place and hadn't been knocked loose when Jeff's head had been smacked with the butt of that gun.

"We can't afford to go any closer. They probably have guards posted," Hershel said.

Morales agreed. "Let's find a place where we can't be seen and wait. When your marshal comes to, he'll make contact. Remember, our objective is to separate Garcia from his men. That's the only way to take him without a bloodbath."

"Yes, and we want him alive. We want him to stand trial for all the American lives he's ruined with his despicable drugs," Bill nodded.

General Morales grunted. "It's not only American lives he's ruined. His drugs have killed many Mexicans as well. I've seen families torn apart. Fathers dead or in jail, leaving their families to go hungry or forced to move in with family just to survive."

He settled against the trunk of a tree. "I would love to see him face justice here in this country. I hate what he's done to his own people. But I agree with my government's decision to extradite him. Sadly, Garcia owns many of our officials. Not only in the police departments but in the judicial as well. He could very well get off. Money is power and he has plenty of both."

While the two men were talking, Cliff had been pressing his earbuds trying to hear any sound from Jeff's end.

Bill was kneeling at the base of a tree, keeping an eye out on their surroundings. He suddenly held his hand up and whispered, "Be quiet. I hear something."

Everyone stopped talking and listened. They repositioned themselves so they were all facing a different direction and had each other's back. They quietly waited and watched. About thirty yards to their left, two men were approaching.

"Guards," General Morales whispered. The others gave slight nods but no one took their eyes off the two guards. If they continued in this direction, their position would be compromised.

Bill shifted but Hershel reached out and touched his shoulder, then gave a slight negative shake to his head.

The men continued for a few more steps. They stopped while one lit a cigarette. His companion leaned against a tree. "Well, what do you think about the guy Ricardo and Javier just brought to camp?"

"I heard he used to be Clint Montgomery's second in command. Montgomery's operation was raided about six months ago. I think he and most of his men were arrested. It's possible this guy got away. The word is, he's looking for a new outfit to hook up with. Could be, but you can be sure Garcia will check him out closely. We've got a good thing going here and I don't see where we need him."

"I heard two of Garcia's generals talking about him. They seem to think Garcia might use him to coordinate things between Mexico and the United States. We have lots of distributors over there. It would be easier for a gringo to cross back and forth over the border."

They stood silent for a few moments. Then the one enjoying his cigarette said, "A lot depends on how fast Garcia takes care of that other matter. I wouldn't say this where he could hear me but the man is absolutely obsessed about it."

"Yeah, but it was his sister. And for him to have seen it made it worse. He isn't going to stop until he gets his revenge. And even then, I'm not sure he'll ever be the same."

"I agree," the other one responded. "I heard he drank himself into a stupor last night and passed out in his cabin. Needed a couple of men to get him in bed. I'd walk softly around him for a while. He's mean but when he's drinking, he's worse and unpredictable as well."

The men turned and went back the way they had come.

When the men were well out of earshot, General Morales turned to Hershel. "I wonder what that was all about? I thought you said Garcia wasn't there when the raid took place. Your report said just some peasants, a few old men and some women. And of course, Garcia's sister."

"I have no idea." Hershel turned to the other marshals but they just shrugged.

"I talked to the girl's mother when I took her body back for burial," Cliff said. "she told me her daughter had been upset because she thought her brother was going to miss her birthday. It was the next day. She figured she ran away to be with him. The mother didn't even know she was gone until I came into their village with her body. Man, I never want to go through something like that again. Just broke my heart."

Hershel nodded. He knew how he would feel if that were his sister or one of his kids or, heaven forbid, Rebecca. He was on the verge of sharing that thought, when he heard a sound coming through his earbuds.

Jeff was coming around. They heard him moan and then something that sounded like "son-of-a-bitch, who hit me?"

Chapter 9

Rebecca ran like she had never run before. He had promised to kill her if she tried to escape again and she believed him. She had weighed her options. They were few. She could let him take her to Garcia, where she would likely be used for bait to lure her husband to his death. After which, she would be killed. Probably in front of Hershel. Or she could run. Easy decision. She ran.

She had checked out her surroundings when they pulled into the gas station. She was in a desert. Which desert she had no idea. If he was headed to Mexico, as she expected he would, she was likely somewhere in Texas.

There had literally been no other buildings in sight. The station was likely the last place to fill up with gas before crossing the desert. She had briefly thought about going inside to beg for help but had instantly rejected that idea. Whoever was working inside would likely have been too afraid of her abductor to intervene. If he had tried, he would have probably been killed for his efforts.

No, as far as Rebecca could see, running was her only choice. The question was, which direction should she go? Everything looked the same. That decision was soon easy to make. The landscape here was flat, which meant nowhere to hide. In the distance she could see a group of very large cactus. She changed direction and headed for them. Even with the hot wind obliterating her tracks, he would know where she had headed. It was the only place she could remain unseen.

Distance was deceiving. It seemed to Rebecca to take forever to reach the relative safety of her destination. She expected every minute to feel his hands grasping her and pulling her back. That image spurred her to run even faster.

To her amazement, she reached the first group of cactuses without being stopped. They were spread out and their tall, narrow shape offered little cover. She moved on until she found several grouped together.

Crouching behind these, she fell to her knees, gasping for breath. The hot air burned her throat and made her eyes water. She crawled between two of the biggest ones, careful not to touch them. Only then did she dare a look behind her.

She let out a sigh of relief. No sign of her abductor yet. She knew it was just a matter of time. If the keys to the handcuffs had been in his pocket, he would have been right behind her. Hopefully they were in the glove box or somewhere else out of his reach.

Rebecca knew she couldn't stay where she was. She searched around for another hiding place. She knew distances were deceptive in the desert. What looked close could actually be miles away. She had just found that out firsthand. While it hadn't been miles to reach her present hiding place, it had taken much longer than she'd expected.

Waiting to fully catch her breath, Rebecca took out one of her bottles of water. She drank slowly. She could have downed half the bottle but knew she needed to ration it carefully. She didn't know when she would have access to more.

Tucking the bottle back inside her blouse, she took another careful look around. Still no sign of her abductor.

She looked in the direction she was headed. Nothing but sand and a few cactuses that were to spread out to provide any cover. She stood up to get a better look. Off to her left, she saw what appeared to be a group of large boulders. She couldn't gauge the distance but what choice did she have? She couldn't stay where she was and they were the only refuge in sight. Having that decision made for her, she started out in their direction.

It seemed she had walked for miles and wasn't any closer to her destination than when she started. She sank down into the sand and took out her water bottle. She sipped carefully, then replaced it. The water was hot, but oh, it tasted so good. She wanted more but knew better than to give in. She had two bottles but how long could she make them last in this heat?

It was daylight and the sun was high in the sky. That meant it must be about noon. She thought back. It had been daylight when they had stopped for gas too. That probably meant her abductor was no longer afraid to travel by day. Was that because they were close to their destination or for some other reason?

She knew from Hershel that the drug cartels had some of the border patrols in their pockets. Not many but a few. Not all of them for money. More likely some members of their family were being held for leverage.

Rebecca tried not to judge. What would she do to keep her children safe? What would she do to keep Hershel safe? She would do whatever it took. Just like she was doing now.

Rebecca got slowly to her feet. She couldn't stay here. She had to keep moving. She stopped looking at the boulders in the distance.

She soon began to feel a difference in the temperature. It didn't seem as hot. She looked up and realized she was in the shadow of the largest boulder. She had made it to her destination. When she was at the base of the huge rock formation, she climbed up so that she was out of the hot sand. She found a place to sit where she could lean back and rest. It felt so good to be in the shade.

She didn't even look to see where she could go next. She didn't look behind her either. Even if her abductor was just feet away, she couldn't go another step. She took out her water bottle and tried to just sip a little. But this time she had no control. Her body was craving water. She didn't stop until the bottle was empty.

For the first time, Rebecca wanted to give in to tears. She was exhausted. She was hot and dirtier than she'd ever been. A bath and clean clothes would be heaven.

She sat up straight. What was she doing? Was she going to start feeling sorry for herself now? She thought of all the children she had stood for over the years. They had been dirty too. Most of them were also hungry and had been horribly abused. They may have shed some tears but they hadn't given up. Well neither would she.

She needed some rest. She was never at her best when she was tired. She looked around for a place she could get out of the open. She climbed a little further up the rocks. She didn't have to go far. She found a place with a deep indentation. She crawled in and curled up. She just fit. She had shade and a place to rest. Someone would have to be on top of her to see her. She would be thankful for what she had. She closed her eyes and felt herself relax. Sleep came before she could think of her next move.

Rebecca was dreaming. She was cold and kept telling Hershel to get up and turn the air-conditioning off. He didn't get as cold as she did. He was more than twice her size. What was wrong with him anyway? Couldn't he tell she was shivering? She reached for the covers, but there weren't any.

Rebecca slowly opened her eyes. She wasn't at home in bed with her husband. She was on a rock in the middle of a desert. But she was cold. She never realized how the temperature dropped in a desert when the sun went down.

She had to warm up. The rock had held the heat from the sun for a while but now all of that was gone. She checked her supplies. She had always been good at improvising but she didn't have much to work with.

She knew heat loss would be greater from her head. She took out the roll of toilet paper she had taken from the bathroom where she had first been held. Starting at the top of her head, she wound the paper around and around leaving only her eyes and mouth uncovered. She kept going until her head and neck were completely covered then tore off a piece long enough to tuck under to keep it all secure. Then she removed her shoes and wrapped both her feet. She was able to cover her feet and halfway to her knees. She tucked these ends as well, to keep the paper in place. She carefully put her shoes back on, taking care not to dislodge any of the paper.

Next, she pulled her arms out of the sleeves of her blouse so that she could tuck them close to her body. She reached and tied the sleeves around her.

She still wasn't warm, just a little less cold. It would have to do. Alright, Rebecca, she told herself. Think warm thoughts. She closed her eyes and drew her legs up, making herself as small as possible, trying to keep as much body heat in as she could.

She let her mind wander. She wondered where Hershel was and if he were thinking about her. She thought of her children. They had done well for themselves. She and Hershel were so proud of them. They had three sons and one daughter. If she didn't make it out of this mess, would they ever figure out what happened to her?

She knew they would look for her. But how would they know to look here? They wouldn't. How could they know to look in this desert miles away from home?

At some point in these disturbing thoughts, she drifted off to sleep. She seemed to be getting warmer so she relaxed and let sleep claim her.

She woke with a start. Had she been dreaming or had she heard a sound on the rock to her left? Had he caught up with her? If so, what was he waiting for?

She slowly opened her eyes. It took her a minute for her eyes to focus and then another for her brain to process what she was seeing. Mountain lion. At least that was what she thought it was. She'd never seen a real one. Whatever it was, it looked hungry. Only Rebecca could feel sorry for something that was fixing to eat her.

Poor creature. She could see its ribs. She could also see its teeth and knew if she didn't do something quick, she was going to be his breakfast. Very slowly, she untied the sleeves of her blouse and slipped her arms back in. She didn't take time to remove any of the toilet paper. If he ate her, he would get paper and all.

She figured the only reason he hadn't attacked her already was because he was trying to figure out what she was. She didn't wait for him to figure it out. The only way he wasn't going to eat her was if she gave him something better.

She felt in her pocket for the candy her abductor had given her at their last stop. She had been saving it for an emergency. Well, this certainly qualified.

The bag contained about twenty pieces. Thank goodness they weren't individually wrapped. She doubted she would have time to unwrap each piece.

When she opened the bag, she got a reaction from the large cat. He was smelling chocolate. It had all melted from the desert heat and then hardened into one solid lump when the temperature dropped at night.

She broke it up into three different pieces.

Slowly, Rebecca took stock of her surroundings to figure out which would be the best way to run. That is, if she got a chance to run.

Her plan was to throw the pieces in different directions, hoping the cat would take time to find each piece before zeroing in on her again. Hopefully she would be gone by then. She tried not to think about the fact he was probably fast enough to catch her even if she got a good lead. Negative thoughts were not her friends.

She waited for the creature to get a little closer, then threw a piece of the chocolate in three different directions as far as she could. The smell of chocolate would have to do the rest.

The large cat hesitated. Obviously trying to decide between her and the candy. The candy finally won.

As soon as he went to find the first piece, Rebecca was up and running. She was off the rocks and back in the sand. She didn't take the time to check out which way she needed to go. She knew that already. Away from the mountain lion.

The pain in her side made her slow down. She finally stopped and looked back. She had come further than she thought. She could see the boulders in the distance. And she could make out the large cat sitting on top licking his massive jaws. He seemed to have lost interest in her.

She understood. Chocolate did that to her too.

Rebecca walked a little further, just in case he changed his mind.

It had gotten hot again so she stopped and unwound all the toilet paper. She folded it as well as possible and stuffed it in her pocket. If she had to spend another night in this desert, she would need it.

She took out the water bottle and slowly drank. It was still cool from the night temperatures. This time she resisted the urge to drink it all. She let it trickle down her parched throat. Trying to savor every drop.

She replaced the water bottle, this time in her pocket with the other empty one. She didn't have a reason to hide them any longer.

She looked around her, but all she saw was sand. Going forward was her only option. The relentless sun was taking its toll. She could tell she was slowing down. She hadn't been looking forward. She had been looking down as she concentrated on each step. Each step she was hoping would take her closer out of this mess she was in.

A movement high up in the sky caught her attention. It looked like a flock of birds. Did birds live in the desert? She didn't know. She looked again to make sure they weren't buzzards.

No, these weren't big enough to be buzzards. That made her feel better. At least they weren't flying around waiting to pick her bones.

But didn't birds need trees to nest in? Trees would mean shade. They also might mean water. A tree needed water to live. Maybe she had found an oasis. Or, she warned herself, maybe what she was seeing was just a trick the desert was playing on her eyes. The heat radiating off the sand made everything appear wavy.

Whatever it was she was heading in that direction. It seemed hours before the trees began to get closer. And yes, they were definitely trees.

When she was close enough, she stated to run. The trees were thick and she was forced to slow down. She finally pushed through into an opening. And there in front of her was a small pond of water.

Nothing had ever looked so good. She ran and fell to her knees at the edge of the water. She didn't wait to fill up her water bottles. She scooped it up with her hands and drank her fill.

When she knew she couldn't drink another drop, she sat back and removed her shoes. Next came her slacks and blouse and then all the rest.

She hunted around for the bar of soap she had taken when she had taken the toilet paper. Slowly, she made her way into the water. She stood for a few minutes just savoring the feel of it against her hot skin.

Then she began to lather up with the soap. She dipped her head under the water and started with her hair and worked down. When she finished, she retrieved her clothes from the bank, emptied out the pockets and gave them a good scrub.

When this was done, she looked around for a limb low enough to hang them on. By this time, the heat had dried her. She found a place in the leaves and lay down just as she was.

Her last thought before drifting off to sleep was that she felt like Eve in the garden of Eden.

Chapter 10

Jeff groaned and rolled over. The last thing he remembered was talking to a lady in a cantina in a shady part of town. Walking out the door behind her was his final memory.

He had been there hoping to make contact with some of Garcia's men. He wanted to infiltrate their camp. Well, he had done that alright. Just not the way he'd planned. He hadn't been expecting to have his head bashed in. He should have. Intimidation was a tactic Garcia used often. It worked for him. Not many were willing to cross him.

Jeff slowly pulled himself up to his feet. His head throbbed like a week-old rotten tooth.

Checking out the room to make sure he was alone, he walked as far away from the windows and door as the small space allowed. He turned his back, pressed his hand against his earbud, and said, "the rat's in the hole, no sign of the cheese yet."

General Morales chuckled. "Only a gringo could make jokes in the spot that you're in, my friend. Better be careful. Those walls may have ears."

Jeff gave a light chuckle. "Why do you think I'm talking about rats and cheese. I'm just standing here in this empty room talking to myself."

Hershel interrupted the light banter. "Stick with the plan. No talking unless relaying important information. I don't want to have to come in with guns blazing to save your sorry ass. Too much paperwork to replace you."

Jeff acknowledged with just a grunt. He knew his boss had his back no matter what the circumstances. He also knew his assignment. He had to separate Garcia from his men so they could get him back to the States to stand trial. If he failed, a bloodbath would ensue.

Time to get this show on the road. Jeff sauntered over to try the door. He slipped into his bad-boy persona. Since it wasn't far from his normal one, it wasn't hard to do.

He tried the nob and to his surprise it turned. He pulled the door open but that was as far as he got. Two burly guards blocked the door.

He knew better than to show fear. "Take me to Garcia," he snarled.

One of the guards put his hand on Jeff's chest and pushed him back into the room. Jeff grabbed the hand and pulled the guard in with him. Someone was going to pay for bashing him in the head. Might as well be this one.

Jeff's left hand was holding the guard as he pulled him into the room. He brought up his right fist and smashed him in the face. Not sure how many times he'd been hit on the back of the head, he hit him again.

Jeff knew this was too good to last. Just as he drew back again, the second guard had him around the neck in a chokehold. Jeff's vision began to dim. He knew if he didn't act fast, he was going to pass out.

Suddenly, it was over. Both guards let go and Jeff hit the floor.

Garcia walked in. "What the hell is going on? You came down here looking for me and now you're picking a fight with two of my men? You want to join up with us and you think this is the way to do it? I should have you shot on the spot."

Jeff struggled to stay on his feet. Gritting his teeth, he said, "And you think sending thugs after me, hitting me in the head and knocking me out cold is the way to welcome me?"

The two men stood toe to toe and stared at each other.

Suddenly, Garcia grinned and slapped Jeff on the back. "Get cleaned up and one of my men will bring you to my office." He turned and walked out. Both his men followed him.

No one on either side of the earbuds spoke but Jeff heard a collective sign from the other side. That initial meeting could have gone either way.

Since he was still alive, Jeff felt like he had won the first round. He cleaned up as best he could and opened the door again. This time there was only one guard who nodded for Jeff to follow him.

Without being obvious, Jeff took in his surroundings. He needed to gather as much information about the layout of the camp as possible. It was important to have an idea of how many men were in the camp and where their barracks were located. Just as important was where Garcia was located. Did he live in the same building as his office? If not, were the two buildings close to each other?

Jeff knew it would take time to gather all the information they needed. If he was not able to get Garcia away from his compound and away from his men, they would have to take him here. That would make this information vital.

The guard led Jeff to a building in the very center of the compound. It wasn't very large. Two rooms at the most and small ones at that. Jeff figured if this was his office, it wasn't his residence as well.

According to their Intel, Garcia liked his comfort and indulgent excesses. He would have much more lavish accommodations. Jeff needed to know where that was and also where the guards were stationed. All in good time. Now all his focus had to be directed toward this meeting.

The guard knocked at Garcia's door and without waiting for an invitation, opened it and ushered Jeff inside. Jeff filed this information away. It could be important. Evidently, Garcia had no secrets from his men. If that had happened in Clint Montgomery's compound, the transgressor would likely have been shot. But then, Jeff's last boss while he was undercover had plenty to hide.

Garcia was sitting behind his desk. He rose when Jeff and the guard entered. He had a variety of papers scattered across the top of his desk but didn't try to move or hide any of them. Something else that was different from Jeff's old boss.

Garcia nodded to the guard and said, "You can leave us." The guard glanced at Jeff before walking out and closing the door behind him.

Garcia walked over to a liquor cabinet and picked up a decanter of amber colored liquid. He held it up and looked at Jeff. "Join me in a drink?"

Thinking it was a little early in the day to be drinking but afraid to offend Garcia, he nodded. He watched as Garcia poured two drinks and walked back to his desk. He handed one to Jeff and then took a healthy swallow of his own before sitting back down. He motioned for Jeff to have a seat across from him. "Now, I would like to hear exactly why you are here."

Jeff chose his words carefully. "After you left Montgomery's compound, we were raided. Montgomery and most of his men were arrested and taken away. Being Montgomery's second in command, I knew a secret way off the island and was able to escape. I made my way here, thinking I could join your operation. It's a little hot in the States for me right now."

Garcia took another swallow of his drink. Most of it was gone already. That fact wasn't lost on Jeff. Could Garcia have a drinking problem? That

70

detail wasn't in any of the Intel they had gathered on him. Could his sister's death have affected him that much?

Garcia leaned back. "I don't need a second in command. We don't operate that way here. I am in command. All my men report directly to me. I like it that way. My men are fiercely loyal to me. They are afraid not to be. They have seen what happens to anyone that crosses me. In fact, I give them a little demonstration occasionally just so they won't forget. So how do you see yourself fitting into our operation?"

"I have no problem with that arrangement as long as you don't use me for that little demonstration. I was just one of Clint's men before Pete got killed. He needed someone to take Pete's place so I got promoted."

Garcia looked thoughtful. "That little promotion didn't have anything to do with your reason for killing him, did it?"

Jeff was taken aback by that statement. How did Garcia know about him killing Pete? Did Garcia have informants they didn't know about? That could be dangerous for all of them.

Jeff looked Garcia directly in the eyes. "I killed that son-of-a-bitch because he tried to shoot me. I would do the same to anyone else who tried that. If you know about Pete, then you have to have a little idea of the caliber of the men Clint hired. Appointing me as his second in command was a no-brainer."

Garcia never took his eyes off Jeff. He walked across the room and poured himself another drink. The look on his face made Jeff's blood run cold.

As Garcia once again took his seat, he smiled and said, "My sentiments exactly."

Jeff didn't realize he had been holding his breath. He wasn't armed. He had thought for a minute that Garcia was going to kill him on the spot. The man not only had a drinking problem, he was becoming unhindered. That was a dangerous combination.

Garcia was once again in control of himself. "Let me think about this for tonight and we'll talk again tomorrow. For tonight, consider yourself my guest."

Jeff stood. "I do have one request. My clothes and all my other gear are in my saddlebags on my Harley. Your men didn't exactly give me an opportunity to gather my things before escorting me here. My bike has probably been stolen or stripped by now but maybe my other gear is still around. I'd like to go retrieve my stuff."

Surprisingly, Garcia agreed. "I'll send one of my men with you. I own that cantina. I think you'll be surprised to find your bike exactly as you left it."

"Appreciate it," Jeff said. "I had my gun on me, I'd like that back as well."

Garcia just smiled. "You are a guest, my friend. You have no need of a gun. Go get your stuff and we'll talk tomorrow."

As Jeff walked out, he saw Garcia turn back to the liquor cabinet.

When Jeff left Garcia's office, one of the guards was waiting. He watched Jeff closely. It was obvious he didn't trust him. "I have been ordered to take you back to town to get your bike and other gear. Follow me."

Jeff didn't speak. He just followed the guard to an old beat-up truck and got in. As they left, Jeff was careful to watch the way they went. He had been unconscious on the trip to their camp. He had no idea where they were in relation to town. That information could be critical if things went south.

His companion hadn't said another word since getting in the truck. That was fine. The less he had to talk to any of the men, the less the chance of him slipping up and saying something to give himself away. He wouldn't have thought Garcia would have known about Pete, but he had. If Garcia truly didn't have secrets from his men, they knew as much as he did. Jeff was uncomfortable with just what else they might know.

As the guard left the road leading to the camp, Jeff was surprised at how close they were to the main road. He would have thought Garcia would have chosen a more isolated spot for his camp. Could it be he wasn't worried about the authorities? He remembered what Garcia said about owning the cantina. Could that apply to the whole town?

He thought about Perez and how things had gone so horribly wrong when they raided the small village where Garcia was supposed to have been. Intel provided to them by Perez.

He remembered how Perez, according to Hershel, had ordered his men to open fire. The other marshals had told him about the confrontation between Hershel and Perez. He hated he had missed that but he had been left behind at Perez's office. They had assumed Garcia was in that village. He could have identified Jeff. Garcia knew him as Clint Montgomery's second in command. His cover would have been blown.

Had Perez known that? Had Perez known Garcia wouldn't be there? Is that why he had tried to blame the botched raid on Hershel? To get them thrown out of Mexico? Was Perez working for Garcia?

If so, where did that leave General Morales? He hadn't court marshaled Perez, just transferred him. Did Garcia own General Morales as well? Is that why the General had insisted on joining them?

Jeff had no way to tell the other marshals of his suspicions without alerting Morales. Whatever he said through the earbuds, they all could hear. He hoped he was wrong. He liked the General. But the others needed to know to watch their backs till they could be sure of him.

All of this was conjecture on his part. But one thing he had no doubt of. If Perez had ordered the raid that had resulted in Garcia's sister's death, he was a dead man. Whether Perez worked for Garcia or not, he would kill him.

It didn't take long for them to reach town. A few minutes later they were pulling into the parking lot of the cantina where Jeff had left his bike. Just as Garcia had said, it was sitting there untouched. Just the way he had left it. Evidently Garcia not only owned the cantina, he owned everyone who patronized it. Either that or they knew his reputation and were afraid of him.

The guard pulled up beside Jeff's bike and cut the motor. He turned in his seat and scowled. "Get out and get your bike. I'll follow you back to camp. If you try anything, I will shoot you or maybe run you over, or both."

Jeff had to think fast. He needed a few minutes to contact Hershel when he could be absolutely certain no one could hear.

"That's fine," Jeff said. "I wouldn't want you to waste any of your bullets on my account." Jeff paused, as a thought came to him. "I do need gas though. I came straight here for a drink when I first got to town. I had planned to have a quick drink, fill up with gas and then find a place to stay. Your boss' unexpected invitation to be his guest changed those plans. I doubt I have enough gas to get back to camp."

"There is a place we can stop on the edge of town. It's on the way. Don't get any ideas. Like this place, Garcia owns it as well. I can shoot you there as easy as I can shoot you on the road. No one there will lift a finger to help you. And wasting a bullet would be my pleasure."

Without another word, Jeff got out. He checked his bike over to make sure it really hadn't been tampered with. He didn't check his saddlebags. He didn't want to draw attention to them. The one on the right had a false bottom just big enough to accommodate a small pistol. Every good law enforcement officer carried a backup weapon.

He started the bike and pulled out onto the road. As promised, the truck stayed close behind him. A little too close. It looked like Garcia had taught his men the power of intimidation.

Jeff pulled into the small station. It was the last building before leaving town. He got out to pay before pumping his gas. His guard got out as well and followed him inside. The guard and clerk nodded to each other. It was obvious they were acquainted.

Jeff paid and walked out, passing the guard on the way. When he got to the pumps, he fumbled around, making it look like he was trying to figure out how the pump worked. He reached up like he was scratching him head and pressed the earbud.

Nothing. Jeff cursed under his breath. He was out of range. It was more than a mile back to camp. Well, at least he had a full tank of gas. If it became necessary, he could make a fast getaway. That is, if Garcia didn't take his key or lock up his bike.

Jeff would have to try and contact the others while he was riding. That would be tricky with the guard on his bumper watching every move he made and the wind rushing by making it hard to hear.

Jeff judged the distance and when he thought he was about a mile from camp, he casually reached up with one hand as if adjusting his helmet.

"Can you hear me?" he said as loud as he dared. The guard had the windows down in the truck and was leaning out just a little. Jeff figured that was to make it easier to shoot him, if he tried to take off. He didn't think the guy smart enough to think a step ahead but maybe he was wrong.

He could hear Hershel through the earbuds, but just barely. "Jeff, where are you? Are you still in camp? You've been out of contact for over an hour. We were worried something had gone wrong. We didn't hear you say the code word. If you had said rocket, we would have stormed the camp but instead there was just silence."

Jeff did something he had never dared before but he was running out of time. He interrupted his boss.

"I only have a few minutes. Just listen. I'll explain more tonight after everyone else is asleep and I think it's safe to talk."

Jeff told them about the layout of the camp and the guards that he had been able to spot. He just had time to fill them in on Garcia's drinking and state of mind when he made the turn leading to camp.

"Later," he said. Afraid to push his luck.

Chapter 11

Victoria and Beth left Hadbury heading for Richmond. They should make it by daybreak. Each was lost in their own thoughts. Both ladies were close to Rebecca although their experiences with her were vastly different.

Beth had met her on an island filled with drug smugglers. She had forced Hershel, Joe and Albert to take her along to rescue Nancy and Mary Alice after they had been kidnapped. Beth had convinced the men her nursing skills would be needed. That was true. However, more important, Nancy and Mary Alice were her dear friends and she wasn't going to be left behind if they were in trouble.

Rebecca had done more or less the same thing with Hershel's marshals that had been left back at the office in Richmond. She knew her husband was in trouble. She coerced Bill, Cliff and Andrew into taking her along to find him. She told them Hershel would be upset if they left her to follow them on her own. He would have been. But he was even more upset when he realized they had brought her into the middle of a dangerous situation.

Beth and Rebecca met on that island and a friendship was formed that could never be broken. If Rebecca was in trouble, she was going to do anything she could to help.

Victoria met Rebecca after Hershel, Joe, Albert and Beth had left to track down Nancy and Mary Alice.

Rebecca and the marshals from Richmond had reached Hadbury in the middle of the night. They had stopped at Victoria's Bed and Breakfast to wait for morning. They needed information that would lead them to Hershel and the others. They were forced to wait till daylight to question anyone with information they could use.

Victoria and Rebecca had made an instant connection. They both were mothers. It didn't matter that Victoria's children were still virtually babies and that Rebecca's were grown. Once a mother, always a mother.

And just as important, Victoria met Andrew. She didn't think she would ever see him again after that night. But the attraction hadn't been one sided. Andrew had found reasons several times to return to Hadbury and Victoria's Bed and Breakfast. After the first return visit, Hershel and Rebecca had found a reason to follow him.

Victoria and Rebecca had renewed their brief acquaintance and became fast friends.

Now Andrew needed her, and her dear friend, Rebecca, was missing. She was going to do anything she could to help.

Beth navigated the early morning traffic in Richmond, as if she did it every day. In reality, Richmond was much larger than the small town of Hadbury. Not much intimated Beth. Heavy traffic didn't have a chance.

Victoria watched as they passed the large buildings. "I don't see how Andrew lives here. Too big, too much traffic, too much everything," she said.

Beth glanced over at her friend. "His whole life has been at the marshal's office for years. From what I hear, he spends very little time at home. He's the first to arrive in the mornings and the last to leave at night. He lives to be a marshal." Beth hesitated. "If you'd give him a little more encouragement, that might change some. I mean, he'll always want to be a marshal but it wouldn't be his whole life. He loves you, Victoria. Anybody can see that."

Victoria seemed to be giving this some thought. Finally, she said, "I don't know. When Gary died, I thought I would never love another man. Now that he's gone, I'm afraid to try. Besides I have the kids to think about. I'm not sure how to introduce another man into their lives."

Beth reached over and patted her friend's hand. She didn't want her words to cause any pain but they needed to be said. "Honey, do you really think the twins remember their dad? They're so young and were just babies when Gary died. And as far as introducing someone else into their lives, you've already done that. Just give it some thought. This is between you and Andrew. He's a good man. The twins will be fine."

Victoria was saved from having to answer. They had arrived at the marshal's office. It was never a question of coming here or going to Andrew's house. They knew where he'd be.

They found him just where they thought they would. He was in his office in front of a bank of computers. On one screen were several blips of light. They moved in various directions and then converged back together. One seemed to be off by itself and never joined the others. By process of elimination, Andrew knew the solitary one was Jeff. He had not activated his device when he had Hershel, Bill and Cliff's. When he had, his blip had appeared in a different location. He wasn't with the others but that was all Andrew could tell. That and the fact all four men were accounted for. On the other screens were words and numbers that only Andrew could decipher.

Beth tapped on the door and walked in with Victoria close behind her. They waited for Andrew to look up. He was so involved with what he was doing, it took him a minute to notice who was standing in front of him.

In his haste to reach Victoria, he nearly bowled Beth over. She quickly stepped to the side.

Andrew gently pulled Victoria into a tight embrace. Finally noticing Beth, he stepped back from Victoria. He cleared his throat. "I don't know how you two managed it, but thanks for coming." He hadn't completely let go of Victoria. He was still holding tight to her hand.

Beth walked over and gave him a quick hug. "You needed us and we came. It's as simple as that. I wasn't going to let Victoria make that drive by herself especially in the middle of the night. Bill and Nancy have the twins and Albert and Mary Alice are minding the Bed and Breakfast. Now. What can we do?"

Andrew looked slightly embarrassed. He didn't normally let his emotions get the best of him. But this was Rebecca, his friend, his boss's wife. "Nothing. You can't do anything. I shouldn't have called you."

Andrew looked so lost; Victoria led him over to a chair. Ever the caretaker, she said, "Where can we get some coffee? It was a long drive and we could use some."

As if just now remembering they had driven all the way from Hadbury, Andrew said, "I can do better than that. Come on, I need to get out of this office for a little while. There is a little diner just down the block. They serve the best breakfast outside of yours." He squeezed Victoria's hand. The one he had yet to let go of.

Andrew locked the door to his office and escorted the ladies out of the building. "My car's over there if you want to ride."

Victoria pulled Andrew to a stop. "Didn't you say it was just down the block? We've been riding for a while. I had just as soon walk if it's all the same to you."

Andrew took each lady's arm and turned then in the opposite direction. "Not a problem. It would do me good to get some exercise. I've been hovering over that computer all night. I am so glad you both are here. There really is nothing you can do. Heck, there's nothing I can do. But at least I'm not by myself. Thank you. Both of you."

Nothing else was said till they reached the diner.

As they entered, they were greeted by the proprietor. "Andrew, so good to see you. It's been over a week. Where have you been?"

Andrew usually stopped in for coffee and a quick bite to eat every morning on his way to the office. He shook hands with the rotund little man and tried to smile. "It's been crazy busy at the office. But I brought two lovely ladies with me to make up for my absence."

Andrew introduced Victoria and Beth to Henry and they were seated at a table with a lovely floral tablecloth with a fresh bouquet of yellow daisies in the center.

Henry took their orders and left to hand them over to his wife, who ruled the kitchen. And Henry too, but he'd never admit it.

After Henry brought them coffee, he left to take care of the other customers, who were beginning to pour in.

While they waited for their food, Victoria turned to Andrew. "Alright, take your time, start at the beginning and tell us everything."

Andrew took a sip of his coffee. He told them about Rebecca stopping by his office. Her frantic call after she had gotten home. His call to the local PD for backup and their search of her house.

Victoria and Beth just sat for a minute without saying a word. Finally, Beth said, "And you found nothing. She was just gone?"

Andrew dropped his voice to a whisper. "I found her phone in the closet where she dropped it."

Victoria took a deep breath. "And no one's contacted you about a ransom or anything?"

"No," Andrew said. "But you see no one would know to call me. If they wanted money, they would call Hershel and his phone is being held at the police headquarters of the small town they are in. He won't get it back till he's headed out of the country. Some weird thing to do with the security of the case he, Jeff, Bill and Cliff are on."

"And there's no way to track her?" Beth knew the answer but had to ask. If there was, Andrew would have already done it.

Before Andrew could answer, Henry was back with their food. After he placed the plates in front of them and left to help his wife in the kitchen, Andrew just shook his head. "Not without her phone. If she had the time and thought to do so, she could have slipped it in her pocket. Then I could use the GPS to track her. But the phone was on the closet floor where she was hiding when she called me."

He pushed his plate back untouched. Victoria nudged it back toward him. "Eat. We don't know what will happen now but If we get a clue and have to act, we need the strength this food will give us."

They all cleaned their plates and stopped on the way out to thank Henry for the delicious breakfast. No one spoke as they made their way back to Andrew's office.

"How do we know this has anything to do with Hershel and the case he's working on?" Victoria said as they opened the front door to the building.

"We don't," Andrew said. "We all know what Rebecca faces every day at work. She faces some pretty bad characters. She gets threats all the time but no one has ever followed through with any of them. The children she represents come from terrible environments. Mostly the parents don't really care if they get their children back. They are just mad because they've been dragged into court. Once they leave the courtroom, they forget all about their threats. Their children too in most cases."

Victoria shook her head. "How can people treat their children that way? The twins are the most important thing in my whole world. I would die for them. I am so thankful for people like Rebecca who are willing to stand up for them."

Andrew and Beth agreed as they made their way back to Andrew's office.

As Andrew took his seat behind his computers, the ladies pulled their chairs up close so they could see what he was doing. He explained the little blips on one of the screens, much as he had to Rebecca.

Beth was looking thoughtful. "Andrew, didn't you say the local police responded to your call for backup?"

Andrew nodded. "They were closer than anyone from here would have been. I know most of those guys. I've helped on some of their cases when my expertise was needed." What he didn't say was that the Richmond Police

Department had tried to hire him away from the Marshals. He had refused and hadn't seen any reason to bring it up to Hershel. No need to stir up hard feelings between the two departments of law enforcement.

Beth and Victoria exchanged glances. They were on the same page. "Well," Beth said. "Have you touched base with them? You said they had called in their crime scene techs. Maybe they found something. You know, trace evidence, DNA. Whatever."

Andrew had to smile a little at Beth's terminology. She was on a roll but her thought process was spot on.

"That's not a bad idea. Hold on. I'll see who's in the office. I wouldn't get my hopes up though. I searched the entire house pretty good myself and didn't see anything. I was thorough."

Beth and Rebecca waited while Andrew made the call. When someone answered, Andrew put it on speaker.

They listened to the detective that had been assigned the case and their hopes plummeted. They had gone over the entire house and found nothing that didn't seem to belong there. They dusted all the doors and windows for prints. They had even dusted the closet door and handle since that was the last place Rebecca was known to have been. Since Hershel was a marshal and Rebecca worked for Child Protective Services, they were able to check the prints they found against the ones in their data base. They were all identified and none of them were suspicious. Either the perpetrator hadn't touched anything or he had worn gloves. The latter was probably the case.

Andrew put his head in his hands. "OK. Thanks for checking and keep me in the loop if anything comes up."

The detective could be heard talking to someone who had just entered his office. "Hold on a minute, Andrew."

They could hear a shuffling sound on the other end of the line. Two voices came through, trying to talk over each other. The detective and a female. The detective said, "Hey, wait a minute. I don't come into your lab and take over your phone calls. Get back."

"You can't get into my office when I'm working. I lock the door," the female voice said.

Finally, the female voice won out. "Hi Andrew. It's Betty. I put you on speaker. I wanted to tell you and this not-head both what I found at the same time. I don't like having to repeat myself. Some people are just so territorial."

"Betty, it's good to hear from you," Andrew said. "I sure hope you've found something that'll help. I have nothing and I've set here all night worrying. This is Rebecca. You know?"

"I know. That's why I came in last night and kept at it until a few minutes ago," Betty said.

Betty was the top forensic scientist at the Richmond Police Department. The Marshals Service had been after her for years. Like Andrew, she was happy where she was.

"Well," she said. "This may not help much but I wasn't given much from the scene to work with."

At this point they heard the detective mutter something they couldn't make out. Betty just kept on talking as if he hadn't spoken. "There was a tiny smear on the carpet just to the outside of the closet. It was almost overlooked. It was really small and almost the same color as the carpet. Shit!" she said.

Andrew loved Betty dearly but he was tired and giving out of patience. "Betty! What did you find?"

"Shit," she said again. "Andrew, I found shit. To be more specific, chicken shit."

Andrew could hear the excitement rising in Betty's voice and knew there was more. "This particular chicken is native to only one place. Mexico."

"Can you pinpoint the region?" Andrew asked, knowing it was a long shot.

"Sorry. They are all over Mexico. I hope that helps a little." Andrew could hear the disappointment in her voice.

"You've been a big help, Betty," Andrew sighed. "If you come up with anything else, let me know." He hung up the phone and slowly looked up at Victoria and Beth. "Garcia has her," he said. "Heaven help us all. Garcia has Rebecca."

Chapter 12

Rebecca woke with a start. Her first thought was that she was naked. She lay still and let her mind wander. She reviewed all the events of the past days. She was safe, for now. She knew it wouldn't last. Her abductor wouldn't let her go that easy. He would have gotten out of the handcuffs by now. He was working for Diego Garcia. Failure wasn't an option. If he went back to Garcia without her, he would be shot. Or worse.

Rebecca got up and made her way down to the water. She drank her fill and then waded out to the deeper water. At its deepest, it only came up to her chest. She sank down till the water covered her head. Another bath would have felt good but she had used up her small supply of soap.

With a sigh, she made her way back to the water's edge. When she was all the way out, she shivered. It was cold but not the bone-chilling cold she had experienced the night before. She wondered if maybe the trees and plants held in more of the days heat than the open desert. She had no idea. She was just thankful.

Rebecca knew she needed to get dressed. She found what remained of the toilet paper she had wrapped herself in the night before and used it to dry off. She had to smile at the thought of what Hershel would have said if he had seen her all wrapped up like a mummy. Well, hard circumstances called for innovative action. She had improvised.

As she pulled her clothes from the branches where she had hung them to dry, she took stock of her meager supplies. She had used all the toilet paper and fed a mountain lion the chocolate. She had used all the soap the day before. *Let's see*, she thought. *That leaves two empty water bottles, a fork, a pencil and a paper bag she had yet to open.* She unrolled the top of the bag and peered inside. A can of fix-a-flat. Well, if she came across a car with a flat tire, she would be all set. You just never knew. She didn't think she would be feeding chocolate to a mountain lion either.

Rebecca finished dressing and stuffed all her supplies back into her pockets. She buried the wet toilet paper. When she left, she wanted nothing to indicate she had ever been here. She didn't know if her abductor would come this way, but she didn't know that he wouldn't.

There were several bushes a few yards further back from where she was standing. Thinking they might help her keep warm till morning, she crawled in among them. It might just be wishful thinking but it did seem to help. That and the fact she was no longer naked.

Rebecca sat with her knees drawn up to her chest. She needed to think. She needed a plan. It had been late afternoon when she found this oasis. She had stayed in the water at least an hour and then washed her clothes and hung them up to dry. It had just been getting dark when she had stretched out and went to sleep.

How long had she slept? She had no idea. It was still dark. When she got home, she was going to buy a watch. She had never seen the need of one before. She always had her cell phone. Well Rebecca, she thought to herself, how's that working out for you?

With no way of knowing how long she had till daylight, she turned her thoughts to what she could do the next day. She had all her pockets packed and ready to go. She couldn't travel in the heat of the day. She was weaker than she was when all this started. Besides she didn't know what resources her abductor had access to. If he could get his hands on a plane, she would be an easy target to spot when it was light. No, it would be cooler and safer to travel at night.

The next question was which way to go. Here she drew a blank. All she knew was she couldn't go back the way she had come. One of Garcia's thugs and a mountain lion lay in that direction. Maybe when it was light, she could see something that would help her decide.

Well, she couldn't do anything else tonight. She needed to sleep. Maybe sleep would help renew some of her strength and give her clarity of mind.

Rebecca curled up on the ground and pulled one of the bushes closer around her for warmth. It was a testament to how tired she was that she fell asleep immediately.

Rebecca woke to the full light of day. Something wasn't right. She lay perfectly still. Afraid to move. She was being watched. She could feel it. Had her abductor caught up to her? What was he waiting for? Cold sweat ran down her back.

She didn't want her life to end this way. She wanted more time with her kids. She wanted more time with her friends back in Hadbury. She and the other ladies had been plotting the best way to get Victoria and Andrew together. They just needed a little nudge. She wanted to be there to help with that. She wanted to see Hershel. Oh, how she wanted to see Hershel again!

OK. If her abductor had found her, she was going to fight. She wouldn't make it easy for him. He had told her if she tried to get away again, he would kill her. Somehow, she didn't think he would. Garcia wanted her alive. If he hadn't needed her alive, the thug he sent would have killed her there in the closet. He could have done that and taken proof back to Garcia that he had completed his mission. But he took her instead. She had no doubt he would hurt her but she didn't believe he would kill her.

With this newfound determination set firmly in her mind, she jumped to her feet ready to fight. She turned in all directions but no one was in sight. But the feeling of being watched was stronger than ever.

Rebecca eased out of the bushes. Then she saw it. A movement up by the tree line. She couldn't make out what it was from here. It didn't look large enough to be a man. Her next thought was the mountain lion. Had he tracked her to this oasis? Was this it's watering hole? Was she going to be its breakfast after all?

Holding on to her determination to fight, she slowly made it closer to the tree line. She picked up a large stick on the way. She wasn't totally defenseless.

She made it to the shade of one of the larger trees and peered around it. What she saw almost made her drop her stick. A rabbit. The largest she had ever seen. His back was to her. Rebecca looked down at her stick. She was close enough to hit him. She was almost hungry enough to do so. Almost.

She watched what he was doing, knowing she would never be able to kill him. No, she couldn't hurt him but she could join him. He was eating some of the biggest berries she had ever seen.

She eased from around the tree. As if just now sensing her presence, the rabbit took off into the underbrush.

Rebecca lost no time taking his place at the berry bush. She stuffed several in her mouth at once. They were delicious. She briefly wondered if they might be poisonous. But just as quickly dismissed that idea. The rabbit had been eating them. They had to be fine.

When she had eaten her fill, she looked down at her hands. They were stained a dark purple. She figured her mouth was too. She didn't care. There was no one to see anyway.

Rebecca made her way back to the water and drank her fill. She was no longer hungry nor was she thirsty. Something was finally going her way.

She took the two water bottles out of her pocket and filled them up. She needed something to put some berries in to take with her.

She found some large leaves and wove them together into something resembling a mat. After making her way back to the berry bushes, she filled it full of the luscious ripe berries. Next, she unwound a long vine from one of the trees and gathering the edges of her makeshift basket together, tied it up leaving enough vine to loop over her shoulder.

She had been a girl scout years ago but never thought these survival skills would actually come in handy. At the time, it had just seemed like play. Now, it might save her life.

With nothing else to do but wait for dark, she walked to the far side of her little oasis. She didn't want to leave and face the harsh desert. But she couldn't stay here. She had to get back to civilization and find someone to help her. She had to get back to Hershel.

Rebecca stood looking out at the horizon. She slowly turned in a circle. There to the south she saw what looked like mountains. She couldn't tell how far. It didn't matter. There was nothing else but desert.

When the sun was all the way down and it was a little cooler, she would head in that direction. With a small prayer, she went back to sit beside the water and wait. She was as prepared as possible.

She found a place she could sit and lean back against a rock. Pulling off her shoes, she dangled her feet in the water. She wouldn't sleep but she would rest. She let her mind wander back to the night she had been taken. Had she left any clues to help Andrew find her? She didn't think so. Her phone had been knocked out of her hand before she could do more than tell him she needed help.

Unless her abductor had left some clues as to where he was taking her, there would be nothing to indicate where she was or where she was headed.

She wondered what Hershel would do when he got home and she was gone. Would he figure out Garcia had sent someone to abduct her? Would he set back out for Mexico? Would he fall into Garcia's trap? Not if she could help it. She would find help. She would get back home and be waiting when Hershel got there.

The light had faded. It was cooling down. It was time to go. She got up and took one last look around her and headed back into the desert.

*

Rebecca's abductor cursed and yanked on the handcuffs that had him tethered to the steering wheel. How had that little slip of a woman gotten the upper hand on him?

He watched as she took off across the desert. Where did she think she was going? He had no doubt he would catch her. He just hoped she didn't kill her fool self before he could capture her again.

He had threatened to kill her, but he knew if he didn't get her to Garcia alive, he was a dead man. Garcia had made that plain when he sent him on this mission.

He tried to reach the glove box. He had thrown the keys in there. She wasn't a complete fool, she had handcuffed his right hand to the steering wheel. No way could he reach the glove box with his left hand.

He tried to twist his body around in the seat but he was too large. He was going to need help from someone else. He took one last look in the direction Rebecca had gone and was surprised to see how far she had gotten. She was almost out of sight.

Finally giving up his struggle with the handcuffs, he sat down on the car's horn. He knew a clerk was inside the station. He was probably too frightened to come out.

Well, he would make him too frightened to stay inside. Taking out his gun, he aimed at the door. He shot twice and then set down on his horn again. Again, nothing. This time he aimed for the windows. He placed a shot in each one shattering the glass. Still, no one came out. But ten minutes later, he heard a motor being cranked on the other side of the building. The clerk was making a run for it.

As the car came careening around the corner of the station, he took careful aim. He needed the clerk to come back. Being careful not to hit the man, he shot out both taillights. He would like nothing better than to aim for the back of the man's head. But a dead man couldn't retrieve the key to these damn handcuffs.

Both taillights exploded. But the man didn't stop. He just stomped on the accelerator, making the car fishtail, before he regained control and careened around a bend in the road putting him out of sight.

The thug slammed his free hand against the steering wheel. This was all that damn woman's fault. She had put him in this mess. He still wasn't worried about catching her. She really didn't have anywhere to go and she wasn't smart enough to survive in that desert.

And that was the problem. She wouldn't survive. He would be forced to face Garcia with only her body. He had seen what Garcia did to men who failed to carry out their mission.

Garcia had always been someone you didn't want to cross. But since his baby sister was killed, he had become vicious. Add his excessive drinking and he was a time bomb just waiting to go off.

No, he couldn't fail. He had to find that stupid woman before she got herself killed. And by doing so sealed his fate as well. He banged his hand against the steering wheel and let loose with another round of colorful words that would have done a sailor proud.

He had no choice but to wait. Someone was bound to stop for gas eventually. And this time he would be careful not to scare them away till he was free.

It had been dark for several hours before a lone car pulled into the station. They must have been stopping for something other than gas because they stopped in front instead of pulling around back to the pumps.

He thought about yelling but didn't want to scare them off so he waited. Surly they would look back here when they couldn't locate the clerk.

That thought had just occurred to him when the back door opened and a small dark-haired boy of about eight stepped through. The boy looked around outside and called over his shoulder to someone inside. "I don't see him. I'll check on the other side of the gas tanks."

When the child was close enough, the thug called out, "Hey boy, I bought this bag of candy inside and it's too much for me. Would you like the rest of it?"

The boy hesitated. He knew better but the lure of free candy was just too much for him. He slowly approached the car. "What kind of candy" he asked as he inched a little closer.

The thug had to think quick. He had to get the boy to come closer. If he bolted and ran back inside, he would lose this opportunity. It might be hours before someone else came by.

"You'll have to come closer and see. I have a bum arm and I can't hand it out the window to you. There're all kinds in there. Chocolate, coconut, caramel. A few of those big all-day suckers."

The boy was just out of reach when the back door to the station opened and a man stepped out. "Joseph, what are you doing? Get away from that car and back in here this minute."

The thug couldn't lose this opportunity. He raised his gun and held it far enough out the window so it could be seen by not only the boy but his father as well.

The man froze where he was. "Don't shoot my son. Please. What do you want? I'll do anything, just don't shoot my boy. If you want money, I'll give you all I have." The man was almost in tears.

The thug was enjoying the man's fear but he didn't have time to play with him. "Come out here and do as I say and nobody will get hurt. Do it now or I'll put a bullet in the kid's leg. The next one will be to his head."

The father needed no other encouragement, he hurried out the door to stand beside his son.

"That's better," the thug smirked. "Now come around to the other door and get the key to these handcuffs out of the glove box and get these things off me." He shook the handcuffs for emphasis. "The boy stays right where he is until I'm free."

The father lost no time doing what he was told. Then hurried back to his son. "I did what you wanted. Can we go now?" He had placed himself in front of his son.

The thug raised the gun a little higher. He loved seeing the fear on the other man's face. Finally, he said, "Alright, get out of here," and for emphasis shot off a round at the man's feet.

The terrified man grabbed his son by the hand and ran. They could hear the thug laughing as they sped away from the station.

The thug stretched and walked over to the other side of the road to look in the direction he had last seen Rebecca. She was nowhere in sight. He shook his head. He wasn't worried. He'd find her in the morning. Probably half dead.

He headed back to the station. Might as well see what was worth stealing inside and make himself comfortable till first light.

Chapter 13

Jeff arrived back in camp with the guard following close behind. When he parked and cut the motor, the guard let his truck roll forward just enough to bump Jeff's bike.

Jeff tensed but forced himself not to react. He could tell the guard was spoiling for a fight. If the odds were a little more in his favor, he would have been happy to oblige. Leaving his bike parked beside the cabin he'd stayed in the night before, he went inside and shut the door. He figured if they wanted him somewhere different, he'd find out soon enough.

A glance out the window, assured him his guard had resumed his post by the door. Jeff turned his back and facing the opposite direction, touched his earbud. "Back in the nest."

He could hear General Morales chuckle. "I see we're birds today," he said. "Kind of reminds me of the way you went flying by us a few minutes ago. Was all your gear the way you left it?"

Jeff hated to be suspicious of the General but until he was one hundred percent sure where his loyalties lay, he had to be careful. "It seemed to be all there. I convinced my guard to let me stop to fill up with gas. I thought it would give me a chance to talk more freely but I was too far out of range."

Bill spoke up, "Any sign of Garcia since you got back?"

Jeff turned briefly to glance out the window. "No. He's nowhere in sight. In fact, the whole place looks kind of deserted. I wonder if he took advantage of my absence to attend to some business elsewhere?"

Hershel broke in, "Watch for him. See if you can tell if he and his men left the camp. They didn't come by us so if he did, he's got another way in and out. That would be vital information for us to have."

Before anyone else could speak, Jeff heard some shuffling going on with the other men. "What's up?" he said.

"General Morales just got a call and walked off to answer it," Cliff said. "I guess he didn't want to talk in front of us. Whatever it was, it was short. Here he comes back."

Jeff knew he had missed an opportunity to talk to the guys without the General hearing.

When General Morales rejoined the others, it was obvious he wasn't happy. "That was my precinct with some disturbing news. Perez seems to be missing. No one's seen him since yesterday. He was obviously upset when I reassigned him, but I wouldn't have thought he would have just taken off."

"Maybe he didn't take off of his own accord," Hershel spoke up. "If Garcia is gone and Perez is as well, there could be a connection."

Jeff felt chills run down his spine. "Hey guys. Don't forget; he's the only one who can identify me as a United States Marshal. If he's in cahoots with Garcia and he ends up here, I'm as good as dead."

Hershel cleared his throat. He didn't want to split his men up in case they had to go in and rescue Jeff. But Jeff would be in more danger if Perez showed up in Garcia's camp and blew his cover. If that happened, he doubted they could get to him in time. "There's only one thing we can do," he said. "Find Perez. General Morales, would you be comfortable taking Bill and going to find Perez while Cliff and I back up Jeff here?"

Morales looked thoughtful. "I don't think I have a choice. He's, my man. That makes him my responsibility. If he's in league with Garcia, he's dangerous. If he's not, he may be in trouble. In any case, he's, my responsibility."

Bill looked from General Morales to Hershel. "I'm good with that. It's not that far back to the truck. It shouldn't take more than an hour to hike back there. We need to leave the hummer here. If things go bad Hershel; you, Cliff and Jeff need a way to get out of here in a hurry. With us gone you will be badly outnumbered. Running will be your only option."

With that plan in place, Bill and General Morales eased back through the trees, heading back the way they had come. They needed to find Perez and get back as fast as possible.

Hershel looked at Cliff. His youngest, most inexperienced marshal. Cliff blushed as if reading his mind.

"You can count on me, Hershel. I won't let you down."

Hershel nodded at Cliff and said to Jeff, "Don't take any chances. If Perez shows up or something else goes wrong, get out of there. Head back the way you came in on your bike. We're not far away. We'll intercept you."

Jeff nodded his head and then remembering they couldn't see him, glanced out the window again and spoke softly, "Sounds like a plan."

Not knowing if Morales was still in earshot, he was hesitant to voice his concerns to Hershel concerning the man. He would wait. He'd get his opportunity later tonight. Jeff wanted to wait at the window for a sign of Garcia but he was exhausted and his head had begun to ache again from being hit with the butt of a gun. He was a little tired of undercover work. He'd been doing it a long time. He had seen what happened to other undercover marshals when they burned out. Most left the marshals all together.

He didn't want that to happen to him. We wanted to stay a marshal. Just not in this lone wolf capacity. He wanted to work side by side with the other guys. He wanted more of a life. He wanted someone to go home to at night. The way Hershel did to Rebecca.

Jeff stretched out on his cot. What he needed now was sleep. And as if his body agreed, he was asleep in minutes.

Jeff woke to a loud banging on his door. It was dark. Not waiting to turn on a light, he stumbled to the door and threw it open. "What the hell? Can't a man get any sleep around here?"

Jeff expected to see his surly guard. But instead, Garcia was leaning against the porch railing as if he could hardly stand on his own.

He slurred his words only a little. "Come out and celebrate with us, my compadre. We have had much success this night. We will eat the fatted pig, no. Then we will drink to my many successes."

Garcia grabbed Jeff's arm with one hand and shot his rifle into the night sky with the other.

A bonfire had been started in the center of the camp and sure enough a fat pig was slowly being roasted. The aroma reminded Jeff how long it had been since he'd eaten. Bread and liquor had been lined up on a table that had been set up for that purpose.

It looked like Garcia and some of his men had been drinking for quite a while. They stumbled around, talking loudly and randomly shooting their guns into the air.

The guards however, were stone-cold sober. It seemed Garcia wasn't so far impaired that he allowed all his men to let their guard down at the same time. It would be well for Jeff to remember that.

He fixed a plate of roast pig and bread, poured some water into a tin cup and found a place to sit beside Garcia. Looking at the outlaw, he said. "This is some celebration. What's the occasion?"

Garcia took another long drink from his bottle. He hadn't bothered with a cup, nor was he drinking water. "We just acquired some prime product from a competitor. He wasn't happy to let it go but we can be very persuasive. He won't be needing it anymore and it will bring us mucho dinero. Fentanyl brings much profit when we take it across the border to our distributors in your country."

Garcia laughed as he tore off another bite of pork and washed it down with a hefty swallow from his bottle.

Jeff had to reach way down for control. He wanted to kill this man. He thought of all the lives that would be destroyed just to line Garcia's pockets with more money. He vowed that wasn't going to happen if he could help it. The man was dangerous. He had to be stopped.

Jeff knew there were others waiting to take his place. He couldn't stop them all but he could stop this one. Maybe undercover work was what he was meant to do after all.

Garcia slapped him on the back. "Why so serious, Mi amigo? This is cause for celebration. It's good news for you as well. With your ability to slip from one side of the border to the other, your talents will come in handy. I have decided I can use you after all."

Jeff laughed and took a big bite of pork to hide his true reaction. He was afraid Garcia would be able to see the revulsion on his face. He was saved from having to make a reply when the beefy guard, who had been assigned to watching him, bumped into his shoulder, knocking his plate to the ground.

The man had obviously had enough alcohol to make him brave enough to confront Jeff right in front of Garcia. Either that or Garcia had egged him on.

The guard shoved Jeff again and said, "Think you're man enough to take my place? Stand up and we'll see who's the better man."

Garcia laughed and pushed away from the table. He stumbled a little as he slapped Jeff on the shoulder and said, "Looks like you're going to have to earn your place, my friend."

Garcia and the other men stepped back and made a wide circle around the two men.

Jeff just had time to wonder if Garcia had planned this, when he was struck from behind. The guard was drunk but still strong enough to knock Jeff out of his chair.

He hit the ground hard. The breath knocked out of him. Just as fast as he'd hit the ground, he was yanked back up again. This time, Jeff was ready. He came up with a hard fist to the other man's jaw. The man was big and one hit wasn't going to bring him down. It did make him stumble back a step though.

Jeff lunged forward, not wanting to lose his advantage. He drew back and hit the man in the stomach with all the strength he could muster. He wanted to end this as quickly as possible. He had a feeling it wasn't going to end well.

The guard went down but only to his knees. As he fell, he caught Jeff and took him down with him. Jeff rolled and tried to regain his feet but the guard held on. Jeff got in another punch to the man's jaw and tried to twist out of his grasp. The guard fell forward, pinning Jeff to the ground. The man outweighed Jeff by a good forty pounds.

Jeff's head snapped back as he was hit twice in the face. When the next punch came, Jeff was ready. He grabbed the man's fist before he could make contact and twisted, throwing him to the side. Jeff made it to his feet just in time to be hit from behind, knocking both men into the table. Their combined weight brought the table crashing down.

Jeff was on his feet first but the other man came up with the knife that had been used to carve the meat off the roasted pig. The man moved the knife from one hand to the other and back again.

Jeff didn't take his eyes off the knife. He would wait for the man to come at him with it before making his move. The knife had a long-wicked blade and would do a lot of damage if it made contact with any part of Jeff's body.

As the man lunged, Jeff stepped to the side and brought his fist down hard on the hand holding the knife. At the same time, he brought his knee up into the other man's stomach. As he doubted over, Jeff hit him in the back of the head knocking him out cold.

Jeff kicked the knife out of reach of the unconscious man and turned to face Garcia and his men. "Anyone else think they're man enough to take me?"

When no one else moved or spoke, Jeff started back to his cabin. He had enough of their celebration for one night. He had enough of being the main attraction. He needed to wash the blood off his face.

Jeff hadn't made it to the door of his cabin when a shot rang out. He twirled around and crouched. Not sure where the shot had come from. He slowly got to his feet as he took in the scene before him.

Garcia stood drunkenly over his own man, with a gun aimed at his head. He pulled the trigger a second time. The man's head jerked even though he was already dead. Garcia stepped back, letting the gun drop to his side. He weaved a little before looking up at Jeff. "I won't tolerate a loser," he said.

Bill and General Morales made it back to the truck without incident. Bill jumped in the passenger side and waited for the General to back out onto the road. "Do you know where to start looking?" he said to Morales.

The General thought for a minute. "We'll stop by his former office first. I know he cleared out his things when I took over there. He was living in a small house a few miles out of town. We'll check that out and ask around. If we don't get any answers then we'll make our way to his newly assigned office. It's in another town about sixty miles away. Since I was told he never showed up there, that will probably be a waste of time."

Bill thought for a few minutes. "Did he have any enemies that you know of? Was he involved with a woman? Maybe someone's wife?"

Morales snorted. "He was involved with lots of women. The kind that are involved with lots of men. Not exactly the kind someone would kill over." Morales paused. "As far as enemies, I don't know. He didn't have a lot of friends. The other men didn't seem to like him much. I have to admit, I didn't like him much myself. Something about him just didn't sit well with me."

"I know what you're saying, General. Hershel didn't like him either. He said he was a hothead that took too many shortcuts, then wasn't man enough to take responsibility for his actions."

The General laughed. "I guess it's a good thing Marshal Bing and I have been together all this time. If foul play has found its way to Perez's door, your boss would be my prime suspect."

At the look on Bill's face, Morales quickly added, "Calm down, marshal, I'm not serious. Your commander has quite the stellar reputation. I can see Hershel angry enough to beat the crap out of him, but he wouldn't kill him."

Morales paused, "So, you see, a lot depends on whether he's dead or just had the crap beat out of him. Like I said, it's a good thing your boss has been with me all this time."

The General laughed again. Although Bill knew he was just joking, he didn't laugh along with him. His respect for Hershel was just too great.

As they reached the edge of town, the General said. "I think I'll stop by his house first and see if he left anything there before we go on to the office."

They turned down a dirt drive and pulled up in front of a small house. It didn't take long to discover this was a dead-end. Perez hadn't been here in a while.

As they headed toward police headquarters, General Morales' phone rang. He fished it out of his shirt pocket. He pressed the button and accepted the call.

"Morales," he said as he pulled to the side of the road. "Can't you take care of it? I'm kind of in the middle of something. Alright, give me directions." He hung up and returned the phone to his pocket. "We've got to make a little side trip. My lieutenant has stumbled onto something he insists I need to see. It's only a few miles from where we were headed anyway."

Bill only nodded. He was beginning to have a bad feeling about this little side trip. They drove on in silence until Morales made a series of turns, taking them deep into the woods. When Bill was beginning to think they were being sent on a fool's errand, they made one last turn into a clearing and came to a sudden stop.

Three police cruisers were pulled up in front of an old rundown shack. The men were standing beside their cars except for one. He was bent over behind some bushes throwing up what was probably his last meal. No one said a word as Bill and Morales got out of the truck.

As they walked up to the men beside their cruisers, one of them stepped forward. All he said was "inside."

Morales and Bill walked up the three rickety steps onto the porch. They could smell the horrible odor of death before they even opened the door. They both drew their weapons, even though they knew there was no need. Whatever was waiting inside was no longer a threat.

Morales toed the door open and they entered. The place was ransacked. Chairs overturned. Table on its side. Lamps broken and blood everywhere.

Morales stopped and pointed toward the floor where a small amount of a white powder had been spilled.

"Drugs," Morales said. "Looks like fentanyl."

Bill walked to the other side of the over turned table. What had once been a man, lay sprawled on the floor. He had been beaten and tortured. And then he had been gutted.

"General," Bill said, "I think we just found Perez."

Chapter 14

Rebecca had been walking for several hours. She could feel the cold seeping into her bones. She stopped long enough to put her makeshift basket filled with berries on the ground. Slipping her arms out of the sleeves of her blouse, she tied the sleeves into a tight knot around her body.

Sliding one hand out from the bottom, she was able to put her basket back on her shoulder, looping it around her neck to hold it in place. She then wrapped both arms around her middle, under her blouse to keep as much body heat in as possible.

Knowing she had done all she could to keep warm in the cold night air of the desert, she tried to pick up the pace. Walking faster kept her warmer but it also sapped her energy faster. She couldn't think of that. She had to concentrate on putting one foot in front of the other.

She didn't look up at her destination. She didn't want to get discouraged. She would get there when she got there. She hoped. She kept repeating to herself, a watched pot never boils, a watched destination never gets closer.

After several more hours of walking, she knew she was going to have to stop and rest. She hated to take the time. If she was still on this desert when the sun came up, she would be in big trouble.

Rebecca slowly slid to the ground. It felt good to rest her feet and legs but she instantly began to feel colder. She couldn't stay here long. Wiggling her arms out from under her blouse, she opened her basket of berries. She ate a few, savoring the sweet taste. If this was all she had, it was a good choice. The high content of sugar in the berries would give her energy and the high content of juice would lessen her thirst.

She knew she would eventually need to find something to supplement the berries. Her body would need more nutrition than just what they provided.

For now, she was grateful for what she had. She closed her eyes and said a quick prayer. Giving thanks for the resources that had gotten her this far.

When Rebecca opened her eyes, she looked up. The sky looked vast and was covered with millions of stars. It was beautiful. She felt small and insignificant. Small yes. Insignificant no. She looked down at the wedding ring on her left hand. When Hershel had placed it there, he had promised that he would someday replace it with a set, each containing diamonds. She had what she wanted and told him so.

In thirteen years, they had four children. Three sons and one daughter. After each birth, Hershel had wanted to buy her those diamonds. After each birth, she had told him her babies were her diamonds.

No way could she be insignificant when someone loved her that much. Hershel wasn't perfect but, in her book, he wasn't far from it. Thinking of Hershel naturally led to thoughts of the brave marshals who worked under his command.

Bill had been with Hershel the longest. His loyalty to her husband was unquestionable and, by association, to her as well. Cliff was the youngest and lowest in seniority. Thinking of the boyish blush, he had never been able to lose, made her smile. Blush or not, he was all marshal. Any advisory, who came up against him, would do well to remember that. Then there was Andrew. If she had a favorite, he would be it. Andrew was her husband's top IT specialist. Organizations from all over had tried to recruit him. He was just that good. But Andrew wasn't just a tech, sitting in a computer lab all day. Like Cliff, he was also a tough, formidable marshal.

These three men had rushed to Hershel's rescue only six short months ago. She had bribed, threatened and cajoled them into taking her with them. They had ended up on an island inhabited by a band of drug smugglers.

This was where they had met Jeff. They didn't know at first that he was an undercover Marshal out of the New Orleans office. His contacts had gotten killed in a raid and he was on his own. If it hadn't been for his quick thinking, they would all have been killed.

Rebecca shifted, trying to find a more comfortable position and let her mind continue to drift.

Along with the adventure, she'd shared with these brave marshals, she had also acquired a whole new group of friends in Hadbury.

Victoria ran the Bed and Breakfast. She was a young widow with a set of rambunctious twins. She had a soft spot for Andrew too. Then there was Beth. She was a nurse at a local hospital. Bossy but loveable. Mary Alice owned

Bullets Firing Range. She had moved to Hadbury to escape an abusive husband and learned how to shoot for self-defense. Finding she had a talent for it, she opened the Firing Range in order to give lessons to other women who found themselves in similar circumstances. Nancy rounded out the list of her new best girlfriends.

She was retired and trying to live the good life, if only she could stay out of trouble long enough. These ladies along with Nancy's husband Joe and Mary Alice's husband Albert were now some of her closest friends.

Rebecca realized she had been sitting there, letting her mind wander far too long. She had a desert to cross and a vicious thug on her trail. She needed to move. Readjusting her berry basket, she once again started off toward what she hoped was civilization and someone to help her out of this mess.

What seemed like hours later, she stopped for a quick rest and a few swallows of her precious supply of water. This time she let herself look up at the mountain range that was her destination. To her delight, they now looked much closer. She could pick out details, she had been too far away to be able to see when she first left the oasis.

There wasn't just one big range of mountains, as it had appeared before. She now could pick out several different peaks with valleys in between. And the rock didn't just jump up out of the desert as it had appeared to do from further back.

But the best thing of all were the foothills. Small groupings of rock and scrubby looking bushes that stretched out to her like a welcoming hand.

Even if she didn't reach the mountains by daybreak, she could reach the foothills. There she could find a place to rest out of the sun. And if she was lucky, water. And if she was very lucky, something to eat besides berries.

Rebecca started off with renewed energy. She wouldn't reach help by daybreak but she would reach a place she could rest.

It was almost light when she reached the first rocky outcrop. She couldn't go another step. She climbed onto one of the lower rocks. Another larger rock provided some shade. She leaned back to rest, slipping off her shoes. She would only rest a moment, then make her way further up into the foothills. She was soon fast asleep.

Garcia's thug stood at the edge of the oasis. It hadn't been hard for him to pick up Rebecca's trail. He had reached the oasis just before dark and decided it would be a good place to spend the night.

He would have caught up with her by now, if his stupid car hadn't quit on him. He had waited at the station for someone to come by with a more suitable vehicle but that hadn't happened. He finally decided he would have to make do with what he had.

Several miles into the desert, the car started to run hot and finally died. He had no choice but to start walking. He wasn't worried about catching up with her. He knew he would eventually. Besides, she was heading in the right direction anyway. Mexico.

He turned back into the shade of the oasis, where he had left his backpack. It was light enough now to use his binoculars to scan the horizon for any sign of her. He had stolen the binoculars from the station and they were a good pair. In this flat terrain, he could see for miles. She couldn't be that far ahead of him.

He adjusted the magnification. And there she was. Sitting on a rock. Leaning back as if she hadn't a care in the world. Lowering the binoculars, he chuckled to himself. She would soon have plenty to worry about.

Knowing not only the direction she was headed but exactly where she was, made the decision to spend the hottest part of the day, exactly where he was. He would rest and start out again when it was cooler. He had her now. No way could she escape.

Rebecca came slowly awake. It took her a minute to remember where she was. She had crossed the desert. She had reached safely. Of sorts. Her muscles were stiff and her feet and back hurt but she was out of the desert.

The mountains would be cooler and the opportunity to find water and food greater. She had crossed a desert. She could climb a mountain, if she had to. But that was the worst-case scenario. Surely, she would find someone to help her before she had to do that.

No longer having to worry about traveling at night and resting in the heat of the day, she decided to make her way a little closer to the mountains before stopping for a nice long rest.

Leaving her perch on the rock, she set out once again. Now the terrain was rougher. Having been so glad to get off the sand, she hadn't thought how hard it would be to climb over rocks, while the incline got steadily steeper.

She had probably covered only a few miles, when she had to stop and rest. She had long since rearranged her blouse so she could use her hands to help her climb over boulders and through underbrush.

She eased her tired body onto a rock and took out her water. She had been drinking very sparingly. Using the juice from the berries in order to save as much water as possible. She took a few swallows of the precious liquid. She had emptied one bottle and started on another. She would have to find more water soon.

As she enjoyed a few of the berries, she thought about where she was going. It was a short thought. She had no idea. She could have been on the moon for all she knew.

Maybe she had made it all the way to California. Maybe if she made it to the top of these mountains, she would see the ocean. She had never seen the Pacific Ocean. She and Hershel had always planned to take a trip there someday. That someday had never arrived. Between her job and his and raising kids, there had never been time.

Well, when she got home, they were going to do that. Seeing the Pacific Ocean with Hershel was right up there with buying a watch. She was pretty sure she would find other things to add to that list before this nightmare was over.

As she got up and started climbing again, she knew this would be impossible to do at night. She had to make the most of the daylight hours. She pushed on until the fatigue was too much for her. By her estimation, she was about halfway through the foothills. The closer she got to the actual mountains, the more formidable they seemed.

She couldn't think about that now. She had come too far to become discouraged. She would tackle the mountains after she conquered the foothills.

But now, she had to rest. Exhaustion was taking over, making her clumsy. If she fell and broke a leg, she would die here. She had nothing to be ashamed of. She had walked across the desert all night and struggled through the foothills all day. It was almost dusk. Her mind was telling her it was time to rest. Her body was telling her it was past time.

Rebecca came to a small stand of trees. A few rocks were scattered about but it was fairly level and there was grass. It was also a little cooler. It would soon be completely dark. She wanted to be settled for the night before then.

Looking up into the trees, she saw there were plenty of branches low enough for her to reach. She broke off enough to make a bed of sorts, then looked around for something to cover with. She found some bushes with soft branches and feather-like leaves. She didn't know what they were, but they would make perfect cover.

She also found something else. A bird's nest with four tiny eggs in it.

Her hand hovered over them. She looked around. There was no mother bird in sight. Could she eat them? Could she think of them as just eggs and not baby birds?

She ate eggs from the grocery store. She didn't think of them as baby chickens. She wasn't even sure she could eat a raw egg.

She gently took the eggs from the nest and laid them aside. When she had finished breaking off enough branches to cover with, she removed her shoes and sat down on her makeshift bed.

She held the four small eggs in her lap. She hadn't seen the mother bird in all the time she'd been there.

Finally, she gave in to hunger. Her body needed the protein if she was going to make it out of this nightmare and back home. Reluctantly, she broke each tiny egg and swallowed what was inside. She tried not to think about them as babies, only a nutrient her body badly needed.

If a tear escaped and ran down her cheek as she lay down to sleep, well, there was no one around to see.

The thug had rested all day. He slept in the relative coolness of the oasis, much as Rebecca had. He had drunk from the refreshing water of the same pool as Rebecca. He had refilled his canteens, much as Rebecca had her water bottles.

Night had fallen. It was time for him to go. He was confident in his ability to catch up with her tomorrow. She would be in the foothills and her progress would be much slower.

He would catch up to her. He couldn't kill her but she would pay for all the trouble she had caused him. Then he would deliver her to Garcia. After that she would no longer be his problem.

His mission would be complete and Garcia would be pleased with him. He worried only a little that it had taken longer than anticipated. He couldn't let Garcia know that she had escaped and he had to track her down and recapture her. No. Garcia didn't need to know that.

Rebecca came fully awake with a start. She felt something was wrong. She felt like she needed to go, now. She listened, but could hear nothing. It didn't matter. The feeling was too strong to ignore. She put on her shoes, gathered her few belongings, and started up the incline.

Several times she looked behind her, but could see nothing. She didn't have to see to know he was there. He was catching up to her and she had no way to stop him.

Rebecca topped a small hill and stopped. Before her was a narrow valley, but what caught her attention was the small building at the end of a long winding road. She didn't know what it was but she headed for it. As she got closer, she thought it looked like an old school house. It was small. Only one room. It looked abandoned. There would be no one there to help her but maybe she could find something to use for a weapon.

It didn't matter. He was coming and there was nowhere else to run.

Rebecca made it to the door. All was quiet. She pulled it open only wide enough to slip through. The windows were dirty, keeping out most of the light. She hurried over to look out each window. Nothing outside moved but she knew he was there. She turned to hunt for anything that could be used to fight him off.

That's when she heard it. Only a small sound but it was coming from inside the building. Could he have gotten ahead of her? Could she have walked directly into his hands without even knowing it?

It took all Rebecca's courage to move further into the room. There was only one place she couldn't see. At the far side of the room was a large desk. It had probably been where the teacher sat.

She couldn't see behind it and that was where the sound had come from. Very slowly, she approached the desk. If he was there, it would do no good to run. She reached down and picked up a piece of wood. It looked like the leg of a small desk. It wasn't much but there wasn't anything better lying around on the cluttered floor. Rebecca held the piece of wood in one hand and placed the other on top of the desk. She raised up on her tiptoes and looked over the desk, ready to bash whatever was there.

What she saw stopped her cold. Two sets of eyes in the faces of two very scared little girls.

Rebecca laid the wood on the top of the table and calmly walked around to kneel in front of them. She reached out her hand and said, "Don't be afraid. I'm not going to hurt you. How did you get here? Where are your parents?"

The girls just pulled further away. Rebecca stayed where she was but looked them over to see if they were hurt. Other than being filthy, they seemed to be fine.

She held out her hand and tried again. "My name is Rebecca. I help little girls like you."

She waited but still no response. The girls were young. One looked to be about five and the other maybe seven.

She had finally decided they must not speak English, when the older girl spoke, "Please don't give us back to the bad men. They don't want us anyway. They just left us here." The girl reached back and put her arm around her sister.

Rebecca spoke softly, so as not to scare them more than they already were. "What were you doing with the bad men in the first place?"

She thought for a minute the little girl wasn't going to answer. Finally, she looked up at Rebecca again. "Our mother paid the men to bring us to America. She said we would be safe here and have a better life. Our father died last year and she's had a hard time feeding us. I think maybe she's sick. She hasn't looked well since our father died. But the men just left us here."

Rebecca reached out and wrapped her arms around the children. The oldest one clung to her but the youngest kept her arms around her middle and started crying.

Thinking the child might be sick, she said, "It's alright. Does your tummy hurt?"

The little girl just cried harder and kept her arms tightly around her waist.

Rebecca waited for the tears to subside before she spoke again. But when she started to speak, the little girl reached under her dress and pulling something out, said, "I was worried about my mother. When the man with the star wasn't looking, I stole his phone. I just wanted to call her and make sure she was alright. I know it's wrong to steal. My mom is going to be so mad at me." Once again, the child dissolved in tears.

Rebecca reached out and took the phone. She didn't know which shocked her most. The fact that she had a phone or that a man with a badge had been involved in leaving these precious little girls alone to die.

She had to hide these precious little girls and keep them safe. "Listen to me. You're right that it's wrong to steel but these men are bad. I don't think your mother will be mad at you under these circumstances. I have a plan but you've got to be very brave. Can you do that for me?"

Both girls nodded. Like Rebecca, they had no other choice.

Rebecca reached into her pocket and took out the pencil and paper bag with the fix-a-flat. She returned the can to her pocket. On the paper bag she wrote a note to Andrew. She told him to take these children to Victoria in Hadbury. She said they had been abandoned by coyotes and that one of them had worn a star. He was not to trust any official with them until this could be straightened out. The last thing she wrote was—tell Hershel I'm sorry.

She gave both girls a hug. "I'm going to find somewhere for you to hide. Someone will come for you. It will be a man and he will be wearing a star too but he's a good man and will take care of you."

She drew a picture of the badge of a United States Marshal and showed the girls. "His star will look like this. Don't be afraid to go with him."

Next, she punched in the number for Andrew's cell phone. When he answered, she didn't let him get past saying hello. She didn't have time to answer questions.

"Andrew, can you track this phone? Silly question. I know you can. Do it and get here quick. Lives depend on it. Use one of the helicopters that are kept for the emergency use of the marshals."

Rebecca was running out of time. She hung up and turned off the ringer on the phone. She didn't want Andrew calling back and trying to talk her out of what she was going to do next. She took the phone and the note and stuffed them both deep in the pocket of the oldest child.

"Come on, we need to find a place for you to hide." She found what she was looking for out behind the building. It looked like an old root cellar or place to store supplies. It was partially caved in. There was just enough space for the two small girls.

Before she let the heavy door close, she said, "Don't come out until my friend gets here to take you somewhere safe. Give him the note and trust him."

The girls nodded as Rebecca eased the door back in place. She didn't want to make any noise that would give away their hiding place.

Rebecca stood up and carefully made her way to the other side of the building. She stood waiting until the thug broke through the tree line. When she was sure he had seen her, she took off running. Just as she had known he would, he veered away from the school building and followed her.

As she ran, she whispered, "Don't be mad, Hershel. The children had to come first."

Chapter 15

Andrew stood staring at the phone in his hands. "It was Rebecca." As Beth and Victoria crowded around him, he hit redial. A generic voice answered and said to leave a voicemail.

Both ladies started talking at the same time. "What did she say? Where is she? Is she alright?"

Andrew jotted down the last call received from his phone's call history. He held up his hand for silence, as he entered the number into his computer. In under a minute, he leaned back and said, "Gotcha."

Beth, having given out of patience, grabbed Andrew's arm. "Talk. Andrew, talk. Tell us if she's alright and where she is."

"OK! OK! Give me a minute." Andrew entered some commands into his computer, grabbed his laptop, and tucked it under his arm.

In almost the same motion, he picked his phone up and hit a single digit. When the call went through, he said in the most official voice either lady had ever heard him use, "This is United States Marshal Andrew Long. I'm located in the Richmond office. I need a helicopter, fueled and ready to go at this location stat."

Victoria and Beth couldn't make out what the voice on the other end was saying, but they had no trouble hearing Andrew's reply.

"Don't you put me on hold! Damn it! Don't you dare put me on hold! I don't need a damn pilot. I've got this. You just have that bird sitting on the helipad on top of this building immediately, if not sooner!"

Andrew slammed the phone down and turned to storm out the door. But that was as far as he got. Beth and Victoria stood blocking his way.

Beth stepped forward. "Andrew, even if they leave immediately, it will take a while for them to get here. Take just a minute and tell us what's going on. Is Rebecca alright! Where is she?"

Andrew took a deep breath to steady himself. "I don't know."

Victoria moved to his side. "You don't know what? Whether she's alright or where she is?"

Andrew looked at the concern on the faces of both women. "I don't know either. All she said was to ping the phone signal and to get a helicopter and come quick. Lives depended on it. I have no idea where she is."

Andrew couldn't waste any more time. He had failed Rebecca once. It wasn't going to happen again. He moved past the ladies and headed toward the door.

Beth and Victoria glanced at each other. No words were necessary. They were out the door. They caught up with him, as he stepped on the elevator that would take him up to the roof and the landing spot for the helicopter.

Victoria and Beth didn't speak but Andrew said, "You're not going. I don't know what I'll run into. It's too dangerous. You're not going."

Neither lady spoke. They just stepped on the elevator beside Andrew.

"Don't argue with me about this. You're not going. It's too dangerous."

When they reached the roof, Andrew stepped out of the elevator. So did Beth and Victoria. They were right beside him when he reached the helipad.

"Now listen. I'll keep in touch by phone every step of the way. As soon as I have her, I'll call and you can talk to her so you'll know she's ok."

Neither lady said a word. They just stood, one on each side of Andrew, and waited. They stood like that for no more than ten minutes when they heard the whooshing sound of the helicopter blades as it approached the landing pad.

Andrew hadn't dared to look at either lady since they had left the office. "You can wait at the office or go to my place where you'll be more comfortable. Either one will be fine. I can reach you at either place when I have her."

As soon as the helicopter landed and the pilot had stepped out, Andrew climbed in and took over the controls. Beth and Victoria climbed in the rear seat and buckled up. As soon as they were airborne, Andrew said without looking behind him. "You're here, aren't you?"

Victoria reached forward and patted Andrew on the shoulder. "Of course, we are. You didn't for one minute think we'd let you leave us behind. You're going to get Rebecca and bring her home and we're going to be there to see that you do."

Andrew kept checking his laptop and adjusting his course. As the signal pinged from tower to tower, he changed direction. One thing didn't change. They were going west.

Victoria maneuvered into the front seat beside Andrew. "I have a question, Andrew. If Garcia has Rebecca, she'll be in Mexico. How can we get across the border?"

Andrew thought for a moment. "We'll figure that out when the time comes. I don't know where we'll end up, but we're not going home without Rebecca. If I have to get both our governments involved I will. I know I can't fly the helicopter across the border. Our fighter jets would intercept us and we'd be forced to land. I'm hoping they haven't made it across the border yet."

Beth leaned forward so she could hear what they were saying. "We need a plan. I mean, if she has been taken across the border, is there a way to cross over undetected?"

Andrew shook his head. "Now, I want both of you to listen to me. *We* are not crossing the border. If it becomes necessary, *I'm* crossing the border. Don't even think about following me. I can only rescue one woman at a time."

Neither woman spoke but Victoria glanced back at Beth. Again, words were not needed.

Andrew was concentrating on his laptop and on the coordinates he needed to be following. He understood the need to help that his two female companions were feeling. Rebecca was their friend too. Any other time he would have enjoyed their company. Now was not one of those times. He needed them to understand what they might be going up against.

He cleared his throat. "I think we've passed the last tower. We aren't far from the phone's actual location. I'm going to set this bird down as close to where the phone is pinging as I can. I want you two to stay in the helicopter. I'm going to find Rebecca and get her on board. The longer we are on the ground, the longer we are in danger. Do not argue with me over this."

Beth leaned over again from the backseat. "We never argue with you, Andrew."

Andrew didn't reply. Beth was right, they never argued with him. They never listened to him either.

Andrew pointed to a clearing up ahead. As he started to bring the helicopter to a lower altitude, he pointed to a small wooden structure.

"I'm going to set us down as close to that building as I can. According to the pings on my laptop, the phone is inside. That means Rebecca is inside. I should only be a few minutes. Stay put!"

Andrew landed the chopper as gently as possible. The ground was strewn with rocks of all sizes. They were in the foothills of a large mountain range. If they had been any closer, landing would have been impossible.

He didn't wait for the blades to stop rotating. He drew his gun and ducking low, ran for the building. He didn't bother trying to hide his approach. Anyone within a mile could have heard that helicopter land.

Andrew reached the building without incident. He stopped at one of the windows and tried to see in but years of grime kept him from being able to distinguish much.

Making his way around to the door, he hesitated. Rebecca had to have heard them land. Why hadn't she run out to meet them? Only two reasons he could think of. Either she was hurt or someone was preventing her from coming out.

Staying as low as he could, to prevent making himself a target, he eased the door open. He carefully made his way inside, staying close to the wall. Letting his eyes adjust to the dim interior, he checked out the one room building. Nothing. He walked from one side of the room to the other. Then he reversed and walked back, checking for any trap doors in the floor. Still nothing.

She had to be here. This is where the signal was coming from. He looked down at his own phone, this is still where it was coming from. He was hesitant to call out. He didn't want to give away his exact location, just in case she wasn't alone.

OK. He had checked the entire room, the walls for false doors, the floor for crawl spaces. He looked up but he could see through the rafters to the roof.

He checked his phone again. The signal was strong as ever. Well, if not inside, she must have found a place to hide outside.

He went back out and slowly made his way around the side of the building.

Now that the helicopter blades had stopped turning, it was quiet. Too quiet. Something wasn't right. She should have appeared by now.

Checking the signal on his phone one more time, he put it back in his pocket. If she wasn't here, the phone sure was, he thought as he rounded the corner to the back of the building.

And then he saw what he'd been looking for. It looked like a root cellar. One side had caved in. Only someone really small could have fit in what was left of it. Maybe she hadn't been able to hear the helicopter from in there.

He reached for the handle with his left hand, still holding his weapon in his right. He gave the door a tug, but it was heavier than it looked. Holstering his gun, he took hold of the door with both hands and gave a hard tug.

The door flew open and banged back against the caved in wall. It was dark inside and for a minute nothing moved.

Then someone rushed him. Andrew had convinced himself no one was here, so was caught off guard.

He was thrown backwards as two little girls latched on. One had him by the leg and the other around the waist.

They were talking to each other a mile a minute. "I told you it was him. He's got the star and everything. She said he would come and find us. He's not like that other man with the badge, the bad one. The star looks just like the one she drew for us." The older of the two girls held up Rebecca's drawing for comparison. "He's the good one. We can trust him."

Andrew knew when he was outnumbered. "Victoria," he yelled as loud as he could. "I need help. Where are you?"

Victoria and Beth rounded the corner and came to a stop. It was hard to believe what they saw. Andrew was sprawled out on the ground being attacked by two little girls. Well, not exactly attacked; more like attached.

The smallest one was wrapped around his leg and the larger one around his waist. They had stopped talking but were holding on for dear life.

Andrew looked up at Beth and Victoria. "Where were you? Didn't you hear me hollering for help?"

As Beth hid a smile, she said, "We were in the helicopter. Just where you told us to stay."

Andrew was struggling to get to his feet. "Now is a fine time to start doing what I tell you. You never have before. Listen, there are two of you and two of them. Get them off me."

It took some time and a lot of persuasion to convince the two girls to let Andrew go. It was obvious he was their security. Rebecca had only told them about Andrew. They weren't sure of the two ladies.

Beth knelt in front of the oldest girl. "Honey, can you tell us where Rebecca is? When we find her, we can all leave. We can get you somewhere safe. I'll bet you're hungry and tired. We have just the place, but we have to find Rebecca first."

The little girl backed up a step and reaching deep into her pocket pulled out the phone and note Rebecca had written. She turned and handed it to Andrew. Evidently, he was still the one she trusted.

Andrew read the short note out loud. When he got to the last words, he choked up. "She said to tell Hershel she's sorry." He looked up at Victoria and Beth. "She left the phone with the children so we could find them. She left the note to explain. Then she used herself as bait to save the girls."

Beth grabbed Andrew by the arm. "You have to go after her!" She was almost crying now. "You have to go save her! Don't just stand there, Andrew, go get Rebecca!"

Tears were in Andrew's eyes too. "I can't. I can't leave you and Victoria and these children here alone. It's too dangerous. I can't take you with me to hunt for her. That's even more dangerous. I can't send you back, you need me to pilot the helicopter. All we can do is get these children to safety. It's what she wanted. It's what she sacrificed herself for."

Victoria's heart was breaking; for Rebecca and for these two frightened little girls. She was a mother. She understood the trauma these children had been through. And she understood why Rebecca had done what she had. It broke her heart but she understood.

Victoria stepped forward and spoke softly to the two little girls. "I'm Victoria. The lady Rebecca mentioned in the note she left with you. She wanted me to take you to my house and take care of you till we can locate your parents. I have two children at home who would love to meet you."

She held out her hands to the girls. The oldest came straight into her arms. The youngest still clung to Andrew's leg. She wasn't letting go.

Victoria took the girl by the hand and started back to the helicopter. She turned and looked over her shoulder at Andrew. "We need to get these children out of here. But it looks like you're on your own with that one."

Reaching down, Andrew pried the tiny little girl from around his leg. She immediately transferred her arms to his neck and held on. "Victoria's right," he said, looking at Beth. "We aren't safe here. Rebecca's abductor or the coyotes could come back at any time. We need to go."

When everyone was safely buckled in, Andrew started the engine. As they lifted off, Beth was still scanning the ground for any sign of Rebecca.

As they gained altitude, the girls lost some of their fear at the wonder of flying. The oldest sitting in back holding onto Victoria's hand. The youngest wedged in front between Beth and Andrew with her arms still tight around Andrew's neck.

He glanced over at Beth. "Do you think you could help me out a little over here?" He nodded at the little girl.

Beth just smiled. "Absolutely not. I'd never get between a woman and her man."

It didn't take long for the children to relax enough to fall fast asleep. Regardless of what Beth had said, she reached over to take the girl from Andrew. But the child whimpered and just clung tighter.

Andrew reached up and patted her back. "Leave her alone. I've kind of gotten used to having her there."

Victoria watched and listened from the back seat. She smiled to herself. She had always suspected Andrew would make a wonderful father.

Everyone was quiet the rest of the way so the children could sleep.

Toward the end of the flight, Beth said, "This isn't the way to Richmond."

"We're not going to Richmond. There's an open field behind Victoria's Bed and Breakfast. We're going to Hadbury and get these children settled."

As soon as they touched down, Albert and Mary Alice, and Joe and Nancy, were waiting for them. They stood together in a group, waiting for the blades to stop.

The first to speak was Victoria. "Where are the twins? Are they ok?"

She had hurried ahead of the others in her haste to check on her babies. The older child was still clutching her hand.

Nancy spoke up, "Those sweet little boys have been missing their mother but they are just fine. Joe and I just got them to sleep." She bent down to the child beside Victoria. "And who is this pretty young lady?"

Victoria touched the girl on the shoulder, nudging her forward just a little. "This is Maria. She's seven and the one hanging around Andrew's neck is her sister Rosa. She's five."

By this time, the others had caught up with Victoria. Nancy reached for Rosa. "I'll take this one." But Rosa just held tighter to Andrew and buried her face in his neck. "Or not," she said.

Andrew readjusted the child so that she wasn't choking him as much. "Let's go inside and get these kids settled, then we can talk. I'm sure they're starving. I know I am."

Inside, Victoria and Andrew took the girls upstairs. They needed to have a bath and something clean to put on. The others headed for the kitchen. Mary Alice and Nancy had been cooking all morning. The last of the guests had just checked out. There were plenty of leftovers. They just needed to be reheated.

Beth poured herself a cup of coffee and proceeded to fill the others in on what they had found, when they had flown out to rescue Rebecca. She told them about finding the girls in the root cellar and showed them the note Rebecca had written.

Nancy reached for Joe's hand and Albert put his arm around Mary Alice. They all knew how Rebecca felt about children and weren't at all surprised that she would sacrifice herself for the little girls.

Joe cleared his throat. "Let's be positive. At least she was able to get away from her abductor and contact Andrew. If she got away one time, she can do it again. And from the way it sounds she seems to be ok."

They all agreed. No one wanted to think Rebecca wouldn't be coming back.

The table was set and all the food heated and placed in serving dishes, when Andrew entered the kitchen. "Victoria wants to stay with the kids. They're exhausted. I'm going to fix some plates for them and take them up. I'll be back in a few minutes. Don't wait on me."

As in most families, they didn't. When they had finished, Andrew still hadn't returned. The ladies started to clean up the kitchen and the men went into the living room to talk things over. Beth had been quiet throughout the meal. She kept going over and over things in her mind. Finally, she came to a decision. She talked it over with the other two ladies and then slipped out the side door.

As Nancy and Mary Alice finished and joined the men in the living room, Andrew came down the stairs and joined them.

"Listen," he said. "I need to get the chopper back to Richmond. Can I depend on all of you to help Victoria out for a little longer? She's going to have her hands full with the Bed and Breakfast, the twins and the little girls. I'll be back as soon as I can."

The others stood. The men shook his hand and the women hugged his neck. They all agreed to stay as long as Victoria needed them.

Andrew felt a little guilty as he eased out the back door. He didn't like lying to his friends but had felt it necessary. He was in the chopper and had it in the air in only a few minutes. He wasn't headed for Richmond. He was headed west. He was going to find Rebecca.

Andrew had been in the air for about twenty minutes when the hair stood up on the back of his neck. A now familiar feeling that he was not alone.

Without turning around, he said, "You're in here, aren't you?"

"Yes," Beth answered. "You're going after Rebecca, aren't you?"

Chapter 16

Bill stood by as General Morales gave his men instructions. He leaned back against a tree, waiting for the crime scene techs to come and process the scene. He knew Morales would not leave until his captain's body had been removed. Neither man had liked Perez, but as Morales had said earlier, Perez was his responsibility. That wouldn't change just because the man was dead.

Bill jerked to attention and placed his hand on the butt of his gun, when he heard the crunch of tires on the narrow road leading to the crime scene. He was letting his nerves get the best of him. They were operating in a foreign country, with little backup. And at this point, he wasn't sure of the backup they did have.

If Perez was dirty, how many more of Morales' men had succumbed to the lure of riches to be made in the drug trade? How about Morales himself? Bill liked the General, but knew he couldn't afford to let his guard down.

Bill watched as the medical examiner's van pulled to a stop in front of the cabin. A small man, with a shaggy haircut got out and approached Morales. Bill remembered him as the man who had removed Garcia's sister from the camp where she had been killed. Two other men removed a stretcher from the double doors at the back of the van.

When Morales and the medical examiner disappeared into the house, Bill moved a little closer. He had no desire to go back inside but he did want to hear what the two had to say when they came back out.

It didn't take long for them to emerge back onto the porch. Bill had seen what was left of the man inside. It wasn't much. Bill wished he could erase that particular sight from his mind, but knew he would always remember it in detail.

Someday, he was going to ask the psych doctor back at the Marshal's office why bad memories seemed to stick in your mind so much longer than the good ones. Putting that thought on the back burner, he moved closer to where Morales and the medical examiner were standing.

At a nod from the doctor, his two assistants moved forward into the house to bag, tag and remove the body.

"Cause of death is pretty obvious," he was telling Morales. "But I'll wait until my exam back at the office to make it official. He was alive for the beating and even for a portion of the gutting. It was the last few slashes of the knife that finally killed him. Whoever did this has had some practice. It isn't easy to keep a man alive until most of his guts are spilled out on the floor."

When the body was brought out and secured in the back of the van, the medical examiner and his two assistants drove away.

Morales turned and looked at Bill. "Well, he didn't add much that we didn't already know. Maybe the crime scene techs will come up with something that will help. It seems to be drug related but how? Was Perez selling, manufacturing, or taking the crap himself?"

Bill thought of the deceased man's behavior. "Maybe all three, General. If we're finished here, I'd like to get back to the others. Hershel and Cliff will need us if Jeff gets himself in trouble."

General Morales turned back to the truck. "That Jeff of yours looks like he can take care of himself. But you're right. They would be vastly outnumbered."

The ride back to Garcia's stronghold was made mostly in silence. Each man lost in his own thoughts. They returned the truck to its hiding place and carefully made the rest of the way back on foot. A few hundred yards from where they had left Hershel and Cliff, Bill stopped and put his hand on the General's shoulder. "We better let them know it's us. I wouldn't want to get shot." Bill tapped his earbud. "Hey guys. It's us. We're coming in."

"Thanks for the heads up," Hershel responded. "We've had guards pass our location every hour or so. Watch yourselves coming in. It's about time for them to make another round."

No sooner had the words been said, when General Morales grabbed Bill's arm and pulled him down in the underbrush.

Two guards passed within twenty feet of them. They had only gone a few steps further, when they stopped for one to light a cigarette.

"What do you think about last night's events?" one said as he leaned his gun against a tree.

"What I think is that our leader has become a little unhinged. I had no problem with the killing. Getting rid of competition is always a good idea. But the torture was over the top. It wasn't just the torture, but the satisfaction Garcia got from it, that bothered me."

The one who had stopped to smoke, nodded. "Since his sister was killed, he's been different. He's always been mean and someone I wouldn't want to cross, but there's a viciousness that wasn't there before. It's like he wants someone to pay and until he finds that person, he's happy to take his anger out on anyone who gets in his way."

The guard leaning against the tree, crossed his arms over his chest. "What worries me, is when he's drinking, you don't even have to cross him. Just being in his path is enough to get you killed."

They stood there in silence till the one smoking, dropped his cigarette butt on the ground and stepped on it. "Let's finish our rounds and get back to camp. I heard some of the other men talking. I think something's going down tonight."

Morales and Bill waited until they were out of sight to finish making their way back in.

Hershel let out a sigh when he saw them making their way through the bushes to their hiding place. He had been worried what they would run into and also what was happening to Jeff in Garcia's camp.

He had heard bits and pieces of conversation about something that had gone down last night. He hadn't been able to put it all together but it sounded like they had taken out a competitor. What was more concerning, it seemed something might be planned for tonight.

Hershel motioned for the two new arrivals to sit down so they would be better hidden. "Well, General, did you find your man?"

Morales sat down before he spoke. "We found what was left of him."

Then he proceeded to describe what they had walked into. When he finished, Hershel looked at Bill. His marshal hadn't said a word. That spoke volumes. He had been with Bill through some pretty horrific times. They had seen some really bad stuff.

Hershel made a mental note to have him talk to the psych doctor when they got back to Richmond. Some things were just too hard to deal with on your own.

Bill seemed to want to change the subject. "What's been going on in the camp while we were gone? Has Jeff been able to communicate much?"

Cliff, who hadn't spoken since Morales had finished describing the condition Perez's body was left in, spoke up, "He's only mumbled a few words to us all day. It sounds like Garcia's keeping him pretty close. From his one-sided conversation, it sounds like something is happening tonight and Jeff's going to be involved in it."

Hershel nodded his agreement. "Cliff, I want you to go back and move the truck closer. If Jeff leaves camp with them, General Morales and I will try to follow and see where they go. The Hummer would be too conspicuous. They would pick up on it tailing them. The old pick up will just blend in with the dozens of others just like it going up and down these back roads."

Jeff had remained close to Garcia all day. After last night's party, Jeff was more wary of him than ever. If Garcia would shoot his own man in a drunken rage, just because he had lost a fight, Jeff had no doubt he would shoot him for almost no reason. Besides, he had a feeling something was going down tonight and he wanted to be part of it. It might be his opportunity to separate Garcia from his men and get the hell out of here before one of them got hurt. The longer this took, the greater the possibility of that happening.

Garcia leaned back in his chair and seemed to be studying Jeff. It had been hard, but he had tried to leave off the alcohol today. If things went according to plan, he could celebrate tonight. He would also have a better idea of how much he could trust the man sitting across the table from him. He had plans to use him but whether or not he let him live depended on his actions tonight.

"Well, mi amigo, are you ready for a little action tonight? You said you wanted to join us. It's time to find out just how useful you can be."

Garcia watched Jeff's face for any sign of weakness. He knew he would kill him eventually. It was just a matter of when.

Jeff let a little of the disdain he felt for Garcia show on his face. Better that than the utter revulsion he really felt. What he couldn't show was any kind of fear.

"I've been here waiting for several days. You're the one that's been dragging his feet. What's happening tonight that you suddenly decide to include me?"

He knew his fellow marshals could only hear his side of the conversation so he wanted to say enough to give them an idea of what was happening. He knew they would follow, if they could, and be there to back him up.

Garcia stood up and paced the floor. When he reached the liquor cabinet, he paused but turned and came back to his desk without pouring any of the whiskey he so desperately wanted. He would have time for that later.

"All in good time, my compadre. We'll leave as soon as it's dark and I'll tell you everything you need to know then. Let's say this is just a little trial run to see if you're as good as you say you are."

Jeff stood up. "Well, the least you can do is give my gun back. I can't be of much help if I'm unarmed."

Garcia reached into his desk drawer and pulled out Jeff's weapon and handed it to him. "Not a problem. Just watch where you point it. I wouldn't want any of my men to mistake your intentions. It wouldn't go well for you. Now go get ready. It will be dark soon."

As soon as Jeff got back to his cabin, he checked out his gun. He wouldn't put it past Garcia to tamper with it in some way. If he got in a situation where he needed it, he wanted it to work. When he was satisfied it was in working condition, he walked to the far side of the room and touched his earbud.

Hershel responded immediately. "How much did he tell you?"

"Not much," Jeff replied, as he removed his backup weapon from the false bottom of his saddlebags and tucked it in the side of his boot.

Hershel lowered his voice. He thought the guards had moved on but didn't want to take a chance. "Say something that will give us a heads up when you start to leave camp. Cliff has gone to move the truck closer. General Morales and I will try to follow you. If he leaves camp by another route try to signal us in some way. If he goes the back way and it comes out on the same road as the front way, say something that has 'same' or 'different' in it and if you turn, something that has 'right' or 'left' in it. Just be careful and stay on your guard. We'll do our best to have your six."

"Thanks Hershel. I couldn't have better backup. I just wish Andrew was here to join the party."

Having done all, he could to prepare for tonight's mission, Jeff tried to relax. He thought about Hershel and what a great boss he was to work for. When he left the New Orleans office, he thought he would never find friends like the ones he had to leave behind. Of course, two of those friends were left behind in a grave. That too was the result of his last undercover job.

He must have dosed because he was startled by a banging on the door of his cabin. Under his breath, he said "show time" for the benefit of those on the other end of his earbuds.

Jeff was surprised to find Garcia standing there when he opened the door. He had expected to see one of the guards. It looked like Garcia planned to stick close. That had Jeff a little concerned. Was he looking for an opportunity to take him out or just wanting to be close enough to gage his reaction to whatever was going to happen tonight? And even more surprising, Garcia was totally sober.

He backed up a few steps so that Jeff could step out the cabin door. "Are you ready, mi amigo? The night is young but we have a way to go so let's load up."

They made their way over to where two trucks were waiting. The first had three men in the backseat. The second one had an extended cab and held six men.

Jeff stopped and whistled and for Hershel's benefit said, "Wow, two trucks and eleven men including me and you. What are we going to do—rob a bank?"

Garcia just laughed and got behind the wheel of the lead car. Jeff followed suit and got in the passenger side. As they pulled off, Garcia laughed again. "A bank. Now that would be fun, but this will be even better. A lot more entertaining."

Jeff thought he detected a little madness in Garcia's laugh but kept that thought to himself.

As the two trucks made a circle in front of Garcia's office, they started out of camp in the opposite direction of the way Jeff had come in on his bike. To begin with it looked like they were just going to drive through the trees but just as they cleared the first few large pines, a narrow dirt road came into view.

"This isn't the way I came in on my bike. In fact, you wouldn't even know this road was here from inside the camp."

"We have many surprises, my friend. If you don't have more than one way in and out, you may find yourself cornered like a bunch of mice. You surely learned that from your last boss. He had a really sweet setup on that island. That little inlet we went down when we arrived, couldn't have been his only way off the island. If the feds hadn't shut him down, we would have paid another visit and found it. I had plans to take over that operation."

Garcia gave another laugh that made chills go down Jeff's back. Just as Jeff was fixing to reply, they tee-boned into another road. Jeff quickly switched his train of thought. "That's funny. I had the 'same' thought but after the authorities swooped in, there was nothing 'left'." He could hear Hershel chuckle through his earbuds.

Hershel stood up. "Let's go. We don't want them to get too far ahead of us."

Morales followed Hershel through the woods and back to where Cliff had hidden the truck. They didn't speak again until they made a left turn onto the same road, they had taken to the camp several days before.

"Speed up a little," Hershel said. "We don't want to lose them. If they make another turn, Jeff might not find a way to signal which way they are headed."

Genera Morales just laughed. "I didn't think I'd ever say this, but my money's on Jeff."

In spite of the tense situation, Hershel laughed too. "He's a good man. The two of you just got off on the wrong foot." Hershel laughed again. This time from deep down inside. "Don't feel bad. The first time I met him, I thought he was a drug smuggler."

It was good to laugh and break the tension that had been building up since they started out.

It didn't take long for them to catch up. They kept several cars between them and the two trucks. They stayed on a straight course for about twenty minutes.

Finally, General Morales spoke up. "I'm familiar with this road. As far as I can remember, there's not much out here. Most of these roads we're passing, aren't really roads. They're just long driveways that dead-end in someone's front yard."

Hershel didn't take his eyes off the trucks ahead of them. There was only one car between them now. The General had slowed down some and dropped back, so they wouldn't draw attention to themselves. "Do you think a rival gang has set up camp somewhere in this vicinity? It's isolated enough."

Morales shook his head. "There haven't been any reports of any such activity. But you have to remember, until recently Perez was in charge of this area. Now that we know he was dirty, I have to wonder how much he might have been covering up. So to answer your question, I really just don't know."

A few miles ahead, the two trucks made a right. Morales slowed even more to let them get far enough ahead so they wouldn't notice when he made the same turn.

Hershel leaned forward. "Don't lose them!" Morales had slowed even more after making the turn. The two trucks were completely out of sight.

Morales continued on for about half a mile, then pulled to the side of the road. "Calm down, marshal. I know where they're going. Just around that curve, the road straightens out for about 200 yards and then dead-ends into the parking lot of an old abandoned factory. We need to go the rest of the way on foot if we're going to remain unseen."

Jeff was getting nervous. They hadn't seen another vehicle for several miles. For a while, he could pick up Hershel and Morales in his side view mirror but now it appeared Garcia might have lost them.

Before he could question Garcia about their destination, they rounded a curve and Jeff could see a building in the distance. It looked abandoned. The road dead ended into what looked to be the parking lot. The two trucks pulled in one behind the other and stopped. Garcia and his men got out. Jeff slowly joined them. There was no one else around. Jeff had a bad feeling. He sure would like to know Hershel and General Morales were somewhere close.

"What is this?" he said to Garcia. "We're in the middle of nowhere. There's nothing around. Are we meeting someone or what?"

Garcia's men had divided and moved to stand at Jeff's back. Garcia was in front of him but a little to his right. At a signal from Garcia, three men came from around the side of the building. When they got closer, Jeff could see two of the men were dragging the third between them. He had been badly beaten.

When they were about forty feet away, they stopped, as if waiting for something. At a signal from Garcia, the two men stepped away from the one in the middle. He staggered a little but remained on his feet. As badly as he'd been beaten, Jeff doubted he could see them.

Garcia turned to Jeff. "Alright, let's see how bad you want to be a part of my outfit." He motioned to the man standing in front of them. "Shoot him."

Jeff was stunned. He had never killed a man in cold blood. He had killed, yes, but it was always in self-defense. He knew he couldn't just shoot this man standing in front of him. His allegiance to the Marshal's code of ethics along with his own personal code just wouldn't let him. He also knew if he didn't, Garcia was going to kill him.

In his earbud, he heard Morales say very softly, "I know this man. He's a very bad hombre. We've been looking for him for years. Draw your weapon, marshal. When I give the word, shoot just to the left of his head."

Jeff slowly drew his gun. He had his doubts about Morales. If he was dirty, he could shoot the man and leave Jeff to take the blame.

Then he heard another quiet voice. One he trusted completely. "Do it," Hershel said.

At the signal, Jeff aimed and fired, making sure to come close to the man's head without hitting him.

The man dropped. A hole dead center of his forehead.

Garcia walked over to make sure the man was dead. He nudged him with the toe of his boot. Turning back to Jeff, he took out a flask and drank deeply, before saying, "You did good, you passed the test, you are now one of us."

Chapter 17

All Rebecca knew to do was run. Away from the cabin. Away from the children. Away from the thug. She could hear him, crashing through the bushes behind her. That was good. As long as he was following her, it was giving Andrew time to get to the children. He would take the little girls to Hadbury, to Victoria. They would be safe. Between her note and what the girls could tell Andrew, he and Hershel would track down the man with the badge. He wouldn't have that badge much longer. And he certainly wouldn't be dealing with coyotes and abandoning children in the wilderness.

She couldn't afford to think of Hershel. He was going to be so upset that she hadn't waited with the girls, for Andrew to rescue them. But then again, maybe he would. He knew her better than any other living soul. When he saw the children, he would figure it out. Of course by then, it would be too late. Too late for her anyway.

Rebecca came to a clear mountain stream. She stopped, wasting precious minutes. But she needed the water. She drank, using her cupped hands, while she let her two bottles fill from the cold mountain stream.

Then she was off again. She couldn't hear him now, but she knew he was there. It was getting late afternoon. It would soon be dark. If she could elude him till then, she might get away. Rebecca had to be realistic. Get away to where? She didn't even know where she was.

One thing she did know. With border patrols and coyotes in the area, she wasn't headed for California. She was headed for Mexico. About the last place on earth, she wanted to be.

It was almost too dark for her to keep going. She needed to find a place to hide that would give her shelter for the night. She was mostly feeling her way through the stand of large trees.

When she stopped to catch her breath, she strained to hear any sound of the man following her. At first, all she could hear was the normal night sounds of the forest. But then she heard it, a twig snapped and then another.

Rebecca looked wildly around, looking for somewhere to hide. She tried to run, but in the darkness tripped and fell in a shallow indentation in the ground. When she tried to regain her feet, she slid deeper into a hole. She couldn't see. What little light that had been coming from the moon was blocked by something.

As quietly as possible, she felt around with her hands. She felt dirt and roots over her head and dirt under her feet. She figured she had fallen and then slid about four feet down before she had stopped sliding.

She knew where she was and what had happened. She had tripped and fallen into a hole left when a huge tree had fallen, bringing its massive roots sticking up in the air. She was in the hole where the roots used to be.

Rebecca was on her hands and knees, feeling her way. If she could get far enough back, he wouldn't be able to see her. When she was as far as she could go, she propped up against the bottom of the roots and took out a bottle of water. She drank her fill. She wasn't in the desert anymore. Water would be easier to find. When she had enough, she screwed the top back on and returned it to her pocket.

She lay down and curled up, realizing she wasn't that uncomfortable. She was protected on all sides but one by the massive roots. She was tucked way back out of sight. The ground was soft and cool. As hiding places went, she had had worse since this nightmare began.

Rebecca relaxed and lay her head on a flat root still embedded in the ground. There was nothing she could do now but wait for morning. She felt safe, protected by the mighty tree roots all around her. She closed her eyes and slept. And she dreamed. She dreamed of Hershel. He had found her and was taking her home. But even in her sleep, she knew it wasn't so. A few loose tears made their way down her cheeks. She wiped them away, then settled back again to wait for morning.

Coming awake with a start, it took Rebecca a few minutes to get oriented. It was morning. She could hear the birds. So why was it so dark? She felt around with her hands. All she could feel was dirt. Panic started to set in. Was she buried alive? She began to crawl in the only direction her hands didn't encounter dirt.

It took only a moment for her to see daylight in the distance. She must have crawled further back in her sleep. Evidently, she was still trying to hide, even when she wasn't aware of it.

Rebecca stopped and listened as she approached the opening to her hiding place. Silence, except for the birds. She had gone hunting once with Hershel and he had told her birds stopped singing when they felt threatened. If they were still singing, it must be safe for her to come out.

Carefully, Rebecca emerged from her hiding place. Looking around, she seemed to be alone. Could her abductor have passed her by in the night? Could he now be in front of her?

For a few minutes, she thought about going back the way she had come. Was it possible Andrew was still at the cabin?

No. He would have gotten the girls to safety. They would all be at Victoria's Bed and Breakfast by now. Probably eating breakfast. She could almost smell the bacon on the stove now.

Rebecca stopped in her tracks. No. She really could smell the bacon frying. Not Victoria's, but she could definitely smell bacon cooking.

Was it her abductor? Had he stopped somewhere close by to spend the night? Was he even now fixing his breakfast?

Rebecca didn't think so. He wouldn't have carried a slab of bacon all the way across the desert and into the mountains.

That meant only one thing. Someone else was nearby. Maybe someone who could help her. Someone with a phone. If she could call Andrew, he would come back for her.

Rebecca started making her way in the direction of the smell. In a matter of yards, she was out of the forest. Ahead of her was a lush meadow. The grass was a brilliant green, dotted with wild flowers in blues and yellows and purple. And on the other side of the meadow, was the most beautiful sight Rebecca had ever seen, a house. Not just a cabin but a real house.

Rebecca started across the meadow. She stopped when she saw the front door open and a woman with a baby in her arms walk through. The woman opened the rear door of the car. It looked like she was positioning the child in his car seat.

Rebecca started to run. "No!" she screamed. "No! Don't leave! Wait! Please wait!" Rebecca started waving her arms in the air as she ran. She was less than halfway when the car pulled out of the driveway and headed in the opposite direction.

Rebecca didn't stop. She kept running and waving her arms. If the woman would just look in her rear-view mirror, she still might see her.

Rebecca didn't stop until the car crested a small rise and was out of sight. And still Rebecca ran. She would get to the house and wait. The woman would be back. She had to come back. Didn't she?

Rebecca slowed to a walk. There was no hurry now. She studied the house as she approached. It wasn't large, maybe two or three bedrooms. The white siding reflected the morning sun. The starkness of the white was relieved by dark green shutters. A walkway of stepping stones led from the parking area to the front porch. The front porch ran the entire length of the house with wide steps leading from the ground up to the porch. Pots of brightly-colored flowers flanked each side of the steps. The yard was small but well cared for. The grass was cut and the hedges neatly trimmed. This wasn't just a house. It was a home.

Yes, the woman would be back. All she had to do was wait.

When Rebecca reached the front porch, she climbed the steps and was surprised to find a swing tucked all the way over to one end. She hadn't seen it from a distance because a lattice covered with a beautiful, blooming vine nearly obscured it from view. What a wonderful place to sit in the evening and watch the sun go down.

Rebecca eased onto the swing and started it moving with the toe of her shoe. She leaned back and closed her eyes. She let a total peace wash over her. She knew she wasn't safe, but just to sit on the porch where actual people lived gave her such a peaceful feeling.

Until she opened her eyes. She tried to make some kind of rational sense out of what she was seeing. She couldn't come up with an explanation that would relieve the sinking feeling in her stomach.

Pinned to the front screen door was a note. If the woman who just drove off, lived here, why had she left the note on the door?

Rebecca got up slowly and removed the note. She unfolded the single sheet of paper and read:

Hi Ida, came by this morning and watered your inside plants like you wanted. Checked everything inside and out. Everything looked good. Some of your tomatoes needed picking. I didn't think they would last till you got home, so I'm taking them with me. I'll feed Fred tomato sandwiches for lunch. Enjoy your cruise. See you in two weeks. Betty.

Rebecca lay the note on the swing beside her. Two weeks? How long had she been gone? If Betty had taken the tomatoes home with her, that meant it would be a while before Ida came back. She couldn't stay here that long. She needed another plan. This one had just blown up in her face.

Maybe there was a phone in the house. She would have to get inside to see. Even if there was one, she didn't know where she was. If this area had 911 service, they could trace her call and find her. She doubted a rural area like this would have that type service but she was getting ahead of herself. She had to get inside first.

Rebecca got up and replaced the note on the screen door. She didn't want the woman to come home and think someone had stolen her tomatoes. It was bad enough for her to come home and find someone had broken into her house. And that was exactly what she had to do.

OK. She had another plan she would try first. She would search all around the house and yard to see if Ida had hidden a key anywhere. Lots of people did that. Rebecca just left an extra house key with her neighbor. This lady didn't have any neighbors.

Rebecca started with the flower pots. She lifted each one and looked underneath. Then felt around each plant. Nothing. So, OK, maybe that was too obvious.

Next, she walked around the yard, turning over rocks. She tried the front door, just to make sure Betty had remembered to lock it when she left. She went around back, where there was a good-sized deck and checked underneath to make sure there wasn't a nail or ledge where a key could be hidden.

Mounting the back steps and crossing the deck, she tried the back door. Locked. "Shoot," she muttered under her breath.

The windows were next. One by one, she tried to raise them. No luck.

Rebecca backed up and looked at the house. So. How did one go about breaking into a house? She was the wife of a United States Marshal, for goodness' sake. This wasn't in her repertoire of accomplishments.

The only thing she could come up with was to break a window. She needed something she could throw or bash the glass with. Picking up a rock, she hurled it as hard as she could at one of the front windows. It bounced off. Ok. That didn't work.

She looked around for something she could swing with a little more force. She picked up one of the flower pots but couldn't bring herself to throw it. Surely, she could find something else. Breaking into someone's house was bad enough but destroying their flowers just seemed wrong. She would leave the flower pot as a last resort.

She circled the house once more and for the first time noticed an old tool shed at the edge of the grass. Hoping it wasn't locked, she gave the door a tug. To her surprise, it came right open. Stepping over the threshold, she felt along the wall for a light switch. Not finding one, she figured there was no power run to the shed.

Holding her arms out in front of her so that she wouldn't bump into anything, she slowly made her way forward. Encountering nothing but air, she moved a little further into the interior of the building.

All of a sudden, something had her. Rebecca screamed and swung her arms all around her. It was holding on tight. She tried to tug free but it had her by the hair.

She turned and tried to run. She made it two steps and stopped. She was trembling and couldn't move. But the light had come on. She looked around for her attacker but no one was there. She tried to step forward but something still had her hair.

Reaching up, she felt the culprit. She had walked right into the pull cord of the light dangling from the ceiling. It had become entangled in her hair.

Rebecca reached up and untangled the cord from her curly hair. If she had killed her fool self, the obituary would have read death by dangling light cord. She shivered. That wasn't even a little funny.

Now that she could see, she resumed her search for something heavy enough to break a window. The trouble was, anything that was heavy enough, was also too heavy for her to swing with the necessary force.

On a shelf in the very back, she found what she was looking for. A hammer. It wasn't too heavy for her to swing, but hard enough to break glass. It had a long, sturdy, wooden handle and even a claw on the back. It would do.

Armed with her hammer, she stepped back out of the shed. As she made her way to the back deck, she passed the homeowner's small garden. Hanging low, almost on the ground, was a big juicy looking tomato.

Would it be stealing if she picked and ate it, she wondered? The other lady had picked some and taken them home with her. But the other lady was a friend. Here to do a favor. Rebecca was here to break into that lady's house. The fact that she desperately needed to find a phone didn't change that fact. Rebecca was committing a crime. Breaking and entering. If she took the tomato, she could add theft of property to her list of crimes.

Hunger won out. Rebecca made her way into the garden and plucked the tomato from the vine. She rubbed it clean with the tail of her blouse and took a big bite.

She took another bite as she made her way up onto the deck. As her grandmother used to say, in for a penny, in for a pound. If she was going to enter the world of criminals, might as well go for broke. She had always been a law-abiding citizen. This would likely be her only trip over to the darker side. With that in mind, she wondered what was in the refrigerator.

Rebecca looked into both windows facing out onto the deck, to see what was close to the windows on the inside. She wanted to do as little damage as possible.

One had a table with a lamp and a few knickknacks scattered around on it. She rejected that one and moved on to the next. This one turned out to be a better prospect. She could see nothing but a chair and even that set over to one side.

Not wanting to create any more of a mess than necessary, Rebecca tapped the glass with the hammer. It rattled a little but that was all. *This is ridiculous*, she thought, *I've got to get inside.*

With that thought in mind, she drew back and hit the window with all her strength. It shattered on impact, the hammer flying from Rebecca's hands and landing inside, halfway across the room.

Rebecca carefully reached inside and unlocking the window, climbed through. She was in the kitchen. First things first. She found the bathroom, took care of business, and washed the tomato juice off her hands. Then she searched each room, looking for a phone. No luck. She wasn't surprised. A lot of people didn't have house phones anymore and the owner would have taken their cell with them.

She looked around for any type of gun. She hated the idea of shooting anyone but knew she would if her life depended on it. She had taken lessons at her friend's firing range in Hadbury. After the debacle six months ago, Hershel had insisted she let Mary Alice teach her to shoot. She would never be in the league with Hershel but she could hold her own if push came to shove.

As with the phone, she struck out with the gun. If the owner had any firearms, they were probably locked away somewhere.

Rebecca knew she couldn't stay here any longer. She knew Garcia's thug wouldn't go back without her. He would find this house sooner or later. Really, she was surprised he hadn't already.

She went back to the kitchen to see what kind of food she could take with her. The pickings were slim. The refrigerator had been cleaned out the way people tended to do when they were going to be gone for an extended amount of time. Most of the canned goods were too heavy to travel with. Even if she could, the only can opener was attached to the wall.

Rebecca found a few small cans of Vienna sausage with pull top lids and some crackers. She put these in her pocket and set out to find some paper and a pencil.

She would leave the home owner a note: *My name is Rebecca Bing. I broke into your house. I also broke your window and took some of your food. I am sorry and will repay you for the food and the window. My life is in danger. I am being chased by a very bad man. Please call this number and tell Andrew where this is. He will understand.*

She left the note on the door of the refrigerator. The home owner might be gone for weeks but Rebecca was trying to cover all her bases. She would love to spend the night here and sleep in a real bed, but knew it was too dangerous.

She refilled her water bottles one more time and headed back out the window.

Just as she climbed through, she was grabbed from behind. She had waited too late. He had found her.

Chapter 18

Beth climbed in the front seat beside Andrew. She knew he wasn't happy to find a stowaway. She was afraid he might turn the helicopter around and take her back. She cleared her throat. "I had to come. I talked it over with the others. It was a group decision."

Andrew glanced over at Beth, but didn't say a word.

She hesitated then continued, "I was the only one not needed there. Victoria has the twins and now the little girls. They need her there. Bill and Nancy needed to stay and help her. It'll take the three of them to take care of the twins and help get the girls settled in. That leaves Albert and Mary Alice to keep the B and B going. Victoria told me she has six new guests coming in tomorrow. They all agreed I was the best one to go with you to bring Rebecca home."

Andrew looked over at Beth and shook his head. "You know I might have to follow her all the way to Garcia's camp. You know what that means. We may have to cross over into Mexico. I will be going in all on my own, not sanctioned by their government or ours. I have no backup and we will be totally outnumbered."

He took a deep breath and started to continue when Beth interrupted, "See, I told you, you needed me. I was there six months ago, when Garcia crossed over the border into our country. I can speak a little Spanish. I'm not sanctioned either. I can be your backup and with me along, your numbers have doubled. Besides, I'm a nurse. If you get shot, I can remove the bullet."

"Don't push your luck, Beth. If I get shot, it will probably be trying to keep you out of trouble."

"No, no!" Beth interrupted. "I thought about that. I came prepared." And with that, she pulled out a SIG P365.

"Whoa! Where did you get that? Do you even know how to shoot that thing?"

Beth put the gun back in its holster, which fit neatly under her arm. With the vest she wore over her shirt, it was virtually invisible. "I got it from Mary Alice at the firing range. I've been taking lessons using it. I'm really good." She paused. "Mary Alice said so."

Andrew shook his head. "Lord save us all," he muttered. "I know when I'm beat. But you've got to promise me you'll do exactly what I say. No going off on your own and you'll only pull that gun out if it's absolutely necessary. Garcia's thugs won't hesitate to shoot you, just because you're a woman."

"I'll do anything you say, Andrew. Just don't take me back. Rebecca's my friend. I need to go with you to find her."

The tears in Beth's eyes did more than all her words could accomplish.

Andrew reached over and patted her on the shoulder. "Don't worry. I'm not going to take you back. You'd just figure out a way to follow me anyway. At least this way, I can keep an eye on you."

Beth knew when to stop talking. She had really been afraid he would turn the helicopter around and take her back to Hadbury. She decided to change the subject. "I couldn't help but notice how that youngest little girl hung onto you. I think she's claimed you for her own. How are you and Victoria going to handle four kids?"

"What do you mean, me and Victoria handle four kids? When we get Rebecca home, we'll find a way to return them to their parents. And the twins are fine. Victoria does a wonderful job with them."

"Andrew, I talked to those little girls. Their father died last year. The mother is sick. That's why she spent the last of her money to hire someone to bring the girls across the border. I'm a nurse, Andrew. I know when someone is dying. That woman likely won't be alive by the time we get Rebecca home. Like it or not, you and Victoria may well be all those children have."

Andrew didn't speak for several minutes. He'd never thought the girls might be homeless. Something about that, broke something in his heart. His head was reminding him, he knew nothing about raising kids but his heart just wasn't listening. He mentally shook himself. He could only solve one problem at a time. Right now that was finding Rebecca and bringing her home. Besides he didn't even know if the other was a problem yet. Even at that, it worried him that Beth thought that it was.

It didn't take as long to get to the building in the foothills as it had the first time. This time, Andrew knew exactly where he was going. He sat the helicopter down close to the same spot as he had before.

As they exited the chopper, Andrew turned to Beth. "The danger should be passed. If I know Rebecca, she made sure the thug followed her. They should both be long gone. But stay close to me just in case. We'll check the root cellar first and then the building just to rule out the possibility Rebecca was able to double back and is hiding here."

Beth stayed behind Andrew as they approached the building. It looked the same but something felt different. She kept looking over her shoulder but nothing caught her attention.

They made their way around the back of the building and checked the root cellar. Everything seemed the way they had left it. The door was still open and it was empty.

Andrew glanced back at Beth. "I didn't really expect to find anything in there. Rebecca wouldn't have taken the risk that she would lead the thug back here, before we had a chance to get the girls. I'm just crossing off all the possibilities."

They made their way around to the front of the building. Andrew held up his hand. "Stay here until I check out the inside."

Beth nodded and stayed where she was. It only took a few minutes for Andrew to make his way around the inside of the small space and motion for Beth to come inside.

"Everything looks the same to me," he said. "There's nowhere to hide in here. I knew it was a long shot but we had to check."

He turned and started toward the door but Beth didn't move. She was staring at the desk across the room. She raised her hand and pointed.

"Not everything," she said. "Look."

Andrew walked closer to get a better look. He hesitated and then crossed the rest of the way to the desk. He reached down and retrieved a piece of scrap paper from the floor and used it to pick up the object Beth had been pointing at.

He crossed back to Beth and held out the partially burnt end of a small cigar. "Someone's been here since we retrieved the girls. Stay here. I'm going to check around outside."

Beth watched as Andrew went out the door. She wandered over to the window. She could see him walking around the front of the building, checking the ground for any signs of fresh footprints. As he rounded the side of the building, she lost sight of him. She went to the back window and could see him standing at the tree line. From what she could see, he hadn't found anything.

As Andrew made it back to the front, a shot rang out. Beth gasped as she saw him fall. She could see the blood spread across the front of his shirt.

She looked in the direction the shots had come from. She could see two men taking cover behind a giant tree. They still had their guns pointed toward Andrew. They probably thought he was alone.

Looking back at Andrew, she saw him trying to crawl to the door so he could get inside and take cover. Where he had fallen was wide open. He was a sitting target.

Beth knew she had to do something. He'd never make it. She ran to the side window and tugged until it was open enough for her to crawl through. When she hit the ground, she eased around the corner of the building.

It looked like they were arguing but both men still had their guns pointed at Andrew. While their attention was diverted, Andrew had made it to his knees. He got off one shot and it was enough to make one of the men turn and run back into the forest.

The attention of the second one was diverted just long enough for Beth to take aim and pull the trigger. She hit her target and watched as he dropped his gun and fell to the ground.

Running to Andrew, she fell to her knees. "Let me see how bad it is!"

"Beth, go see if he's dead but whatever you do, don't get close to him. Kick his gun away and bring it to me."

Beth hesitated. She wanted to see how bad Andrew was hurt. The blood on his shirt was now dripping down his arm.

"Do it now, Beth. You wanted to be my backup. Well, that's what backup does. If you just winged him and he's able to get to his gun, we're still in danger."

That got her attention. She left Andrew and sprinted to the man just inside the trees. As she approached, she slowed down and finally came to a stop about six feet away. The gun had fallen out of his hand, but still easily within his reach. If he was conscious, he could reach out and grab her.

Keeping her gun trained on him, she picked up a stick and pulled the gun toward her. Then the nurse in her kicked in. If he were still alive, her oath wouldn't allow her to just walk away. Placing both guns out of reach, she leaned over and felt for a pulse. It wasn't strong but it was there. She rolled him over to check his wound. She needed to know where she had hit him.

It was when she rolled him over that she saw it. A badge. This was the man who had left those two precious little girls alone to die. This was the man who had shot Andrew.

Yes. She was a nurse and she would do all she could to keep this man alive. Not because her oath demanded it but because she wanted him to sit in a cell for the rest of his life. She wanted him to have a lifetime behind bars to think about what he had done. She hoped he lived to be an old, old man. And when he died, she hoped he would…well, she couldn't say she hoped he burned in hell. But if he did, he would have only himself to blame.

Beth reached down and unbuckled his belt. Rolling him back over to his stomach, she used it to secure his hands behind his back. That and the fact he had been shot, would keep him from going anywhere.

Retrieving both guns, she hurried back to Andrew. He was sitting exactly where she'd left him. Reaching for the arm on his good side, she helped him to his feet. He staggered a little but managed to stay upright.

When she got him inside, she ran to the helicopter to retrieve the first aid kit and several bottles of water. She carried them back to where Andrew was waiting. Putting her supplies on the teacher's desk, she helped him take his shirt off. She cleaned and bandaged his shoulder. "At least I don't have to dig the bullet out. It went straight through."

Andrew grunted. It felt like his whole arm was on fire. "Good," he managed to say. "We've still got to find Rebecca."

Beth backed up a few feet. "The only thing we're going to find is a hospital. I patched you up, but you need some stitches in the back where the bullet came out. If that wound gets infected, you won't be any good to Rebecca or anybody else."

Andrew opened his mouth to argue, but Beth continued, "Besides, that man I shot is in pretty bad shape. My bullet is still lodged somewhere in his body and from the way his pulse felt, he wouldn't survive me trying to remove it. You both need a hospital. If you can still fly, we can get to the nearest hospital and both of you can get the help you need. And after you turn him over to the authorities, if you want to call in real backup, I understand."

Andrew didn't try to interrupt her again. When she finally stopped talking, he stood up. He knew she was right. "Do you think you can help me get him on the helicopter? There's a hospital about thirty miles to our north. I can fly but as far as the backup, I've got all I need."

When Andrew and Beth made their way back to where the other man lay, Andrew added his belt to the one Beth had secured his arms with.

Turning him over, he saw the badge for the first time. "Damnation," he said.

"My thoughts exactly," Beth muttered. "Well, close enough. He looks heavy. How are we going to get him to the helicopter? If you try to carry him, you're going to start bleeding again. I've been working out at Albert's gym, but I don't think I'm strong enough to carry him."

"Neither of us are going to carry him. We're going to drag him."

Beth hesitated. "Is it going to hurt him?" At Andrew's nod, she said, "Good, let's go."

Between the two of them, they were able to get him secured in the backseat of the helicopter.

As they took off, Andrew said, "Hang on, Rebecca, we're coming back."

It took the rest of the day to reach the hospital, turn the prisoner over to the correct authorities and get Andrew patched up. By then, it was dark.

"We can't track Rebecca in the dark," Andrew told Beth. "Let's see if the hospital can accommodate us for the night."

"Check on that, Andrew. I'm going to see about replenishing our medical supplies."

Andrew watched her walk to the nurse's station and speak with the lady at the desk. It was only a few minutes till an older lady came out to talk to Beth. Then they both disappeared through the door of what looked to be the supply room.

Now, I wonder what she's up to, Andrew thought. From the determined look on her face, he didn't think it was a social visit. And he would bet his next paycheck, she would come out with more than just replacement supplies for their first aid kit.

While Beth took care of her business, Andrew found them accommodations for the night. The hospital had several rooms reserved for resident doctors who needed to spend the night.

The first thing Andrew did when he shut the door to his room was to call Victoria. He wanted to be the one to tell her about getting shot. If she heard it from him, she would know he was alright. Besides, he wanted to check on the kids. He didn't know how or when those four little ones had claimed his heart but they had. Andrew had always liked his life just the way it was. He had his job with the marshals. He had his friends and his own private space when he went home. Now, all that just seemed empty without Victoria and the kids. When Victoria picked up on the other end, the first thing Andrew said was, I think I love you.

In the other room, Beth was talking to Mary Alice, who had put her on speaker phone so Nancy could hear. "Yes, I did! I shot him. Just the way you taught me. You would be so proud. I'm glad I didn't kill him but I'm not sorry I shot him. He shot Andrew and left those poor little girls to die." After twenty more minutes of catching up on what the children had been up to and Beth assuring them Andrew was going to be alright, Beth hung up and headed to the shower. She had no doubt she was going to sleep well tonight. After all she wasn't just Beth, the nurse anymore, she was Andrew's backup. At least for this mission. She had done good. He had said so.

Andrew finished his shower and stretched out on the bed. His shoulder hurt but he took only one of the pain pills. He needed to be alert in the morning. They were going back and this time they weren't coming home without Rebecca.

They would go back to the abandoned school house and track her from there. No doubt Garcia's thug had caught up to her by now. She would be no match for him.

At some point, he fell asleep, but even in his dreams, he couldn't let it go. He dreamed Rebecca was standing on the porch of the school house. He could see her but couldn't reach her. Garcia and his men had her surrounded. They were drinking and laughing. One of them lit a match and threw it on the porch where Rebecca was standing. The dry timbers of the old porch caught and Rebecca was surrounded by fire. She had no way out. She grabbed the pull cord of the old school bell and rang it over and over, trying to summon help.

Andrew suddenly set up in a cold sweat. It had been a dream. Just a dream. They weren't at the school house and there was no fire. But the ringing was very real.

It took him a minute to come fully awake. What he heard wasn't a school bell ringing, it was his phone.

He fumbled around on the bedside table where he had left it after talking to Victoria. He pressed the connect button and said hello.

There was a pause and then a lady said, "I'm sorry to call you so late at night but I think this might be important. Do you know a Rebecca Bing? I think she might be in trouble. I've been on a cruise and decided to fly home early. When I got here, I found my home had been broken into. I found a note. She said to call you. It sounds like this lady is in a lot of trouble. I decided not to wait till morning but to try to reach you tonight."

For a moment, Andrew was speechless. Rebecca had been at this woman's house and left a note?

"Please," he said, "read me the note."

He could hear the lady fumbling around on the other end of the line. When she finished reading, the lady said, "My front window is broken out and something wet has seeped into the boards on the front porch. It might be blood."

Chapter 19

Hershel put his hand on General Morales's shoulder. "Let's get back to camp. I think the action for tonight is over. Garcia will want to get back and celebrate."

Morales nodded and they made their way back to the truck. As they backed out of their hiding place, Morales spoke, "I know you're wondering how I could have shot that man in cold blood. Here in Mexico, we live by a little different philosophy than in your country. We do our best to stay within the law, but when circumstances call for it, we do what is necessary. The man I shot was a very bad man. He has killed many innocent people. He not only dealt in drugs but in prostitution and human slavery. We have been after him for years but he's always been just out of reach. It looks like Garcia was able to accomplish what we could not. I don't know what Garcia's beef with him was and I don't care. The world is a much safer place without him in it."

Hershel took a deep breath. "I'm not judging you, General. You saved my marshal's life. For that, I am grateful. I gave Jeff the order to obey your instructions, so I am as guilty as you. If you have to put our actions in a report, I'll gladly take my share of the blame."

"There will be no need for that," Morales said. "I will, however, notify my superiors. They will need to know that particular threat has been eradicated."

They road on for a few more miles in silence. Hershel was thoughtful. Finally, he turned to Morales. "Maybe we've been going about this the wrong way. We've been waiting for Garcia to get far enough away from his men, for us to grab him. That hasn't happened. According to Jeff, he never leaves the camp without a contingent of his men with him. The longer Jeff stays in that camp, the greater the chance his cover will be blown. That or something else, like what happened tonight, will force him into a situation, which will compromise him emotionally."

"For all his tough guy demeanor, Jeff has a very strong sense of right and wrong. So far, he has been able to skirt the edges, without crossing the line. That came very close to changing tonight. I'm not sure he could kill someone in cold blood, even to save his own life."

Morales agreed. "So, what are you suggesting? A diversion that will allow us to slip into his camp and take him or a situation that will force him to leave his camp without the majority of his men? Either will be hard to pull off."

"Think about it, General, you know him better than I do. What are his weaknesses? What can we use on a psychological basis, that would cause him to deviate from his normal cautious behavior?"

General Morales sighed. "His sister was his biggest Achilles heel. Now that she's gone, I'm not sure he has another. He puts money in an account for his mother but I don't think she touches it. As far as he's concerned, all his men are expendable. He's killed more of his own men than anyone else has been able to do. His drinking makes him more vulnerable, but only if he's separated from his men."

"What about his business?" Hershel checked behind them to make sure they were far enough ahead of Garcia, to remain undetected. "You know, his warehouse of drugs, his suppliers, his distributors. What if there was a disruption in one of those? Would it draw him out, make him careless?"

"Possibly, but he would take all his men with him. He wouldn't venture out on his own, even for those things."

Both men fell silent, trying to think up a scheme that would separate Garcia from his men and in the process allow them to take him down without unnecessary bloodshed. As they came upon their turn, Hershel checked behind them one more time to make sure they weren't being observed.

Hiding the truck in the same place as before, Hershel tapped his earbud to alert Bill and Cliff that they were back. Luckily, this time there were no guards in sight.

"Things have been really quiet here," Bill said. "I started to do a little reconnaissance into the camp but wasn't sure how many guards were left behind. If they had caught me, Jeff's next assignment might have been to shoot me. Then you would have to make a choice whether to shoot him to save me or just to sacrifice me for the greater good." Bill laughed. Hershel and Morales did not. When they relayed what had happened after following Garcia and his thugs, Bill understood why. He slapped Morales on the shoulder. "Thanks for saving my friend. I wouldn't want you to have to make that kind of decision between me and Jeff."

Only half joking, Morales said, "Me either. I've found myself rather partial to your friend."

They made themselves as comfortable as possible, while waiting for Garcia and his entourage to return to camp. While they waited, Hershel and Morales continued their discussion on the best way to separate Garcia from his men.

Cliff listened to the other three men discuss possibilities. Finally, he spoke up, "When I was at the academy, there was this one guy that was a real bully. No one would confront him because he was always surrounded by a bunch of guys who would do anything to stay in his good graces. They were afraid of him too, but—"

Bill interrupted; he punched his fellow marshal in the arm good-naturedly. "Cliff, we all went to the same academy. We don't have time for your stories, however entertaining they may be."

Bill thought highly of the junior marshal but loved to rib him every chance he got. Usually, Cliff would blush and try to stutter an explanation, ending with everyone having a good laugh at his expense. Normally, he would laugh along with the others. He understood, as the youngest marshal and not all that long out of the academy, this was his right of passage.

But this time, it was different. He had a point to make. Cliff punched Bill back and spoke up, "Let me finish. One day a couple of us got tired of being bullied. We knew we couldn't take them all on so we decided to divide and conquer. If the bully didn't have his backup, he was nothing. So, we decided to take out the backup instead of the bully. They weren't so tough; they were just afraid of him like we were. All we had to do was make them more afraid of us than they were of him. Well, it worked. Without his backup, he was nothing."

As soon as Cliff paused, Bill spoke up. He just couldn't help it. "Well," he drawled, "even a blind hog gets an acorn every once in a while."

Cliff pushed him off the stump he had been sitting on. This time everyone laughed but it was at Bill's expense. Maybe the young marshal was coming into his own. Bill laughed along with the others as Cliff reached his hand down to help him up.

"So, what you're saying is that if we eliminate some of his men, it will give us a better opportunity to get to him." Morales looked thoughtful. "You know, Hershel, he might be on to something. Let's talk with Jeff in the morning to see if any of Garcia's men leave camp for supplies or anything. We need to know that and how long it would take for them to be missed. If they are missed right away, the others would be on guard and our plan would be halted before it even got started."

Hershel agreed. "Jeff could tell us when they leave and how many go at a time. If we can take them out in small groups, they might not be missed for a while." He looked at Morales. "If we can pull that off, General, do you have enough men that you trust explicitly, to come pick them up and make sure they are locked down tight? If even one gets back to Morales, our plan will blow up in our face."

Morales nodded. "I have enough men that I have complete confidence in, to make that happen."

Jeff was momentarily stunned. It had all happened so fast. He wasn't sure he had actually believed Morales would shoot the man. Garcia gave the dead man one more kick and recapped his flask. "Let's get back to camp and celebrate. We'll leave this one just where he is so his men can see what happens when someone goes up against me."

Jeff followed along with the others. He'd sort this out later. He needed to talk to Hershel. Morales had shot the man in cold blood. Yes, he had done it to save Jeff's life. Yes, Garcia would have killed the man anyway. Yes, the man probably deserved to be killed. Still, what did that say about Morales?

They piled into the cars and headed back to camp. Garcia had taken several more swallows from his flask. "Tonight, we celebrate," he said. "I'll send a couple of men out to bring in some women. We'll roast a pig and drink to our success. You proved yourself tonight, mi amigo. You will be rewarded."

Jeff tried to play the part. "Sounds like a good plan to me, my friend. But first, I need to wash some of this blood off. A woman wouldn't want to be within ten feet of me."

"Don't worry about that. The ones we bring in have no option but to cooperate. They're too afraid not to. If they give us any trouble, I'll make an example out of one of them and the others will fall in line."

By the time they got back to camp, Garcia had finished off the last of the liquor from the flask. When he got out of the car, he stumbled and had trouble staying on his feet.

"As good as that sounds," Jeff said. "I think our celebration may have to wait till tomorrow. I want my money's worth, my compadre, and right now, I don't think you're up to it."

Garcia pushed Jeff away and drew his gun. "What are you saying? You don't think I can hold my liquor? Or you don't think I can handle the ladies? I ought to shoot you where you stand. Don't forget who's boss. You did good tonight or you would already be dead."

Jeff backed up. Garcia's emotions were volatile. "Hold on! I am well aware who runs this outfit and I just appreciate being part of it. I didn't mean any disrespect. I just thought we would have a better time if we got some rest tonight and left the celebration till tomorrow. By the time we clean up, dig a pit, and get a fire started for the pig, it will be nearly morning. Besides, your men need time to find some senoritas. But if tonight is better, let's go for it."

Garcia didn't lower his gun. He looked at Jeff through bleary eyes. He stumbled a little, then righted himself. He looked down at Jeff's gun.

Then just as quick as it had started, it was over. "Alright, my friend, maybe you're right. The night is nearly gone. We will save the celebration for tomorrow."

Garcia started toward his quarters but went only a few feet before he turned back. "Do not mistake my capitulation as weakness. I assure you it is not."

Jeff watched Garcia walk away. One day Garcia wouldn't be able to rein his emotions in. He would explode and there would be no going back. Jeff turned and made his way back to his cabin. He needed to talk to Hershel and this time he didn't care if General Morales was listening or not. He needed some answers.

Jeff entered his cabin and shut the door. He waited at the window to see if his guard would appear. If not, it would be the first time since he had been in Garcia's camp that a guard had not been posted outside his door.

When no one appeared, he made his way to the other side of the room, taking his bloody shirt off as he went. He washed up at the basin, then tapped his earbud. "Hershel, you there?"

"Now, where else would I be? What took you so long? We've been back for a while. We left as soon as we were sure Garcia was convinced you had carried out his orders. We didn't want to take a chance you might overtake us back to camp."

"Yeah, well, we had to wait for Garcia to have a few drinks to celebrate his victory over an opposing drug lord. And once we got back, he was all set to have another celebration here. He wanted to roast a pig and bring in some girls. When I suggested we wait till morning, I thought he was going to shoot me. He drew his gun and it was touch and go there for a few minutes. The man's unstable. I don't know how much longer he will be able to hold it together."

Hershel sighed. "I've been afraid of that. We did some brainstorming while we waited for you to check in. I think we have a plan to move things along a little faster and get you out of there."

Bill spoke up, "You'll never guess who came up with this idea. Our young friend fresh from the academy. You know. The same academy we all graduated from."

Jeff laughed. "Now you're scaring me. I want to hear about this plan but first I need to ask Hershel a question."

"Go ahead, Jeff, I'm still here."

"I'm kind of a sitting duck here, so I need to know that you all have my back. That was a pretty slick trick Morales pulled back there. I'd really like some assurance that he's really on our side."

Morales started to respond but before he could, Jeff continued, "You have to admit it's unusual for a law official to kill a man in cold blood. And Perez was dirty but he reported to the General. In fact, it seems a lot of the businesses in town belong to Garcia and that town is in Morales's providence. Now all that's circumstantial but in this case, it's my life that's on the line."

Finally, Morales was able to speak. "I don't blame you for being suspicious. I would be too in your situation. As far as killing that drug lord, we have been after him for a very long time. When it came to your life or his, it wasn't a hard decision. Besides it was the only way I could keep your boss from charging in there to save you. As far as Perez and the businesses in town, money talks, and down here money is synonymous with drugs. I'm sure you see some of the same in your country."

"Besides," Hershel spoke up, "Bill, Cliff, and I have your back and we've got him outnumbered. Seriously, don't worry about the General, he's one of the good guys."

Jeff would have to be satisfied with that. He trusted Hershel and if Hershel trusted Morales, that would have to be good enough for him.

"OK, let's hear this plan our young friend came up with." Like Bill, he would never miss an opportunity to poke at Cliff. They just had to cure him of that boyish blush. Other than that, he was an outstanding marshal.

They all started talking at once, when Hershel called for silence. "Since this is Cliff's plan, let's let him explain it to Jeff."

When Cliff finished, Jeff had to admit the plan had merit. They weren't getting anywhere the way they were going. If they couldn't separate Garcia from his men, then separating his men from Garcia seemed like a workable plan.

"All right then," he said. "We've got the perfect place to start tomorrow. I don't know how many men he'll send to fetch the women but I assume at least two. If I know Garcia, he'll start drinking as soon as he gets up. He probably won't even remember who he's sent. If you can intercept them, put the women in protective custody to make sure they don't talk and detain Garcia's thugs, that will be at least two down. I'll keep my eyes open and let you know if any of the others leave camp."

Bill spoke up, "You do know if this works, Cliff will never let us hear the last of it."

They all groaned in unison.

Chapter 20

Rebecca couldn't move. She could barely breathe. How had she allowed herself to become so distracted? He had not only found her, he was holding her arms so tightly to her sides, she couldn't move them high enough to fight.

The thug leaned his mouth closer to her ear. His hot breath made her shiver. "You didn't really think you could get away from me, did you? You have caused me a lot of unnecessary trouble. Whatever Garcia has planned for you, I just might stick around long enough to watch."

He tightened his grip so that she could hardly breathe. He knew he was hurting her and took pleasure in it. Slowly, he started dragging her backwards.

Rebecca tried to think of all the self-defense moves Hershel had taught her. She tried to jab back with her elbow, but he was holding her arms too close to her sides. She tried to kick back with her foot or stomp on his instep. He just laughed and pulled her off her feet, so they were dragging along the wooden porch. She tried going limp, to throw him off balance but he was so strong, it had no effect whatsoever.

They had almost reached the steps. Gravity did what Rebecca had failed to do. The thug stumbled on the top step, causing him to release Rebecca just long enough to regain his balance.

She threw herself forward, trying to break the hold he still had on one arm. She pulled and tugged but couldn't break his hold. She fumbled around in her pocket with her free hand. She pushed the small cans of Vienna's and the sleeve of crackers to the side.

The thug had followed her back onto the porch and had a better grip on her arm. He was trying to recapture her other arm, when Rebecca found what she had been searching for. She came up with the fork that she had carried with her from the first time he had captured her and chained her to a wall. It had settled to the bottom of her pocket and she had thought to begin with she had lost it. When she had hidden it, she had wondered if she could actually stab someone with it. Now she had no hesitation.

Holding it in her fist, she came down as hard as she could on the hand holding her arm. He yelled and jerked his hand back, only to grab her with the other one. Rebecca immediately stabbed that one as well. He backed up a step and Rebecca advanced. She stabbed toward his face, but he pulled back his head at the last minute.

She struck his shoulder instead and this time her force had been so great, the fork was embedded to the base of its tines.

The thug screamed and reached for his shoulder. He grasped the fork and tried to pull it out but his hands were so bloody from where she had stabbed them, they just slid off the handle of the fork. Rebecca knew she had to do something else. She had hurt him but knew she hadn't stopped him. A fork wasn't going to keep him from grabbing her again.

She tried to think. It would do no good to run. She couldn't get a head start and he would easily overtake her. She fumbled in her pocket, for anything else she could use as a weapon. If she could get back in the house, she might find something. She knew she would never make it back through the window though, before he had her again, so she backed up all the way to the wall. She had nowhere else to go.

Still fumbling in her pocket, while never taking her eyes off her assailant, she came up with the can of fix-a-flat. She had no idea what it would do. She depended on Hershel and her car club for all things automotive.

Shaking the can, she aimed for her assailant's face. She didn't know what she had expected. She thought it was a liquid but it quickly turned into a foam. She covered both his eyes and when he opened his mouth to curse at her, she filled his mouth full. She kept spraying till the can was empty.

The thug was gagging and clawing at his eyes. This was her chance. If she could get to the tree line before his vision cleared, she might have a chance to hide. Rebecca side-stepped her assailant and made it off the porch. She slowed down and took one look behind her. What she saw assured her, the thug was still fighting with the foam in his eyes and mouth.

She took off at a full run, not bothering to look behind her again. She didn't stop till she made it to the first line of trees.

He wasn't after her yet. But he was no longer on the porch. She finally located him at the back of the house. He had found the outside faucet and was no doubt trying to wash the foam out of his eyes and mouth.

Rebecca made it further into the forest. She kept herself hidden in the thick underbrush, trying to be as quiet as possible. Her plan, such as it was, was to follow the narrow dirt road that dead-ended in the front yard she had just escaped from. It had to lead somewhere. The woman she had seen this morning had come from this location. Her only chance was to find help before he caught up with her. She stayed well off the road. It would have been easier going but would leave her too exposed.

Rebecca had been moving as fast as she could, without making any noise. She was beginning to tire. Her arms ached where the thug had held her. She would have bruises but that was the least of her worries. Finally, she had to stop and catch her breath. She figured she would have heard him by now but all was quiet.

When she was satisfied he hadn't yet caught up to her, she forged ahead once again. The road seemed to go on forever. She was getting tired and it would be dark soon. What if it was miles before she found another house? For all she knew the house she had just left could be the only one on this road.

Just as she was starting to lose hope, the road curved and about a mile further on was what she had hoped to find. At least she hoped it was. She couldn't see a house, but a driveway with a mailbox beside it. She would have to cross the road to get to it. Checking behind her, she decided this was as good a time as any.

She took a deep breath and darted to the other side of the road as fast as she could manage. Just as she thought she was about to reach the safety of the other side, she fell and went headfirst into a ditch she hadn't noticed before. It wasn't deep but as she fell, she caught her leg on a sharp rock, protruding out of the ground.

She could feel the sharp pain as the rock dug into the flesh of her right leg. Rolling over to check the damage, she saw blood seeping through the material of her pants leg. Sitting up, she tore what was left of the material away so she could see the damage. It wasn't as bad as she'd feared but her pants were ruined and she needed to stop the bleeding.

Rebecca ripped the material in half. Taking her water bottle out, she soaked one piece and used it to wash away the blood. No, it wasn't too bad, if she could just stop the bleeding. Wringing out the wet material, she held it against the wound, applying pressure. When the bleeding had nearly stopped, she tied the other piece of material around her leg and knotted it as tight as she could. That was as much as she could do. Maybe whoever lived at the end of that drive would have a first aid kit.

Rebecca pulled herself to her feet. Looking around to make sure she was still alone, she edged back into the tree line. If her abductor had witnessed her crossing the road, surely he would be on her by now. She stayed hidden and watched for any sign he had caught up to her. Again, she saw nothing so she started forward again.

Finally gaining the drive, she eased around the mailbox and was able to see a house way down at the end. She couldn't tell if anyone was home or if, in fact, anyone even lived there. Not having any choice, she started down the drive, still keeping well inside the tree line.

As she got closer, her hope of finding someone soared. At the back of the house was a clothesline filled with freshly washed laundry. Carefully, Rebecca made her way around to the front of the house. This one was much smaller than the last one. It didn't have a porch. The front door opened right out into the yard. Trying not to make any excess noise, she knocked. When she got no response, she knocked again.

Next, she tried the door. It was locked. She knocked again, this time a little louder. Still no response. She tried the back door, with the same results. She thought about trying a window but they were too far off the ground for her to reach.

Walking around the house, she could see no sign of a vehicle. It looked like no one was home. Walking once again to the backyard, she stood looking at the clothes on the line. Did she dare take some? What she had was ruined and bloody.

But that was stealing. Wait! She was already guilty of that. She had stolen food back at the other house. She was also guilty of breaking and entering back there but didn't have time to try that here. Besides, she couldn't reach a window.

Not waiting to second-guess herself, she walked up and down the clothes line, trying to find something that would work. Rebecca was a small woman and everything looked a mile too big. She wasn't concerned with what she looked like but with whether or not she could keep them up.

Finally, she decided on a peasant blouse and long gypsy skirt. She could work with those. Quickly removing them from the line, she took off her blouse and ruined, blood-soaked slacks. Pulling the skirt on, she rolled the elastic waistband up to match her shorter height. That also took up some of the extra space at the waist.

The blouse was too big as well, but because of the style, it didn't really matter. She left it untucked to hide the roll at the top of the skirt.

Looking down at herself, she decided it would have to do. Looking down the clothesline, she saw one more thing she could use. Not so much to add to her clothing, as to further disguise herself.

Hanging on the end post of the clothes line, was a hat, or rather a sun bonnet. Probably left there by whoever had been hanging up the clothes.

Rebecca stood on tiptoes to remove the hat. She put it on. It not only covered her head, but also the sides of her face. Tying the strings under her chin to secure it, she walked over to a small pond to look at her reflection.

Startled was an understatement. She would not have recognized herself. Hershel would not have known it was her. Rebecca smiled. She had not only solved the problem of her ruined clothes; she had disguised herself as well.

If she couldn't outrun her abductor or out fight him, maybe she could fool him long enough to find someone to help her.

Feeling slightly better, she started toward the drive. She needed to keep going before she lost what little lead she had.

Rounding the house once again, she stopped. She couldn't believe she hadn't seen it before. Leaning up against a tree by the house was a bicycle. She checked it out. The tires looked good and were fully inflated. She rolled it back and forth a few times and it rolled smoothly. The only problem—it was a boy's bike. But maybe in this case, that was a good thing. The extra bar from the seat to the handlebars would help hold up the long skirt so she could pedal.

It was almost dark now. Should she stay where she was till daylight? No. He was too close and would find her. She had to keep moving. Since she couldn't ride or push the bike through the forest, she jumped on and rode it to the end of the drive. She had no way to leave a note this time but when she came back to repay the woman at the first house, she would stop by and settle up here as well. Hopefully, when she explained the circumstances, they wouldn't have her arrested.

She sat at the end of the drive, looking both ways. She wasn't looking for traffic. She would have been thrilled to see some. No, she was checking to see if Garcia's thug was anywhere in sight.

Rebecca pedaled out into the road trying with all her might to look like she belonged on this bike, on this road, at night, in the dark. She adjusted her bonnet. The road was rutted and every time she hit a bump, the bonnet shifted.

The going was slow, hardly any faster than she could walk. But at least she was sitting down. It felt good to be off her feet, although the movement of keeping the pedals going made the fresh abrasion on her leg ache.

She tried not to think about it. After all, she could have broken it. One more thing to be grateful for.

Rebecca rode on for about five more minutes, before her luck ran out. She could see him from the corner of her eye, but there was nothing she could do.

He ran out from the opposite side of the road just ahead of her. Evidently, he had thought she would have kept going instead of investigating the driveway. Now, she wished she had.

She tried to speed up and go around him. It didn't work. He grabbed the handlebars and knocked her off the bike. He started to jump on the bike and ride off, when her bonnet once again fell to the side, revealing her face. Her luck had just run out. He had only been going to steal her bike. He hadn't recognized her.

The thug lay the bike to the side of the road and turned back to her. "Well, who do we have here? I think we have a little unfinished business."

Rebecca was able to get her feet under her and turned to run. She made it as far as the first group of trees before he caught her. Grabbing her with one hand, he slapped her with the other. "Garcia said to bring you back alive. He didn't say what shape you had to be in. Now you're going to pay for all the trouble you've caused me."

He drew back his fist and hit her upside her head. Rebecca almost lost consciousness but was still lucid enough to try to run. It did no good. He pushed her to the ground and kicked her in the ribs. Rebecca doubled up from the pain. She curled her arms over her head, trying to protect herself. It did little good.

He yanked her to her feet and slapped her again. This time she didn't go down, but stayed on her feet. She backed away from him but had nowhere to go. She stood her ground and faced him. "I don't know why Garcia wants me, but if he sent you all this way, he must have a really big reason. If you kill me, it's not going to go well for you. And if I'm all beat up, I may not be any good to him. You'd better think about what you're doing."

The thug just laughed. "I just had to get that out of my system." He grabbed her arm and started pulling her into the woods. "What I have in mind for you now won't leave any marks. At least not visible ones."

Rebecca felt herself grow cold. He was going to rape her and there was nothing she could do to stop him. He had only drug her a few feet, when a voice came out of the dark from behind them.

"That's enough. This isn't what Garcia sent you to do. He sent me to find out what's taking you so long. You should have been back with her days ago."

Rebecca and her abductor had stopped in their tracks. Rebecca was terrified. This man was not here to help her. He was here to help her abductor.

Finally, he spoke, "You have no idea the trouble this bitch has caused me. She deserves everything she gets. She needs to be taught a lesson."

The man facing her abductor said, "So do you. Garcia said when I caught up with you to use my discretion."

Rebecca hadn't seen the gun in his hand but she heard the noise when he pulled the trigger. Her abductor fell forward. There was no doubt he was dead.

Her new abductor didn't touch her. He just nodded to the truck idling in the road behind them. "Get in," he said.

Rebecca complied. She was out of options.

Chapter 21

Andrew fumbled around for the rest of his clothes. He stuck the phone in his shirt pocket and bolted out the door of his room. Beth was just next door but it seemed to take forever to get there.

Banging on the door, he barged in without giving her a chance to answer. "Beth, get dressed and meet me at the helipad. Now! We've got to go."

Beth sat up. As an emergency room nurse, she was used to being summoned from a deep sleep because she was needed. But now she was a little confused. She wasn't in Hadbury and she wasn't at Memorial General Hospital. She was miles from home in a strange hospital with Andrew trying to find Rebecca and bring her home. Rebecca! She jumped from the bed and grabbing her clothes headed for the bathroom to get dressed.

Andrew was already gone. He knew she would follow as soon as she was dressed. He needed to get to the helipad and do his preflight check. Thank goodness he had requested the helicopter be serviced and refueled when they had first landed.

Beth reached the helicopter and threw her stuff on board before Andrew could finish. She didn't bother to question him. She could sense his urgency. Something had happened and he would explain as soon as they were airborne.

When Andrew finished and climbed in the helicopter, Beth took her seat beside him and waited till they were in the air. "Well!" she almost shouted. "Tell me!"

Andrew banked the helicopter to the left and headed west. As he did so, he told Beth about his telephone call from the concerned woman. "That means she escaped her abductor at least for a while. She must have seen the house and went there for help. The house was empty because the lady that lives there was off on vacation."

Beth interrupted. She couldn't contain her questions any longer. "So, she broke the front window to get inside? Was she trying to find a place to hide or looking for something to eat? Didn't she know he wasn't far behind her and she would be trapped inside? Why didn't she just hide somewhere and wait for someone to come home?"

Andrew held up his hand in the universal sign to stop. "Beth, I don't know the answers to any of those questions. I'm sure she knew she couldn't hide in the house without getting trapped in there. After all, the front window was broken out and Rebecca was the one to do it. All the thug had to do was walk up to the porch to see that. He wouldn't even have to break in a locked door. He could just climb in the window like Rebecca had done. My guess is she was looking for a phone to call for help or some kind of weapon to defend herself with."

Beth sucked in a deep breath. "And all she'd been able to do was leave a note. She must have been so scared. And the woman said there was blood? Did she say how much?" As a nurse, Beth knew the amount of blood a person could lose and still be alive. She didn't even want to go there. Rebecca had to still be alive.

Andrew touched Beth's hand. "We can't assume the worst. We don't know yet if it's blood on the porch. These helicopters are equipped with crime scene kits. We'll be able to tell if it's blood or something else. You can help me work the scene. If they're any clues to what happened and where she went, we'll find them."

They both were silent then. Each lost in their own thoughts. Andrew going back over everything the woman on the phone had said. Had he missed anything? He had been sound asleep when the phone had rung. He had been dreaming of Rebecca and her being surrounded by Garcia and his thugs. Was he confusing anything from the dream with the actual phone conversation? He didn't think so but at this point every clue was important. The one fact he kept holding on to was that Rebecca was alive when she left that note.

As all these thoughts went through Andrew's mind, Beth was lost in her own. She and Rebecca had only been friends for six months but it didn't take long to bond with someone who had so many of the same characteristics. They were both strong women. They were like minded when it came to helping others. She, as a nurse and Rebecca as a child advocate. They both could be fearless when it came to the welfare of others. That was what made them so good at their jobs. She had sat in on a hearing once when Rebecca had been representing an abused child. She had removed the child from the home and was petitioning the court to place the child in the custody of her maternal grandmother. It looked like the child might be sent back home, when Rebecca took control of the hearing. By the time she finished presenting her evidence and calling witnesses on behalf of the child, the judge reversed his decision and the child went home with her grandmother. Beth's easy-going, mild-mannered friend had turned into a fierce defender. Thinking about that made her feel better about Rebecca's present situation. She was smart and resourceful and not easily backed into a corner.

As Andrew changed course, Beth again started to pay attention to her surroundings. In the distance, she could see the small building where the two young girls had been abandoned. How fitting that Rebecca was the one to find them and make sure they were taken to safety.

"Are we going to land there again? I don't think Rebecca would have come back this way. Unless of course, she was being forced."

"No," Andrew said. "I just want to fly over and take a look. We captured one of the guys, thanks to you, but the other one got away. I don't think he'd come back but I'm just making sure."

Andrew did a low flyover and hovered for several minutes over the forest; in the area the man had fled. Seeing nothing new, he changed course and headed in the direction of Rebecca's last known location.

They flew over the forest and across the meadow but Andrew chose to set the helicopter down well shy of the yard. He didn't want to do any damage to the ladies' scrubs and flowers. It appeared she spent a lot of time tending to both. He also didn't want to destroy any evidence of what went on here between Rebecca and her assailant.

As Andrew and Beth exited the helicopter, an older lady stepped through the front door. It was barely daylight but it looked like she had been up for hours.

She waited for them to get closer, then walked down the porch steps. Holding out her hand, she said, "Thanks for coming so quickly. That poor woman must be terrified. I called our local sheriff too, but he hasn't arrived yet. He has quite a distance to come. I called you first so you would have time to see everything just the way I found it. When you told me you were a United States Marshal, I figured you would have more resources to handle this than our local authorities."

Andrew and then Beth reached out and shook hands with the lady, introducing themselves. They learned the Good Samaritan's name was Ida Grantham.

Andrew stood holding his crime scene kit and taking in the porch and broken window. "Mrs. Grantham, before we do anything else, would you mind walking us through the house and yard and pointing out anything out of place? If I can get an overall picture of everywhere Rebecca might have been, I may be able to piece together a picture of what happened here."

"Certainly dear, let's cover the outside first. You can see where she broke the window. I left the glass and everything else just as I found it. I know better than to disturb a crime scene. The hammer she used is inside the house on the kitchen table. She must have laid it there after climbing through the window. Something wet has seeped into the porch. Some of it looks like blood but some spots have a peculiar smell. Not that I got down and smelled it. I didn't have to; the odor is strong."

Next, they made their way around to the back. She motioned to the utility building at the very back of the yard. "That's where the hammer came from. I didn't see any disturbance in there, but you're welcome to look."

At Andrew's nod, she opened the door and reached for the pull cord to turn on the overhead light.

"Hold on," Andrew said, before she could touch the cord. He took a small flashlight out of his pocket and focused it on the pull cord.

Beth gasped. "That looks like Rebecca's hair."

Andrew nodded and pulling on a pair of disposable gloves, unwound the strands of curly hair from the cord. Beth held an evidence bag, while he dropped it in.

He was following all crime scene protocol. This was not his jurisdiction and knew he might face an inquiry for not waiting for the local authorities.

He stood for a few minutes looking around the inside of the utility building. "Ma'am, does anything look disturbed in here to you? Anything missing or out of place?"

Ida slowly looked around the building. She was studying it intently, wanting to be as helpful as possible. "No. I don't think so. There's so much junk in here, it's hard to tell. My late husband didn't get rid of anything and since he passed away, I haven't had the heart to clean out in here."

Ever the nurse and nurturer, Beth stepped forward and placed her hand on Ida's shoulder. "We're so sorry for your loss. It must be lonely living way out here by yourself."

"Oh no. I keep busy. I have a wonderful group of friends. We have a sewing circle and Bible study group. We meet on Thursday evenings and play cards. The cruise I just came back from was to celebrate Jolene's birthday. My husband's been gone several years now. This is home. I wouldn't want to be anywhere else."

Andrew had walked to the back of the building, while the ladies were talking. "Is this the table where the hammer came from. Most men keep their tools in some kind of order and there's an empty spot where something used to be."

Ida looked back to where Andrew was standing. "Yes, that's where Herbert always kept it."

Andrew made his way back to the front of the building. "Alright, I think that's all I need to see in here. Let's go back out and finish looking around outside and then I want to take a closer look at the porch and window."

Ida led the way back out but stopped halfway to the house. "Now this is probably nothing. I hesitate to even mention it because an animal could have wandered through my garden and left this but it is out of place."

Andrew and Beth looked where Ida was pointing. On the ground lay what was left of a mostly eaten tomato.

Beth held out another evidence bag and Andrew dropped it in. "Just to be thorough, I'll bag and tag it. The local authorities may want to see if they can get DNA off of it. I'll leave that up to them."

Ida led the rest of the way back to the house. She stopped beside the outside faucet. "Now next to the broken window, this was the worst. It was turned on and left running. If I hadn't come back early, it could have caused the water level in the well to get low enough to burn up the pump. Now that would cost a pretty penny to replace."

Andrew knelt on one knee and examined the ground. Most of whatever was here had been washed away by the running water. But over to one side, some kind of residue clung to the grass. He took a sample and placed it with the others.

Ida stood by, watching him work. "That's about all out here. Do you want to see the porch and window now?"

Andrew nodded and they all made their way back to the front of the house. As they started up the steps, Andrew held out his hand for the others to stop. "It looks like a lot went on up here. Would you ladies mind waiting on the steps while I check this out and take some samples?"

Both ladies complied, took a seat on the steps, and watched Andrew as he studied the scene under the broken window. He bent down and opened his kit. He took several samples, then took out a small device and attached it to his phone. He was muttering to himself but not loud enough for the ladies to be able to understand what he was saying.

Finally, he walked back to where the ladies were sitting and joined them. "I've seen all I need to. I think I can piece together what happened. Rebecca was running for her life. She saw the house from across the meadow. Hoping to find help, she came here. No one was home. Out of desperation, she found the hammer and broke the window to get inside. She probably hoped to find a phone and call for help. Maybe she even looked for a weapon to defend herself with."

He paused and looked at Ida. "Would she have found either of those things inside?"

Ida shook her head. "No, all I have is a cell phone and I had that with me. I don't like guns and wouldn't know how to shoot one anyway. My husband had a shotgun but I gave it to our oldest son after he passed away."

"Ok then," Andrew continued. "Not finding anything inside that would help her, she probably searched your cabinet for food that would be easy for her to carry. Knowing the thug couldn't be far behind her, she wouldn't have stayed any longer. My guess, from the looks of the porch, he grabbed her as she was coming back out the window. Scuff marks indicate a struggle. There is some blood but it's not Rebecca's."

Beth let out a shuddering sigh. She hadn't realized she'd been holding her breath. "How do you know it isn't Rebecca's blood?"

Andrew studied Beth's face before he spoke again. She had turned pale at the mention of blood that might belong to her friend. Beth was a nurse and so competent, he sometimes forgot she was still just a civilian.

"We have a database with the blood profiles of all our marshals and their families." He cleared his throat. He knew Beth would be all over what he was going to say next. "Just in case we need to identify them."

But to Beth's credit, she didn't speak. Ida, however, was a different matter. "You mean to identify their remains, if they aren't identifiable by any other method?" She stopped as if suddenly remembering they were talking about a close friend.

Andrew jumped in to fill the awkward silence. "The important thing is that the blood is not Rebecca's. Therefore, she must have found a way to injure her assailant. It wasn't a little nosebleed. Too much blood for that. She got in some good jabs with something. I'm not going to look for what she used as a weapon. I'll let the sheriff do that.

"It doesn't surprise me she would find a way to fight. She is after all Rebecca. What surprises me is what else I found. I knew it smelled familiar but until I tested it, I couldn't place what it was. HFC-134a."

When he noticed the blank look on the faces of the two women, he explained further, "It's the chemical name for the propellant in fix-a-flat. I'm familiar with the smell because like most teenage boys, I hung around our local garage when I wasn't in school. I'm guessing that's what was at the back faucet as well. I don't know where Rebecca got it but she was smart enough to hold on to it. It's my guess when she hurt him bad enough to draw blood, he opened his mouth to scream and probably curse at her, she filled his mouth and eyes full. While he was trying to wash it off, she ran."

Andrew looked down the road that led to Ida's house. "I'm betting she followed that road, hoping to find another house with someone at home. Ida, how close is your closest neighbor back that way?"

"Well, I don't know exactly. It would be a long walk but not impossible. Especially if you didn't have another option."

Andrew gave Ida a hug. "I'm not going to leave you with an open window. I know the sheriff is on his way but you said yourself, it might take him awhile. If you have some loose boards, I'll nail it up for you. I don't think that thug will come back this way, but I'll feel better if I know you're tucked safely inside until the sheriff gets here."

After taking care of Ida's window, Andrew and Beth climbed back into the helicopter and followed the road until they spotted the next house. Ida was right. It would have been a long walk, but flying took only minutes.

They weren't able to land close to the house so they circled and found a spot wide enough in the road to set down. Andrew didn't figure much traffic came this way, but he left room to get by just in case.

As they started walking back to the house, Beth suddenly stopped. She fell to her knees, grabbing something off the ground. She bent over in tears, rocking back and forth.

Startled, Andrew dropped down beside her. "Beth, what in the world? What is it?"

Beth continued sobbing, but held up the bloody piece of cloth to Andrew. It was soaked in blood. "This is Rebecca's. I remember it. Andrew, she's hurt. He must have caught up to her and hurt her."

Andrew reached and took the bloody material from Beth. He got up and examined the road and ditch they were standing in.

Coming back to Beth, he knelt down. "Beth, look, this may be Rebecca's and this may be her blood, but he didn't catch her here. Look, there's only one set of footprints leading up to this spot and only one leaving this spot. She may be hurt but not so bad that she couldn't keep going. Come on. Let's get to that house and see if she stopped there."

Beth quickly got to her feet and they hurried on. Rebecca had to be close and if she was hurt, she needed them more than ever.

By the time they made it to the driveway, a man and woman were approaching from the direction of the house.

The man hurried forward. "What took you so long? We called hours ago." Suddenly, he stopped. "You're not the sheriff! Who are you?" The man stepped in front of his wife as if to protect her.

Andrew stepped forward and introduced himself and Beth. He explained about the break-in at Ida's and their search for Rebecca. "What happened at your place that caused you to call the sheriff? Ida said he was on the way so I'm sure he'll swing by here first."

The man explained about the missing clothes and bicycle. Andrew thanked the couple and taking Beth by the hand hurried back toward the helicopter.

"We have to be close. She has disguised herself and has a bike to ride. She can move quicker now but we can catch up if we hurry. This is as close as we've been to finding her."

They had been airborne only a few minutes when Andrew sat the helicopter down. This time he didn't look for a convenient place. He sat it down directly in the middle of the road. He didn't care if he was blocking traffic. He had seen the bike Rebecca had been riding, flung to the side of the road and only a few yards from it lay a body.

When they had landed, he touched Beth on the shoulder. "Stay here and let me check this out."

But Beth shook his hand off and was out and running. She was a nurse. If this was Rebecca, she needed her. Reaching the body, she stopped just ahead of Andrew. It wasn't Rebecca but if this was the thug that had abducted Rebecca, where was she? Why hadn't she gone back to one of the houses and waited? The threat would have been over.

Andrew knelt by the body. "This man's been shot. Rebecca didn't have a gun." He got up and grabbed Beth by the arm. "Come on, let's go, hurry."

Beth did as he directed but when they reached the helicopter stopped. "Go where, Andrew? We don't know where she is now."

Andrew got the helicopter in the air. "Yes, we do. She's headed for Mexico."

Chapter 22

To Jeff's surprise, the rest of the night was peaceful in Garcia's camp. Evidently, Garcia had consumed enough liquor to allow his tormented mind to sleep. The rest of the men always followed Garcia's lead.

Jeff took this time to try to unwind. Having a man shot between the eyes while standing only a few feet in front of him, had been unnerving. Especially when he had to act like he was the one who shot him.

He thought about his fellow marshals, so close and yet so far away if trouble broke out inside the camp. He could handle himself but was vastly outnumbered. It would take only one bullet to take him out and there would be plenty of guns pointed his way. Jeff couldn't let his mind dwell on that. Being undercover was always risky. This time was no different.

Just at dawn he saw Garcia emerge from his office. He must have slept there. He talked to two of his men briefly, then went back inside. He seemed to be sober but Jeff knew that wouldn't last. Garcia wanted a celebration. A celebration meant drinking. Drinking meant trouble. But in this case, it could also mean opportunity.

If any of the men drank enough to wander away from camp, Hershel and the others would be ready.

Jeff watched as the two men headed out of camp. Jeff tapped his earbud.

Hershel responded immediately, "You're up early. What's up?"

Jeff laughed. "The early bird gets the worm. And two of them are wiggling your way now. If you catch them on the way out, you won't have to deal with the women they're going to fetch."

"Understood. Going fishing now," and Hershel was gone. He turned to the other men. "Get up, we've got two coming our way."

Bill groaned. "I was having the best dream. You remember that nurse back in Hadbury? I think her name was Beth. Well, I've only seen her briefly in the past six months but she seems to be stuck in my mind."

"Well, unstick her and get up. We've got two coming our way." Hershel briefly wondered why his senior marshal hadn't already made a move in that direction. The man wasn't getting any younger and he wouldn't find a better match than Beth.

Cliff spoke up, "She's a little old for me or I'd give you a run for your money." At Bill's look, Cliff decided to change the subject. "I sure could use a good breakfast. Eggs, sunny side up, crisp bacon, grits, and a big fluffy biscuit. These rations we've been eating are getting old."

Before he could say anymore, Hershel interrupted, "Sounds good to me. When we round these two thugs up, you can go with General Morales to hand them over to his men. On your way back, stop and get some of that breakfast for all of us."

The General and Cliff went to take care of business. Bill and Hershel settled back to wait. They set in silence for a few minutes, then Hershel spoke up, "Bill, did you do much fishing when you were growing up?"

Bill didn't have to ponder an answer. "Shoot, yea I did. My dad would take a group of us nearly every weekend in the spring and summer. Those were some of the best days of my life."

Hershel nodded. "Where'd you get your worms?"

Again, Bill didn't hesitate. "Get the worms? Why, the bait shop, of course. Where else would you get worms?"

Hershel chuckled. "You are a city boy. Didn't you ever grub for worms?"

Bill looked mystified "What's that?"

"Well Bill, you drive a wooden stake in the ground, then take a piece of metal, maybe a pipe or whatever's available, and rub it across the top of the wooden stake. The worms come to the top of the ground."

Bill was into it now. "And then you get the worms to fish with. Who would have thought they had hearing that good?"

It took Hershel a minute to pick up on what his marshal had said. "No Bill, they don't hear what you're doing, they feel the vibrations in the ground. They come up because of the vibrations."

Bill looked confused. "Alright. You want to hunt some worms? I'd just as soon wait for Cliff to bring us back some breakfast."

Hershel couldn't tell if Bill was messing with him or serious. He decided to give him the benefit of the doubt.

"If we moved a little closer to the edge of Garcia's camp, we might catch one or two of his men separated from the others. We could stay back a little and rattle the bushes. If we can get him to come investigate, we might whittle the odds down a little more. Kind of like grubbing for worms."

The look on Bill's face was like someone had turned a light on. "Oh, I get it. You want to go grub now or wait for Morales and Cliff to get back?"

"I think we'd do well to wait. It's always a good idea to have backup. But we can let Jeff in on our plan."

Hershel tapped his earbud and explained to Jeff what he and Bill were planning.

Jeff listened. "I'm not sure I'm comfortable with my backup grubbing for worms. Just make sure they're well out of camp before you grab one and he's not able to sound the alarm. I may even be able to help a little. I was fixing to walk around to see if Garcia is out and about. If I see any possibilities, I'll think of a way to let you know."

As Hershel and Bill settled back to wait for Morales and Cliff to return, Jeff stepped out of his cabin. The sun was bright. Jeff had to wait for his eyes to adjust. It didn't look as if Garcia had made an appearance yet. He counted the men he could see. He counted only twenty but knew Garcia had many more than that in his organization. They just didn't all stay in Garcia's camp. They were spread out all over the region and performed many jobs inside the organization.

Still, twenty was too many. They wanted to take Garcia with little to no bloodshed. Besides, the fewer people who knew the exact details of what happened to him, the better. It would also be good if Jeff could get out of this mission with his undercover status intact. It might be useful later on down the road. There was always one more drug lord to be taken down.

Jeff walked around the perimeter of the camp. No one challenged him. That must be due to his new status. He hadn't had a guard at his door last night either.

Jeff didn't think for one minute Garcia trusted him. He just distrusted him a little less. He also knew Garcia would kill him for next to no reason. Especially if he was drinking.

As Jeff made his way around the perimeter of the camp, he came across two men standing by the back road to the camp. They weren't guarding. They were smoking. He stopped to talk to them.

"You wouldn't happen to have a spare cigarette, would you, mi amigo?"

One of the men reached in his pocket and offered the pack to Jeff. "Garcia doesn't like us to smoke in the camp. Better stay to the edge if you don't want to bring his wrath down on you and if he's drinking, better not to light up at all."

Jeff accepted the cigarette and a light before thanking the man for the cigarette and the advice. He moved on toward the other side of the camp as if that had been his purpose all along. When he was sure no one was looking, he reached up and scratched the side of his head, tapping his earbud in the process.

"Go ahead," Hershel said.

Jeff spoke quietly, "Two worms by the backdoor."

Hershel chuckled. "Good timing. Morales and Cliff just got back. Bill and I are going fishing. I'll let you know if we catch anything."

Jeff didn't respond. He just moved on the way he'd been going. After a few yards, he threw the cigarette down and ground it with his heel. He hated the things. It had been all he could do not to choke on the nasty thing. He headed back to his cabin to wash his mouth out.

Garcia watched Jeff from his window. Just what was the gringo up to now? Garcia couldn't put his finger on it, but he didn't trust his new recruit. Something about him was off. Yes, he thought, as soon as his usefulness was over, he would have to take him out. If Garcia took pleasure in the thought, he wouldn't let it show. At least not yet.

Jeff watched from the other side of the camp as the two men he had been talking to eased back into the woods. He silently wished Hershel good fishing.

Jeff entered the cabin and went straight to the lavatory to wash his mouth out.

It was an hour later when Jeff heard Hershel whisper, "Fishing was good. Two more in the freezer. Before long, we'll have enough for a fish fry."

Jeff whispered back, "Eighteen to go by my count."

Jeff rolled over and closed his eyes. He thought Garcia would be chomping at the bit to get this celebration started. It was just ten o'clock but still, what was he waiting for?

Jeff must have dosed. He sat up with a start when someone banged on the door to his cabin. His hand automatically going to his gun. He had to get better control of his emotions.

He got up and opened the door to find one of Garcia's men standing there. "The boss wants you to join him for a drink," he sneered, and walked away.

Jeff could see Garcia sitting at one of the tables in the middle of the compound. He had a bottle and two glasses. He held one up and motioned for Jeff to join him. Closing the cabin door behind him, Jeff made his way over to the table and took a seat across from Garcia.

Pouring liquor in the two glasses, Garcia handed one to Jeff. He motioned to the other side of the camp where two men were digging a pit to roast the pig.

"As soon as the women get here, we can get this party started. The pork will be ready by nightfall."

Jeff took a small sip of his drink. If this was going to go on all day, he had to be careful not to drink too much. Until Garcia was too drunk to notice, he had to at least appear to be drinking as much as Garcia.

Garcia emptied his glass and refilled it from the bottle. "What happened to the rest of Clint Montgomery's men?"

That took Jeff by surprise. Other than the first day in camp, Garcia hadn't mentioned his former boss. "I don't know. It was my understanding they were all arrested. I didn't exactly stick around to find out."

Garcia took another swallow of his drink. "What about that United States Marshal, Hershel Bing? I heard he was the one who brought Montgomery down."

Jeff had to be careful. Why was Garcia asking about Hershel now? Did he suspect something or just making conversation? "Like I said, I didn't stick around and I don't exactly run in the same circles with U.S. Marshals." Jeff wished Garcia would change the subject.

But when he did, Jeff was even more uncomfortable. "That's a nice gun you've got there. Mind if I take a look?"

Jeff could do nothing but hand over his weapon. Garcia had kept it when he was first brought to camp. Why did he want to see it again? Not having any reason to refuse, Jeff took it out and handed it to Garcia.

Garcia examined it like he'd never seen it before. He got up and, aiming it into the woods, fired off a round. For a minute, he just stood there. Finally, he turned back to Jeff, still holding the gun, now pointed at Jeff's head. Pausing for only a minute, he turned the gun butt first and held it out to Jeff.

Jeff took the gun and placed it in its holster. What had that been all about? Had Garcia been trying to make a point or had he actually been thinking about pulling the trigger?

Garcia seemed to remember the celebration. "Where the hell are those women I sent for?" He yelled for two of his men, who came running. "Go check on the women. What's a party without women? And liquor," he added as he drained the bottle. Giving Jeff just a glance as he walked off, he said, "I'll get another bottle."

Jeff watched as Garcia walked back to his office but what his attention had really been on was the two men leaving camp to help fetch the women.

Jeff casually touched his earbud. "Two more worms wiggling your way."

Jeff heard a soft laugh. This time, it was Morales. "At this rate we'll have a stringer full."

Jeff answered, "You may have a stringer full, but they're just minnows. The big bass is still in the pond. With me," he added.

Morales just laughed again. "Patience, my friend. Patience."

Jeff didn't answer. What could he say anyway? Until they could end this, he had no choice but to be patient.

Garcia chose that moment to emerge from his cabin. He had a bottle in each hand. From his unsteady gait, he had taken a couple of drinks before he came back out.

Looking around to make sure no one was watching; Jeff lowered his glass between his knees and poured the rest of his on the ground.

Garcia staggered toward Jeff. "I see I'm just in time. Your glass is empty. You can't have a celebration with an empty glass." He reached over to fill Jeff's glass, splashing it on Jeff as he did so.

Jeff clenched his teeth together. He would like nothing more than to put his fist into this blowhard's face. It took all he could do to hold back.

Garcia didn't even notice—the spilled liquor or Jeff's reaction. He was too far gone. A few more drinks and Garcia would pass out. Jeff would just have to wait it out. Garcia wasn't too drunk to shoot him and he would if Jeff tried to leave the party too soon.

Garcia turned and shot his gun in the air. He screamed out several obscenities and walked drunkenly toward the roasting pig.

Jeff thought for a second he was going to shoot the pig but instead he grabbed a knife and cut off a piece. The meat wasn't done but that didn't stop

Garcia. He stuffed it in his mouth and chewed. The fact that blood was running down his chin didn't seem to faze him.

Jeff had to turn away. He could feel his stomach roil.

Garcia was making the rounds of his men, offering each a bite of the meat. Nobody refused. Jeff didn't think he could do it but knew what would happen if he didn't. Hoping to avoid the inevitable, Jeff stood up and, picking up the knife, cut a piece of meat that was nearly done and at the same time rubbed his hand in the bloody part. Walking over to Garcia, he slapped him on the back and at the same time put the meat in his mouth and chewed. Being sure to let Garcia see the blood now running down his arm.

Garcia nodded his approval and held up Jeff's hand to show the others the blood. They all cheered and Jeff finally allowed himself to take an easy breath. If Garcia had been sober, Jeff would have never gotten away with it. If any of the others noticed, no one was brave enough to bring it up. That told Jeff that not only were the other men afraid of Garcia, they were beginning to fear him as well.

Garcia went back to the table to wash his meat down with another drink. This time Jeff joined him. He felt like he needed it. It wouldn't be long now. Garcia was hardly able to sit up. Jeff could be patient now. This celebration was coming to an end.

Jeff thought things had gone better than expected. The celebration was about over and no one had been killed. And better yet, they had taken out some of Garcia's men.

Jeff looked around to see if there were any more possibilities but all the men had settled down well within the parameter of the camp. They were enjoying the food and liquor and weren't likely to wonder off anywhere tonight.

Jeff unobtrusively touched his earbud. "Fishing's over for the night. Worms gone to earth."

In his ear he heard his boss say, "You did good. Tomorrow's another day."

Just as Jeff had expected, Garcia had passed out. Without being told, two of his men picked him up and took him to his bed. Jeff took the opportunity to make his way back to his cabin. He was exhausted and ready for this assignment to be over. He was ready to go home.

Jeff shut the door of his cabin and taking his gun and holster off, placed them close to the bed. Removing his clothes, he stretched out on the bed. He hadn't drunk much of the liquor, but what he had was sitting heavy on his stomach. For all his tough guy appearance, he wasn't much of a drinker.

Just when he thought he might dose off, he remembered Garcia holding his gun. Reaching over, he removed it from the holster. As soon as he started checking it, he noticed the damage to the firing pin.

He was right to be cautious. He wasn't going to shoot anybody with this gun.

Chapter 23

Getting in the truck, Rebecca dared a side glance at this new threat. She had not seen this coming. It had never occurred to her that Garcia would send a second thug. Why did he want her so bad? It had to have something to do with Hershel. Was he going to use her as bait? She couldn't let that happen. Hershel would do whatever he had to, in order to save her. Even if it cost him his life.

She had gotten away from the first thug, she would figure out a way to get away from this one. She took a deep breath and turned slightly in her seat. "Where are you taking me?"

At first, she thought he wasn't going to reply. Finally, he glanced in her direction. "I think by now you know the answer to that question. I'm taking you to the same place your other escort was taking you. I'm delivering you to Garcia. What happens then is not my concern."

"I know that. I guess I mean, are we going all the way to Mexico? Does Garcia have a camp on this side of the border?"

"You ask too many questions. What difference does it make? You'd do better to worry about what's going to happen once you get there."

Rebecca knew he was right but she figured the more she knew, the better. She couldn't make a plan without some information. "It makes a difference to me. Garcia has no reason to take me over into Mexico. How would you even get me there? It's not like you can just drive across the border. I have no passport or papers of any kind. The border patrol wouldn't let you take me across."

"Don't you worry about how I'm going to get you there. That's my job and I know what I'm doing."

Rebecca gave his words some thought. "I'm not going to just sit quietly while we cross over. I'm going to scream and create a commotion. If I'm going to die, I'd just as soon be killed at the border than in Garcia's camp. You'll be arrested and put in jail. I may be dead, but you won't go free."

A cold smile came over her abductor's face. "You can scream all you want. Nobody's going to hear you. Only the snakes and lizards. I don't think you'll find any help in that direction. You look pretty beat up to me. I don't figure you'll be much trouble."

Rebecca remained quiet. What had she learned? Evidently, they weren't going to cross the border at any of the conventional border crossings. The thug wasn't worried about her calling any attention to them.

She knew if Andrew hadn't been notified of her note, he eventually would. He would follow her trail. The note, the broken window, the bloody piece of her clothing on the side of the road, the missing clothes and bike from the second house and most important of all the dead man just off the road. Those were not exactly subtle clues. Andrew would have no trouble up to that point. But what about now? She had to figure out a way to leave a trail for him to follow from this point. It was her only hope.

Rebecca reviewed her resources. They weren't many. She had used up all the stuff she had hoarded in her pockets. They had all come in handy but now she had nothing left.

She looked down at her borrowed, or if she was going to be honest, her stolen clothes. There had to be something. The blouse was full and the skirt was long. Both blouse and skirt were brightly colored. The bottom third of the skirt was red.

Rebecca fingered the hem of the skirt. She eased it up so she could see the underside, being careful not to call attention to what she was doing. Just as she hoped. The skirt was hemmed with bright red thread.

Glancing at her abductor, to make sure he wasn't paying any attention to what she was doing, she started to pick at the thread. If she could break a piece lose, she could work the thread out of the hem and use it to leave a trail for Andrew to follow. As a plan, it wasn't much, but it was all she had.

They rode on in silence for the next couple of hours. Her abductor didn't seem to be in any hurry and that was fine with Rebecca. She needed time to work as much of the thread lose as possible. When she had reached as far to both sides of the hem as possible, she knew she needed a reason for him to stop so she could readjust her skirt. She needed more thread.

Shifting in her seat, she looked at the thug. "How much further do we have to go? I really need to use the bathroom. I've been trying to hold it but I can't much longer. If I have an accident in your truck, it's going to make you mad.

If you can stop for just a minute, I can step behind some bushes by the road. I promise not to try to run. There isn't anywhere for me to go anyway."

Evidently, the thug understood the wisdom of this, because he pulled over and stopped. "Go just behind those bushes. Do what you need to do and come back. If you try to run away, I'll shoot you in the leg. I won't kill you but you'll never be able to run again either."

Rebecca just nodded. She wouldn't try to run. She knew he would shoot her. As soon as Rebecca felt she was far enough behind the bushes to afford the privacy she needed, she found a spot and took care of business. She really did need to go.

Having gotten that necessity taken care of, she pulled her skirt around so she had access to the back hem. The good thing about these gypsy skirts, there really wasn't a back and front. They were the same all the way around.

Like most hems, one long piece of thread went all the way around. All she had to do was tug on the thread and it released its hold on the material. Because of the fullness of the skirt, Rebecca ended up with a lot of loose thread.

Hunting around on the ground, she found a twig that had broken free of the bush she was behind and quickly wound the thread around it. She had seen her father do this with fishing line to keep it from getting tangled.

After stuffing all but one piece of thread in her pocket, she realized she had another problem. Her skirt was now two inches longer than it had been before. It would drag the ground when she tried to walk. Reaching under her blouse, she rolled the skirt up at the waist to shorten it. If the blouse hadn't been so loose, it would have been obvious, but the extra material hid the roll.

Rebecca checked herself over to see if anything else she was wearing could be used to leave a trail. All she had was the skirt and blouse and her underwear.

She dismissed the idea of using her underwear as soon as it crossed her mind. She had been raised a Southern Baptist and Southern Baptists did not go around without their underwear.

She had taken too much time anyway. She heard the truck door open and then close and his boots crunch on the dirt and gravel on the side of the road. He was coming to get her. She let him get a little closer, then started out from behind the bushes. She wanted his back to her as they walked back to the truck.

"I'm coming. I didn't mean to take so long." She met him halfway back to the truck.

He didn't speak, just turned around and headed back, knowing she had no choice but to follow him. He had no way of knowing but that was exactly what Rebecca wanted him to do.

As they reached the edge of the road, Rebecca took her piece of bright red thread and wound it several times around a tree branch hanging from the roadside. She left about four inches to dangle in the breeze. She hoped it would be like a signal, if Andrew made it this far.

As they drove off, Rebecca tried to engage the thug in conversation. She didn't want him to look in his rear-view mirror until they were down the road. It was only thread but it was bright red and waving in the slight breeze.

Her attempt at conversation fell flat. The thug was not paying any attention to her. Neither was he looking in his rear-view mirror. Instead, he was zeroed in on the dashboard of the truck and seemed to be listening intently to a small knocking sound.

For the next five miles, this stayed the same. Rebecca watching the thug. The thug watching the dashboard and listening to the knocking.

When smoke started to billow from under the hood of the truck and the knocking got louder, he was forced to pull to the side of the road. He leaned his head back and muttered something in Spanish. The few words Rebecca understood made her thankful she wasn't more affluent in his native language.

Finally, he turned his head in her direction. "Get out. We walk from here."

Without saying a word, Rebecca got out. As she rounded her side of the truck, she surreptitiously draped a piece of red thread under the windshield wiper.

Seeming to talk more to himself than to her, the thug muttered, "We would have ditched the truck up ahead anyway."

Rebecca didn't speak. She had no way to know what was going to happen next. Why would they have ditched the truck anyway? They weren't even in Mexico yet.

Shoving her in front of him, they started down the road. After only walking for about an hour, he grabbed Rebecca by the arm and pulled her roughly off to the side. Taking a bandanna out of his back pocket, he tied it around Rebecca's mouth so that she was unable to make a sound.

He leaned in close to her face. "We're going to stay well off the road for a while. Up ahead is a border crossing. It is in a very rural area and only manned by two guards. If you make a sound, I will shoot them. Nod if you understand me."

Rebecca vigorously nodded her head. For some time now, she had been able to hear running water. Maybe a river or wide stream. They had been too far away for her to see anything. Surely, he didn't intend swimming across whatever it was. Rebecca could swim, only not very well and not very far.

They made their way slowly and silently past the border crossings and the two guards. About fifty yards down and around a bend in the road, they started making their way out of the trees and brush. While her captor checked to make sure they were out of sight of the guards, Rebecca wound a piece of red thread around one of the bushes at the side of the road.

She was sure Andrew would stop and talk to the guards. She just prayed he would continue on this way far enough to see her sign. Surely, when the guards said they hadn't seen anyone come this way, he would continue at least for a while down the road to see if they had skirted around the guards to keep from being seen.

If he found her red thread on the truck, he would know they were on foot and he was still on the right track.

Rebecca knew she was putting a lot of faith in Andrew's ability to read her signs. What was obvious to her, might mean nothing to him. Still, he was a United States Marshal. He was trained to be observant.

Her abductor reached over and removed the bandana from around her mouth. "Remember, stay quiet. I will shoot anyone trying to come to your rescue."

Rebecca only nodded her head. She knew if he worked for Garcia, he was a killer. Was she leading Andrew to his death by leaving a trail for him to follow?

Having to have faith that Andrew could take care of himself, she had no choice but to follow her abductor when he once again started off down the road. At one point, she lagged a little behind so she could drape a piece of her red thread around a bush growing a little out into the roadway.

They seemed to be veering away from the water as the road wound around an outcropping of rock. As they were halfway around the rocks, her abductor grabbed her arm and pulled her across to the other side of the road. Her abductor stopped and studied the face of the rocks bordering this side of the road.

Rebecca watched but could see nothing. She took the opportunity to tie off another piece of thread to let Andrew know they had crossed to the other side of the road.

She couldn't understand why they were just standing there. There really wasn't any direction to go but to follow the road.

Her guard walked down a few feet and then back, still studying the rock. At last, he grunted with satisfaction and moved some bushes aside.

Rebecca gasped. He had uncovered the opening to a cave. She didn't like where this was going. If they went underground, Andrew would never find her.

She quickly unwound some of her thread. She was getting short but left a longer than normal piece, hoping he would understand that this location was more significant than the others.

Not able to hold back any longer, Rebecca looked at her abductor. "Where does that go? We aren't going in there, are we?"

"You ask too many questions but yes, we're going in there and it leads to Mexico, where I'll finally be rid of you."

Rebecca pulled back. "But we have to cross the river, don't we? How are we going to do that from inside this cave?"

The thug pulled harder. "This isn't a cave, it's a tunnel and it goes under the water."

Rebecca was really fighting now to get free. She screamed, "I'm not going in there!" Finally, Rebecca had found something that really frightening her. She couldn't do this. She couldn't go under the river in this tunnel.

The thug yanked her forward with one hand and rearranged the brush over the entrance with the other.

"You will do this, if I have to carry you." Once again, he tried to pull Rebecca forward but fear had given her new strength. She pulled back and dug in her feet. He finally stopped fighting with her. "Listen to me. The river is very shallow at this point. It's no more than seven feet deep and thirty feet wide. We will be well under the water and as soon as we are across, the tunnel starts back up."

Rebecca was past listening. She didn't care if he was the one with the gun. She wasn't going.

"Let me put it another way," he said. "You either come without a fuss or I will knock you unconscious and drag you."

That got through Rebecca's fear. She didn't want to be unconscious. How would she be able to leave her trail for Andrew? She stopped struggling. "Alright, but I can't open my eyes until we get to the other side. Let me hold on to you so I won't fall."

The thug just sighed, took Rebecca's hand, put it on the back of his belt, and started forward. They almost immediately started to descend. Rebecca whimpered but didn't speak. Nor did she open her eyes. If she had, it would have been too dark to see anyway. This crossing was too close to the border patrol's crossing. Any small light shining through the ground before they got to the river would have alerted the guards.

Rebecca stumbled but kept going. The ground was uneven but didn't seem to be wet. For that she was grateful. Finally, the ground under her feet seemed to be leveling out. They must be under the river, but Rebecca couldn't let herself think of that now. If she did, she would panic.

She couldn't hear the water and that in itself was a blessing. Of course, she was humming loud enough to drown out any other sounds. She stumbled again, but now they seemed to be climbing. "Are we across the river yet?" she ventured.

She thought he wasn't going to answer but finally he stopped and turned so she could hear him better. "Yes, we are on the other side but the tunnel goes on for several hundred more yards. When we emerge, we will be well past the border patrol's crossing. It will do you no good to try to get their attention."

Without another word, he turned and started walking again.

Rebecca took a deep breath. She was ok now, but didn't let go of his belt. She still couldn't see, but wasn't afraid any longer. At least not as afraid as she had been. With her eyes open, it was a little easier. She could see a light coming from in front of her. Not exactly a light, as a lessening of the darkness.

And then they were there. The thug was pushing through bushes that concealed the opening of the tunnel. When they were finally in the clear, Rebecca reached in her pocket to retrieve her red thread. She would leave a sign for Andrew, just in case he had been able to follow her this far.

But just as Rebecca pulled the thread from her pocket, she was pulled forward, causing her to drop all of it. She couldn't pick it up without her abductor seeing it. She would have to leave it. But that thought was secondary to what she was seeing in front of her.

The thug was moving brush and limbs to the side, while pulling her forward. As he continued, she was able to see a truck emerge from its hiding place. He opened the door and pushed her inside. As he pulled off, she could see her supply of red thread, lying on the ground just outside the tunnel.

Chapter 24

Beth looked at Andrew in puzzlement. "Why are we going back the way we came? He wouldn't have taken her back that way."

"We don't know what kind of vehicle they're in. Nor how much of a head start they have. Heck, we don't even know the direction except back that way."

"Alright," Beth said. "But why are we going back the way we came?" she insisted.

Andrew was as frustrated as Beth. "The one thing I'm sure of are the tire marks. The people in both the houses we stopped at drive cars. But back there where we found the body, was a very distinct set of tire tracks made by a large truck. Probably a 4 x 4. They didn't come this way. They turned around where we found the body and went back the way they came from."

Beth was gritting her teeth. She didn't care about tire tracks. She cared about what was happening to her friend. "Andrew, I'm going to ask one more time, why are we going back the way we came?"

Andrew was setting the helicopter down close to the last house where the bike had been stolen. He turned and looked at Beth. She had been such a trooper and so savvy on everything up to this point, he was temporarily speechless that she had to ask.

"We can't follow those tracks from the air. We need another vehicle. One that's on the same level as the truck that left those tire tracks."

All Beth could say, as she suddenly was on the same page as Andrew, was "oh".

Andrew was out and running up the driveway, as soon as the helicopter was settled. Beth was right on his heels. By the time they reached the house, the man and his wife were waiting for them in the front yard.

The man stepped forward. "What's wrong? We thought you were close to finding your friend?"

Andrew had to bend over and catch his breath. "We need your car," he gasped.

The man backed up a step. "Now wait just a minute. First, a strange lady steals my wife's clothes. Then she takes our son's bicycle. Now you want to take our car? I don't think so!"

His wife stepped forward and placed her hand on his arm. "Let him have it."

Turning to his wife, he shook her hand off. "No, they're not taking our car!"

"James, a woman's life is at stake. Let him have it. We can manage."

They stared at each other and Andrew held his breath. He could commandeer the vehicle, but wanted it to be their choice. He waited.

Finally, the man pulled the car keys out of his pocket and handed them to Andrew.

The woman spoke up, "Do what you have to and good luck finding your friend."

Andrew was touched. He figured the car was the only transportation they had. "I'll see you're compensated." He shook the man's hand and hugged the lady's neck. "Thanks."

He jumped behind the wheel and Beth climbed in the other side. He raced down the driveway and onto the road, not slowing down till they were back where the truck tire marks started. Andrew got out of the car and took a closer look. He took a couple of pictures with his phone. He was familiar with this brand of tire but if there were any irregularities in the tread, he wanted them documented.

After all, if they got in a more congested area, they might run across a lot of trucks with this same brand. He wanted something that would distinguish this particular set of tires from any others.

When he returned to the car, he showed the pictures to Beth. "I'm going to drive slow. You look out the window on that side and I'll do the same on this side. We follow these tracks and we'll find Rebecca."

What he didn't say was, what they would really find was the truck. Whether or not Rebecca would still be in it or not, was yet to be seen. He couldn't bring himself to take away what little hope Beth had of finding her friend.

They drove on for several miles without speaking. Beth finally broke the silence. "Thank you."

Andrew took his eyes off the side of the road just long enough to say, "you're welcome." He didn't have to ask what for.

Neither spoke again for several more miles. Andrew pressed on the accelerator a little. No reason to keep to this slow pace. The tracks they were following, were now the only ones on the road.

Suddenly, Beth was shaking Andrew's arm. "Stop! Back up!"

Andrew slammed on brakes. Beth was out of the car, running back the way they had come, almost before the car had stopped.

He backed up to where Beth was standing on the side of the road. When he joined her, she said, "Didn't the lady back there say the clothes Rebecca took were multicolored? And didn't she say they were gypsy style with a lot of red?"

"Yes, she did. Why's that important now?" Andrew was trying to follow Beth's train of thought, but was coming up blank.

"Andrew, look! That's red thread wound around that bush. I almost missed it. I was looking down at the tire tracks and not at the side of the road. I happened to glance in the rear-view mirror and it caught my attention. The wind was making it more. Don't you see! Rebecca left us a sign."

Andrew moved closer so he could get a better look. The thread did indeed look as if it had been placed there. It wasn't merely caught on a branch. It was wound around several times, as if someone put it there and didn't want it to blow away.

"Beth, you may be right. Stay alert for any more signs like this, especially red thread."

Jumping back in the car, they once again stuck to their slower pace. If Rebecca was trying to leave signs for them, she was using the only thing she had at her disposal. Red thread from her clothes.

They drove on in silence. Each lost in his own thoughts. Andrew thinking what a good marshal Rebecca would make. She was smart and resourceful and good at using whatever was at her disposal. Beth was thinking, as soon as they had her friend back home, she was taking her shopping. She had certainly earned some new clothes. They would each buy a red outfit and go out to eat at a fancy restaurant to celebrate.

About five miles down the road, Andrew pulled in behind a truck sitting on the side of the road.

He put his hand on Beth's arm. "Stay in the car and keep the doors locked until I check this out. I think this is the truck we've been following but until I get a closer look at the tires, I can't be sure. If something's wrong with the truck, they may be hiding nearby to commandeer another ride."

Beth waited, but if Andrew was right, Rebecca could be close. She scanned the area all around the truck. But if Andrew was right, Rebecca wouldn't be alone. That thought was the only thing that stopped Beth from leaving the car to search for her friend.

She watched as Andrew examined the inside of the truck and then knelt down to look at the tires. When he gave her the signal that it was safe, she got out and joined him. As she approached, he reached out and pulled something from under the windshield wiper. When she was close enough to see what he was holding, she stopped and gasped. A piece of red thread.

"You were right," Andrew said. "She's leaving us a trail to follow. And since there are no other tracks going forward, it's safe to assume they're on foot."

Beth reached and took the red thread from Andrew. She put it in her pocket with the other one. She didn't know why but she couldn't leave the thread behind. She wanted to be able to give them back to her friend when they were all safe again. It was her way to prove to Rebecca that they had followed her signs.

Andrew motioned toward the car. "Let's go."

Once again, he and Beth slowly drove down the dry dusty road. Both keeping a lookout for red thread or other signs Rebecca had passed this way.

They had been driving for about fifteen minutes without any further sightings, when Andrew pulled over and stopped. Beth followed him when he got out and walked to the side of the road and then a little way into to brush.

She turned around in a circle. "I don't see anything, Andrew. What am I missing?"

Andrew pointed at the grass and weeds around them. "Someone came this way and not very long ago. See how the grass is mashed over. It's bent but it's still green. If this had been done for a while, the bent grass would have died and been brown."

Beth pushed ahead of him and started following the damaged grass.

"Wait, Beth. Let's think about this. Rebecca has been smart enough to leave a trail for us. And yet she didn't leave her signature red thread at this point. It's almost as if she's telling us not to go this way."

Beth wasn't convinced. "Or maybe she ran out of thread." She wasn't ready to abandon the trail she was following. But even as she said that, she could see the wisdom in what Andrew was thinking. She came back to stand beside him. "So what are you thinking?"

Andrew hesitated, as if working something out in his mind. "We have only two choices, follow this path or follow the road. Wait here a minute, Beth. Let me check something."

Walking back to the road, Andrew started forward on foot. He walked several hundred feet and then stopped and cocked his head to one side. Obviously hearing something Beth could not, he nodded to himself and started back toward the car.

Beth looked at him questioningly but didn't speak. Andrew leaned against the car.

"Ok, this is what I think. Let's check out my theory and if I'm wrong we'll come back here and follow this lead."

"Tell me," Beth said.

Andrew nodded. "Look around you. There is nothing within sight. What would cause them to suddenly leave the road and take to the bushes? When I walked up the road, I could hear water. If my guess is right, Mexico is on the other side. There's something up ahead, he's trying to avoid. Since we can't see where they came back on the road, I say we drive a little way up the road and see what's there. If I'm wrong, we'll come back here and follow this trail. I'm trusting Rebecca and her red thread to guide us."

Without speaking, Beth climbed back in the car and waited for Andrew to follow.

It didn't take long to prove Andrew's theory. Around the next curve in the road was a border crossing, manned by two guards. Andrew pulled up to the crossing and got out. After showing the guards his credentials, he explained their situation and questioned the guards on anything they may have seen.

They assured him no one had come their way. He didn't mention his theory of someone slipping past them to try to cross further down. He respected their authority and the fact this was their jurisdiction but he couldn't afford to let them slow him down. They were close to catching up to Rebecca and her captor. He could feel it.

Andrew pulled the car back onto the road. They had only gone a little way when there was a sharp bend in the road, putting the border guards out of sight. About fifty yards into the curve, Andrew saw what he had been looking for. Hanging on a bush beside the road was a piece of bright red thread. He had been right to trust Rebecca.

A little further down the road they found another piece of thread. The road curved again to skirt around a large outcrop of rock.

About half way around the outcropping, Beth gasped. "Andrew, stop! Look, they've crossed the road." She was pointing at the opposite side from where they had been looking.

Andrew stopped the car and looked in the direction Beth was pointing. The piece of red thread was dangling from a low branch. And then he saw another. Rebecca had been trying to direct their attention to this spot specifically. She wouldn't have wasted her precious supply of red thread by leaving two pieces otherwise.

Pulling the car off the road, they both got out. Andrew walked in one direction, Beth in the other. They were both examining the side of the road and the rock. Trying to figure out what Rebecca had been trying to show them.

Andrew was the first to see it. "Beth, come look at this. When I moved some of this loose brush, I uncovered the opening to a cave or maybe a tunnel. This is what Rebecca was trying to tell us. They went this way and she didn't want us to miss it."

Beth stuck her head in the opening. She wasn't crazy at the thought of going in there, but if Rebecca had, she would too.

Andrew moved ahead of her and drew his weapon. "Let me go first. We don't know how far ahead of us they are. They could still be in the tunnel."

Beth nodded and drew her gun as well. Andrew groaned. He had forgotten she was packing the gun. "Please put that up. I don't want you to stumble and accidentally shoot me in the back."

He waited as Beth hesitated. She didn't want to put her gun up but saw the wisdom of what Andrew was saying. Finally, she put it back in the shoulder holster. Andrew waiting while Beth eased around him into the tunnel. Then he pulled the brush back in place. He didn't want some curious passerby seeing the opening and try to investigate. They all would be in trouble if they walked up behind Beth and scared her. If she pulled that gun and started shooting, the bullets ricocheting off the walls of the tunnel could take them all out.

When the bushes were back in place, he again took the lead.

It was dark and they had to feel their way along. When they started down, Beth didn't stop but she did hesitate. "We're going under the river, aren't we?"

Andrew responded, "I would expect so. I can't see any other reason for this tunnel to be here. The coyotes use it to bring people over from Mexico. There must be hundreds of similar tunnels along the border. They dig them faster than the border patrols can shut them down. It seems like we're fighting a war we can't win. But if we didn't stop at least some of them our country would soon be overrun with people who have no way to support themselves. They come here looking for a better life but most end up being used for free or cheap labor. The migrants can't report them for fear of being deported. And yet, they still come."

He knew he was talking mainly to keep Beth's attention off the fact they were now probably directly under the river. If he were being honest, he'd have to admit it freaked him out a little as well.

Finally, they started to climb. They both relaxed a little and Andrew stopped so they could catch their breath. "Now Beth, when we get to the end of the tunnel, I want you to stay put until I check things out. I'm sure they've gone by now, but just in case, stay inside the tunnel."

Bet nodded, then realized Andrew couldn't see her. "I'll stay put, Andrew, until you give me the all clear."

Not long after their rest break, they were able to see light up in front of them. When they reached their destination, Beth was true to her word and stayed put while Andrew eased outside the tunnel to check things out.

"Alright Beth, you can come on out."

Anxious to be out of the tunnel, Beth pushed past the brush into the fresh air.

She felt herself relax, until she saw what Andrew was holding in his hand. Not just a piece of red thread, as Beth would have expected. But a small stick with all of Rebecca's thread wound around it. How would they follow her now?

Chapter 25

Jeff woke from a troubled sleep. He could sense Garcia was becoming more unhinged. The alcohol wasn't causing it but it was definitely contributing to his erratic behavior. They needed to bring this mission to an end, and soon.

Looking out his window, he noticed things seemed quieter than normal. He imagined Garcia and most of his men were sleeping off last night's festivities. He tapped his earbud. Hershel responded on the other end. "Sounded like quite a party last night. Everything ok this morning?"

Jeff sat down on the edge of the bed to put his shoes on, making sure his backup weapon was firmly in place. It was the only workable gun he had now. He wondered if Garcia disabling his primary weapon at this particular time had any significance.

"Everything seems quiet here so far. Except for the perimeter guards, everyone else seems to be sleeping in."

Bill spoke up, "Garcia's getting careless. It wasn't that long ago he wouldn't have tolerated such lax behavior from his men."

Jeff stood up, making sure his pants leg covered the top of his boot where his gun was nestled against his ankle.

"Careless is a mild term to describe Garcia's behavior. The man is getting absolutely unhinged. I don't think he's going to be able to hold it together much longer. And his men are taking their cue from their leader. Things are going downhill fast."

Hershel spoke up again, "Don't take any unnecessary chances, Jeff. Get out if you feel it's too dangerous. If you can't, we can bring in reinforcements. I wanted to bring Garcia to justice without excessive bloodshed but not at the risk of losing one of my best marshals."

Bill and Cliff spoke up at the same time. "I thought I was your best marshal."

Hershel chuckled. "It depends on which one of you happens to be in the most trouble. Right now, it's Jeff."

General Morales took this time to cut in on the light-hearted banter. "I have some men that are totally trustworthy. If we have to come in and get you, Jeff, it won't be just us. We can get you out."

Jeff's opinion of General Morales had changed somewhat. He had more trust in the man but not as much as he did his fellow marshals.

"No offense, General, but unless your men are faster than a speeding bullet, they won't be much help to me if the lead starts flying around here."

Morales didn't take offense. "You're never going to forgive me for taking your gun away from you back at Headquarters, are you?"

Jeff thought back to that particular conflict with the General. It still didn't sit well with him, to have another man take his gun. Especially another law enforcement officer.

"I have to admit, that's not one of my favorite memories. However, in your shoes, I would have done the same thing."

Morales spoke again, "Good to know. But I'm serious about the backup, Jeff. I can have my men in place just in case they're needed. Unlike Garcia's, my men are fit and ready to go."

Jeff had been looking out the window as he talked. "I'll have to get back to you on that, General. Garcia just left his office and it looks like he's heading this way."

Jeff opened the door to his cabin and went out to meet Garcia. He looked to be sober but something about him was off. Jeff couldn't put his finger on it, but there was a look in Garcia's eyes that wasn't quite sane.

They met in the middle of the compound. Garcia put his hand on Jeff's arm and pulled him to the side. "I have something for you to do. I considered sending one of my other men, but in this particular situation, you would be better suited."

"I'm one of your men now. What do you need me to do?" Jeff had a feeling he wasn't going to like what he was fixing to hear.

Garcia started walking again, he was trying to decide how much to reveal to Jeff. This mission was just too important to take any chances. He still had reservations about this gringo. Garcia stopped. He had made up his mind. After all, he wasn't going to let him live after this mission anyway.

"I just heard from one of my men. He's been gone on a special assignment and it seems he's had some success. He should be here late this afternoon. I need some information and I think you may be the one to get it for me."

"Tell me what you need and I'll see what I can do."

Garcia stopped walking and turned to face Jeff. "I have very reliable information that United States Marshal Hershel Bing is in this area. I need to know exactly where he is and if I should happen to need to contact him, how's the best way to do that. I want this to be done quietly without him knowing anyone's asking questions."

Jeff took a moment before he answered. Had Garcia somehow discovered his connection to Hershel? If so, he would surely be dead by now. He decided to play along.

"And you think I would be the best man to get this information for you? Why is that?"

"Simple; you are a gringo. If one of my men started asking questions about a United States Marshal, it would raise questions. On the other hand, if another gringo started asking the same questions, it would probably go unnoticed."

Jeff wondered what Garcia was up to. He wasn't surprised Garcia knew that Hershel had been in the area. After all, Hershel had been part of a raid on a village where Garcia was supposed to have been. The same raid in which Garcia's sister had been killed. What surprised him was that he seemed to know that Hershel was still here. General Morales had been careful to put out the word that Hershel and the rest of the marshals had gone back to the States after the failed raid.

"I can be very discrete but what makes you think he's still around here? From what I heard, he and his men left the area weeks ago."

Garcia just smiled. "Let's just say a little bird told me. A little bird that doesn't sing anymore." Now Garcia let out a full-blown laugh, evil in its intensity.

Jeff immediately knew he was talking about Perez. If Perez had revealed that much information to Garcia before he was beaten and gutted, what else had he said in an effort to save his life?

"I'll get right on it. Where's the best place to start? After all, I don't run in the same circles as lawmen."

Garcia seemed to consider this for a moment. "It is my experience most men at some time or other frequent the bars. Some to have a drink, some to

190

pick up a willing senorita. Now maybe this marshal wouldn't talk so freely in such a place. But he cannot isolate himself. People around him see things and hear things and just maybe they aren't so careful when they go into a bar for a drink after work. I don't care how you get the information, just get it."

Jeff nodded. He knew he wasn't going to get any more information out of Garcia. He would have to play this out and see where it went.

"I'll leave right away. I may have to hit several bars to get the information you want. I'll try the ones closest to Police Headquarters first. If he's still in the area, that seems the best place to start."

Garcia watched Jeff walk away. He waited while he retrieved his Harley and rode out of camp. Yes, he thought, the gringo would be useful but not for much longer.

As soon as Jeff was outside of Garcia's camp, he tapped his earbud.

Hershel answered immediately, "I was able to pick up part of that. Start from the beginning and tell me everything Garcia said and exactly what he wants you to do. It sounds like this is all fixing to blow up in our face."

Jeff rode slowly. He had to talk fast before he was out of range. After he had repeated all of his and Garcia's conversation, he said, "What should I tell him? I already have the information he wants but I can hardly tell him that you're just outside his door waiting to take him down. Neither can I go back with no information."

Hershel understood the situation his marshal was in. "Stay in town as long as you can. That will buy us a little more time to come up with a plan. When you get back, tell him that I sent the others home but I stayed back to tie up some details with the Mexican authorities."

Jeff had just turned onto the road leading to town.

Hershel continued, "But Jeff, if you feel it's too dangerous, don't go back to Garcia's camp."

But Jeff was already out of range and didn't hear Hershel's last statement.

Jeff reached town and took the opportunity to ride around and get a better idea of the layout. When they first got to town, he had been restricted to police headquarters to keep from blowing his cover. When he had assumed his bad-boy persona, looking to hook up with Garcia, he had been sent to a cantina known to accommodate thugs and drug lords.

He wanted to see how the town was laid out. In his experience, the more information he had the better. He never knew what little detail would save his life.

The town wasn't large so it didn't take long to ride from one end to the other. He counted five bars. He would visit them all. He needed to kill as much time as possible. Maybe Hershel and General Morales would come up with a plan. He would give them as much time as he could, without raising Garcia's suspicions.

Since it didn't matter where he started, he pulled into the parking lot of the bar closest to the Police Headquarters. Securing his bike with a chain and lock, he checked it from the outside. It looked like a relatively mild place. Probably its proximity to the Police Headquarters had something to do with that. It was early in the day, so it was almost deserted.

He walked up and took a seat at the bar. When the bartender wandered over, Jeff ordered a beer. After he was served, he left the bar and took a table where he could keep his eyes on his bike.

Being this close to the police department, he wasn't too worried. Still, it was his only transportation. What self-respecting bad guy allowed his bike to be stolen? His fellow marshals would never let him live it down.

He stayed about an hour, nursing his one beer. Only three other men came in while Jeff was there. He didn't try to make conversation with any of them.

Finishing his beer, he made his way outside. He stood for a few minutes before removing the lock and chain from his bike.

The next bar was only a block away. He debated leaving his bike and walking but decided against that idea. He might be next door to the police department, but that was no guarantee. Guiding his bike out of the parking lot, he headed for the next bar. It looked much the same as the last one. As before, he locked his bike down before going inside.

He was still within view of the police department, just not quite as close.

Several other patrons came and went but all was quiet. He had been there about thirty minutes, when two guys came in and took a seat next to his table.

They both ordered whiskey. Jeff privately wondered how anybody could drink whiskey this early in the day. He couldn't help overhearing their conversation.

One guy was asking the other a question. "What's going on at the police department? I passed by on the way here and I saw a large contingent of officers leaving. It looked like they were in a hurry."

The other man just laughed. "Who knows. Something's always going on around here. I learned a long time ago to keep my head down and my mouth closed."

They both laughed and started talking about someone's uncle getting caught with his wife's best friend.

Jeff angled away from the men. He wasn't interested in their new topic. He did however, wonder what was up at the police department. Had General Morales called in reinforcements? Had he and Hershel come up with a plan or were they just hedging their bets? He'd have to wait till later to find out.

Right now, it was time to hit the next bar. This was number three. It was a little further across town and a little livelier. Whether it was the later hour or the distance from the police, it was packed.

Jeff stayed at the bar just long enough to order his beer, then took a seat by the front door. He didn't want to get caught in the back incase a fight broke out and he didn't want to have his back to the room.

He watched as two men on the other side of the room confront another guy, who looked to be minding his own business. The two seemed to be wanting something from the man who was now trying to leave.

Jeff could only hear part of the conversation but it sounded like the two were either trying to start a fight or take the man's money. The lone man finally made it as far as the door, in his effort to avoid a confrontation and get out with his money intact. The other two were right behind him. Jeff knew if they all made it outside, the single man wouldn't have a chance.

It wasn't his fight. He couldn't blow his cover. He also couldn't stand idly by while a man was robbed, beaten and maybe even killed. Jeff was a marshal first and an undercover marshal second.

He waited for the lone man to clear the door, then stood up just as the other two reached the door. He blocked the door, seemingly by accident. The two tried to shove Jeff to one side so they could get out of the door. Jeff stumbled back in front of them as if he were intoxicated.

Watching out of the corner of his eye, he saw the lone man make it to his car and drive off.

He stumbled out of the other's way and muttered an apology. The two men trying to get out the door shoved Jeff back into his seat and went back toward the bar.

Any other time, a shove like that would have ended up with fists flying, but Jeff had accomplished his purpose. He waited for the men to return to the bar where their backs were to him, before he slipped out the door.

By the time he got to the fourth bar, it was almost dark. He secured his bike and went in. Making his way to the bar, he ordered his beer. He had no intention of drinking this one. He couldn't afford for his senses to be dulled. He knew things in Garcia's camp were coming to a head. He would need all his faculties sharp to stay alive.

He watched the other patrons for a while but nothing much was happening. A group in the corner were in a poker game but it seemed friendly enough.

Jeff left his beer on the table and was on his way to the last and final bar. After this, he was going back to camp. He would tell Garcia the story they had agreed on. 'All the marshals had gone home, except for Hershel and he had stayed behind to tie up all the paper work. He could be found around the police headquarters and it would be easy to find him.'

Jeff pulled up at the final bar just in time to see a group of women being loaded into a wagon. It looked like they were going to a party. They were dressed like dancers. They seemed fine with the arrangements so Jeff just passed by them and entered the bar. This one was the noisiest yet. Music was blaring from a sound system. Couples were dancing and a lot of liquor was being consumed.

Jeff had been here before. This was Garcia's bar. The one Jeff had been bashed over the head and abducted from. He didn't stay here long. He had no doubt he would be recognized and his activities reported back to Garcia. He had no reason to stay anyway. He had his story down pat.

He ordered his beer and taking it with him, went back outside. He poured the contents on the ground, chucked the bottle in the bushes, and got back on his Harley. Just as he started the bike, he thought he heard someone calling his name. He looked around but didn't see anyone so he pulled out of the parking lot. Again, he thought he heard someone calling his name. He hesitated but thought he must be mistaken. Who here would be calling him?

Jeff hit the clutch and sprayed gravel as he sped out of the lot. He had been gone long enough. It was time for him to get back.

As he neared the camp, he contacted Hershel just to let him know he was back.

Hershel waited for Jeff's brief report before speaking, "You better get the lead out. It sounds like you're missing the party. Things sure have been loud since you left. Looks like Garcia finally got his women."

Jeff rode into camp and parked his bike beside his cabin. Something was happening alright. The women he had seen at the last bar had arrived and the party was in full swing.

But that wasn't what had Jeff's attention. A truck was pulling into camp from the other entrance. He was close enough to see a man and woman. Garcia met them before they were completely stopped.

When the woman got out and was handed over to Garcia, Jeff couldn't believe what he was seeing. He wasn't sure what to do first, but one thing he knew, he was going to need some help.

He tapped his earbud but instead of reporting what was happening in camp, he asked General Morales a strange question. "How close to Hershel are you?"

"I'm standing right beside him, why?"

"And the others?" Jeff asked. "Where are Bill and Cliff?"

"We're all right here, you idiot. What is it?" That was Hershel and he didn't sound happy. Well, he was fixing to be a whole lot less happy.

Jeff spoke again, "Guys, I'm going to ask you to do something. Please don't question me. Just do it and then I'll explain."

For a minute, no one spoke. Then something must have clicked with Bill, because he said, "Sure Jeff, what is it?"

Jeff took a shaky breath then said, "Grab and hold Hershel and no matter what he says or does, do not let him go."

Jeff could hear a scuffle on the other end. Finally, amid a lot of heavy breathing, he heard Hershel's outraged voice, "Jeff, you'd better explain yourself pretty damn quick or your career as a marshal is over."

And then Jeff said the words he knew would rock Hershel's world. "Garcia has Rebecca."

Chapter 26

Andrew and Beth had no choice but to start walking. They had emerged from the tunnel in a forest. They could follow the path the truck had taken but if it came out onto a well-traveled road, the changes of following the tire marks were slim to none.

Beth held back the tears. She would not cry. If she cried, it would be a sign, she had given up. And she refused to give up, therefore, she would not cry.

Andrew wasn't going to cry either but not for the same reason as Beth. Andrew was too mad to cry. This shouldn't have happened to Rebecca. She didn't deserve this. She was a good person. She helped people for God's sake. She had removed hundreds of children from abusive situations and placed them in loving homes. She had sacrificed herself for the two little girls his sweet Victoria was looking after now.

Beth couldn't stand the silence any longer. "It looks like the thug was well prepared. He knew he would have to leave his truck at the other end of the tunnel. He must have left this second one so he could pick it up when he came back through."

Andrew didn't speak immediately. He was trying to come up with a plan. "The coyotes who bring these illegals across the border are usually well prepared. The concealed tunnel and the hidden truck, tell me this is a well-used crossing for them. I would guess this thug has friends in that business or either he is involved in it himself."

Beth snorted. "Don't these people ever do any honest work? Are they all thugs, drug smugglers and coyotes?"

Andrew knew she was looking for something to vent her anger on. "Most are honest, hardworking people just trying to make a living. Would you judge all Americans by the bad ones Rebecca faces in court every day?"

Beth sighed. "Of course not. I'm just frustrated, that's all. Just when we think we're close to catching up, we hit a brick wall. I just want to find my friend and go home."

Andrew didn't answer. What could he say? He felt the same way.

They made their way on through the forest in silence. It was easy to see where the truck went through. Suddenly, Andrew picked up the pace. It looked like they were going to catch a break. A small one anyway. They were coming to the edge of the tree line.

Andrew and Beth stood at the edge of a narrow, dirt road. They had no idea where it led. The good news was that there was only one way to go. The road ended right where they came out of the forest.

Andrew examined the tire tracks. The tread had been impossible to see through the leaves and rotted vegetation on the floor of the forest. Now it was easy to distinguish the pattern of the worn tread. It was also the only tire tracks on the road. That told Andrew not many people came this way.

With no other option, they started off at a brisk pace down the road. They didn't bother staying in the tree line. No one was around anyway. That made Andrew wonder just how far they were from civilization. Not that it mattered. They had no choice but to keep walking till they got somewhere, wherever that somewhere might be.

After several miles, the road widened. Surely, they were getting close to a town or at least a more populated area.

When they finally came across some houses, maybe they could talk someone into giving them a ride to the nearest town. Talk was all Andrew could do. He couldn't commandeer a vehicle on this side of the border like he could on the other. His status as a United States Marshal didn't carry any weight here. He was not only out of his jurisdiction, he was out of his country.

He also wouldn't stoop to using his weapon to take what he wanted. That would put him on the same level with the thugs he was sword to take down. He had a little money, so he wasn't completely unprepared. A couple of hundred wouldn't buy much but if he could just get them to the nearest town, he would check in with the police there and see what they could do to help.

He would also be taking the chance that they would be escorted right back over the border. He had no papers giving him authority to be here at all. He would cross that bridge when they came to it.

The first house they came to was vacant. From the looks of it, no one had lived here in a long time. Walking up to what was left of the front porch, Andrew hesitated. "Beth, stay out here. I want to see if there's anything inside we can use."

Beth didn't go any further. She was too tired to argue. Beth wasn't like other women, who dissolved in tears when they got overly tired. When Beth got past tired, to the level of exhaustion, she got mad. The administrators back home at Memorial General knew better than to ask Beth to work one minute over a double shift.

The one time they had, all hell had broken loose. Before the dust had settled, two doctors had walked out, both janitors were found hiding in the third-floor closet behind the mops, and three other nurses were in tears. No, Beth didn't cry when she was overly tired but others did.

Andrew came back out and found Beth leaning against a tree in the front yard. He sat down beside her. "Let's rest for a while. I'm tired of walking and I know you are. There's nothing in the house we can use. We'll find help further down the road. If we have to, I'll hire someone to drive us to the nearest town."

Beth didn't speak, she just got up and headed back to the road. Andrew fell in step beside her. He didn't speak either. After all, what could he say?

What seemed like hours passed before they came across another house. Unlike the first one, this house appeared lived in. A dog met them in the road but seemed friendly enough. Andrew scratched the dog's head as he walked up to the porch. He knocked and waited. No one came to the door but he could hear movement inside.

He knocked again and this time heard a small voice say, "no one's home."

He couldn't help but smile. Evidently, the child had been told not to open the door to strangers. He remembered being told the same thing when he was small. He also remembered what had happened the one time he'd forgotten that rule. He hadn't made that mistake again. He had been raised by loving parents. Loving parents who believed in following the rules. Following the rules laid out by his parents probably had a lot to do with him becoming a marshal.

Beth stepped in and saved the day. "I can see no one's at home but if a passerby happened to need to talk to an adult, where would they find one?"

The screen door opened just wide enough for one little arm to come through and point across the road.

Beth turned around and for the first time noticed a man working in the field on the other side of the road. He had two donkeys hitched to a wagon and seems to be planting something.

Beth started in that direction. "Come on, Andrew, we'll be sure to explain that we knocked at the door, but no one was home."

They crossed the road and started toward the man in the field. When he saw them, he stopped what he was doing and waited beside the wagon. When they were close enough, Andrew reached out to shake the man's hand. After introducing himself and Beth, he asked the man if he could drive them into town.

The man shook his head. "I'd be glad to help you but I don't own a car. Besides, I have to finish planting this field. It may rain tomorrow and I have to get these seeds in the ground."

Andrew nodded his head. He had to stay on this man's good side. They needed his help. "I understand. Can you tell me then how far it is to the next town?"

"Well, I'd say a good fifteen miles. Maybe more. I've never checked to see."

Andrew knew Beth would never make it that far. He had to think of something. "You must go to town for supplies. How do you get there?"

The man looked at Andrew as if he was mentally defective to ask such a question. He nodded toward the wagon and two donkeys.

Andrew knew it was pointless to ask, but he had nothing to lose. "I don't suppose you'd give us a ride into town?"

The man just shook his head. "Sorry, I've got to finish planting. We eat what I grow and if I don't plant before the rain, I won't be able to feed my family."

Andrew changed tactics. He mentally calculated how much money he had in his billfold. "Well, you don't seem to be using the donkeys to plow. Looks like they're just pulling the wagon with the seed. Can I buy them from you?"

The man hesitated. It was obvious he could use the money. "I can't sell my burros. I need them on the farm. How about I rent them to you? They'll get you to town. When you get there, just turn them loose. They know the way home."

Andrew and the farmer came to a fair price for renting the animals, then walked back to the house where he found bridles for the two donkeys.

Andrew walked to the road holding the bridles and leading the burros. He helped Beth up on the back of one and he climbed aboard the other. He had never ridden a donkey and doubted Beth had either. He was surprised she hadn't made a comment since crossing the road to talk to the farmer. Her silence bothered him.

"I know you didn't sign on for this, Beth, but I told you when we started out, I didn't know what we'd run into. It was your choice to come."

Just when he thought she wasn't going to speak, she turned in his direction. "I don't regret coming with you, Andrew. I was just imaging explaining to the folks back home about me and this jackass."

"It isn't a jackass, Beth. It's a donkey."

This time, Beth didn't hesitate. "Who said I was talking about the animal?"

As transportation went, it wasn't the most comfortable Andrew had ever experienced but it sure beat walking. And even more important, it was faster. Just barely.

Andrew's mind wondered back to Hadbury and Victoria and the kids. He smiled. When had he conformed from confirmed bachelor to family man wannabe? It hadn't been a gradual process, more like a lightning bolt. One minute he was absorbed in his work and happy to go home at night, alone, to the solitude of his apartment. The next, he was only really happy when he was with Victoria and the kids. Of course, the little girls hadn't been with them very long, but somehow it just seemed right that they were there. He knew their future wasn't settled. They had a family back in Mexico that were probably worried sick about them. He knew their father was dead and their mother had been sick when she arranged for the coyote to bring them across the border. According to Beth, the mother was most likely dead by now too. But even if she was, there would be aunts and uncles.

His daydreaming was interrupted by Beth. Her mood had not been improved by sitting on a donkey for the last two hours. "What are you thinking about Andrew? First, you're smiling, then you're frowning. Every time we pass someone, they look at you like you're demented. It's bad enough to have to ride into town on a donkey, but it's worse to have people thinking I'm doing it with a crazy man." No, her mood definitely had not improved.

For the first time, Andrew noticed they were passing other people. A couple walking along the side of the road, nodded in their direction. Beth nodded back, like she had been doing it for a while now.

A car came up behind them, then eased around and sped on by. The donkeys showed no reaction. They kept plodding along like they were the only ones on the road. It was obvious that this wasn't their first trip to town.

"Sorry Beth. I guess I've been lost in my thoughts. It looks like we're getting close to town."

"That's alright. I've been passing the time talking to the donkeys. They've been better company than you."

No, Beth's mood definitely hadn't improved. As soon as they got to town, he would find a place for them to rest and get something to eat. Then he would find the local police station and try to solicit their help. If they were sent packing, at least they would be rested and have a full stomach.

He didn't even want to think about Beth's reaction if she was told she had to go home without finding her friend. The Bible said not to borrow trouble from tomorrow. Today has enough of its own. Andrew couldn't agree more.

Finally, they made it to the outskirts of town. One of the first buildings was a cantina. It was getting later in the day and business was picking up.

Andrew needed to go inside to inquire as to the location of the local police station but he didn't want to take Beth inside with him. It looked like a pretty rough place. He also didn't want to leave her outside alone.

The decision was taken out of his hand. Beth had climbed down off the donkey and made her way to the side of the building. She was sitting on a bench under a shade tree.

He walked over to where she sat. She seemed to be settled in. Maybe he could leave her to her own devices for a few minutes without her getting in trouble.

"I'm going in through the back door. No need calling undue attention to ourselves. I'll get the bartender's attention and find out where the local police department is and where we might be able to find a room for tonight. Will you be alright here while I'm gone?"

Bet nodded. She wasn't really paying attention. "Sure, go ahead. I'm fine."

After Andrew walked away, Beth returned her attention to the group of women waiting beside a wagon. It looked like they were going to a party. They were dressed for dancing. Beth could only hear snatches of their conversation but she heard enough. They were headed to Garcia's camp for a party. He had been waiting for a big deal that had just come through. Now he wanted to party.

Beth instinctively knew the big deal was the arrival of Rebecca. She had to do something. They were fixing to leave and Andrew hadn't come back out. If she went in after him, they might leave before they got back out.

Making a split-second decision, which she knew Andrew wouldn't agree with, she studied all the women waiting to load up in the wagon. She picked out one that didn't seem particularly happy to be there. Pulling her to the side, Beth whispered something to the woman. When the woman eagerly nodded her agreement, Beth led her around to the other side of the building where they quickly exchanged clothes. If the woman was surprised to see Beth's shoulder holster and gun, she didn't show it. She was just glad to escape the party, which she knew wouldn't end well for the women now loading into the wagon.

Beth led the woman, now dressed in her clothes, back around to the bench she had been sitting on. "In a few minutes, a gringo will be coming out of the cantina. Tell him where I've gone."

The woman nodded her agreement but Beth was already gone. The others were already in the wagon. She wasn't going to be left behind.

Inside the cantina, Andrew waited for his eyes to adjust to the dim light. As he looked over the crowd, he thought he saw a familiar face but quickly dismissed it. He had never been here before. It wasn't possible for someone he knew to be in this bar.

He watched as the bartender filled several orders. At the first opportunity, he approached the bar. As he talked to the bartender, his eyes were following the man that had caught his attention when he first came in. He was moving toward the door. Something about the way the man moved kept Andrew watching him.

As the man turned his head, Andrew got a better look. Jeff! Not waiting to hear the rest of what the bartender was saying, Andrew tried to catch up to his fellow marshal. The crowd dancing in the middle of the floor got in the way.

Andrew got to the door just as Jeff was pulling out of the parking lot on a Harley. He called out to him but Jeff couldn't hear over the noise of his bike. Andrew ran behind him but couldn't catch up and couldn't get Jeff's attention.

Having failed in his pursuit of Jeff, he turned back to the cantina. He had to get Beth. He didn't know how they would catch a Harley on two donkeys but they had to try. As he rounded the side of the cantina, he saw Beth where he had left her. Only it wasn't Beth. The woman was wearing Beth's clothes but it wasn't Beth.

As he approached her, the woman stood up and explained what had taken place between her and Beth. Andrew turned cold and could barely breathe. Beth had gone to rescue her friend. She was going to try to take Garcia down in his own camp.

He turned and ran back to the donkeys. He untied both and slapped one on the rump, hoping he would indeed find his way home. He got on the other and started off in the direction Jeff had gone. Which was also the way the woman in Beth's clothes told him led to Garcia's camp.

Pushing the donkey as fast as he dared, Andrew made several turns still following the directions he'd been given. As he made the last turn to the camp, he dismounted and sent the donkey on its way home. He would go the rest of the way on foot. If he ran across any of Garcia's men guarding the perimeter of his camp, he wanted to see them before they saw him.

Several hundred feet down this narrow dirt road he stopped and listened. He could hear faint sounds coming from his left. He silently made his way through the trees and brush. Whoever was there was well hidden. If not for the muffled sounds, he would have passed by without knowing anyone was there.

About fifty feet off the road and well hidden, he came across four men. They seemed to be in a scuffle. They were all armed but none of them were going for their weapons. It looked like three of the men were trying to hold down the fourth.

All of a sudden, two of the men were thrown to the side and Andrew could get a better view. He didn't know what shocked him most. Seeing a large man he didn't know sitting on top of Hershel trying to hold him down by the shoulders or seeing Bill and Cliff waiting for a chance to jump back in the fray. And unless his eyes were deceiving him, they were helping the stranger sitting on top of Hershel.

He didn't know what was going on but he'd figure it out later. Right now, his boss was in trouble and he wasn't going to stand by and watch.

Andrew stepped out from his hiding place and drew his gun. "Stop or I'll shoot."

The shock of hearing Andrew's voice stopped all four men. He looked at the stranger. "Get off him or you won't be breathing much longer."

The stranger complied. Bill and Cliff were apparently speechless. Hershel was momentarily distracted from his struggle to get to Rebecca. He sat up. Instead of thanking Andrew, he said, "What the hell are you doing here?"

Chapter 27

Beth unloaded with the other women. It looked like the party was in full swing. She assessed the situation and realized she didn't know what Garcia looked like. She gritted her teeth when she was grabbed from behind by a pair of rough hands. She didn't struggle as she was pulled into the center of the camp where the dancing was taking place. She had to play the part for now.

Beth was passed from partner to partner. There was no rhythm to this dancing. All the other women were just tapping their feet, swaying their arms in the air, and wiggling their hips. So, Beth tapped and swayed and wiggled with the rest of them.

Until she could figure out if the thug had arrived with Rebecca, all she could do was keep dancing. When she had traded clothes with the woman back at the cantina, it had been a spur of the moment decision. She hadn't had time to make a plan. Well, she needed one now.

Beth had not been paying much attention to her partners. She was being passed from one to another at a pretty fast pace. At least until this last one. He must have felt something he liked because he was holding on pretty tight and his hands were getting a lot more personal.

Beth's reaction was instinctive. She didn't stop to consider the consequences. Easing one of the hypodermic needles from her pocket, she moved in even closer. After one quick jab, the thug slowly slid to the ground. She was immediately grabbed and danced away by another partner. She watched as two men laughingly pulled her victim to the side and left him there. She realized they thought he was drunk and had passed out. Well, okay, now she had a plan.

Not wanting her actions to be too obvious, she didn't take out every thug she danced with. Only the ones with roaming hands.

Beth had been passed from partner to partner and managed to take out another one without raising any suspicions. She now found herself at the opposite end of the clearing and face to face with someone she knew. It took her a few seconds to realize he didn't recognize her.

When she was finally able to catch his attention, she managed to wink and smile, before she was pulled into another pair of eager arms and danced away. She had no idea if her not too subtle signal had registered with him or not. But one thing she did know; if Jeff was here, he was working undercover and Hershel, Bill, and Cliff were nearby. If the woman back at the cantina had stayed around long enough to give Andrew her message, he was also somewhere nearby. She felt a lot better knowing the odds were more in her favor.

Beth tried to maneuver her current partner back to where Jeff was standing but when she managed to get close enough, she couldn't get his attention. It was riveted on something happening on the other side of the compound. She swiveled her head, trying to see what he was looking at.

When there was finally a break in the other dancers, she gasped and stumbled over her partner's feet. Rebecca! She had just emerged from a truck and was being handed over to a man with one of the evilest smiles she had ever seen. No one had to tell her who he was. Garcia.

She watched as Rebecca was led away. Looking back at Jeff, she tried once again to get his attention. But his eyes were on Rebecca and the man leading her away. Finally, his gaze found hers and this time there was shock and recognition in his eyes. He had recognized her.

Beth hesitated. She was unsure what to do. Then her concern for her friend took over. She had to get to Rebecca before something horrible happened to her.

Beth pulled out another hypodermic and stabbed the man holding her. He fell to the ground. She didn't wait to see if anyone noticed. She moved on to the next man standing between her and Rebecca and repeated her elimination process.

On the other side of the compound, Jeff understood what Beth was doing. He had seen her in action before. He had to get to her before she got herself killed. He had made contact with the other marshals just long enough to tell them Rebecca had arrived in the camp and to hang on to Hershel until he could get a read on the situation.

Now, he frantically tapped his earbud as he tried to make it over to where he had last seen Beth. He could no longer see her, but the trail of fallen bodies was enough to let him know where she had gone. She was following Garcia and Rebecca.

It was at this precise moment that the other men noticed the number of their fellow comrades that were out cold on the ground. It finally seemed to penetrate the alcohol-induced fog in their brain that something was wrong. Not able to discern where the threat was coming from, they drew their guns and started firing at anything that moved.

Outside the camp, the other marshals were facing their own situation.

Hershel got up off the ground and the others stepped back. "Put the gun down, Andrew. We're good here. This is General Morales of the Mexican Police. He's on our side."

Andrew didn't lower his weapon. "If he's on our side, why was he holding you down and why were Bill and Cliff helping him? I'm not putting this gun down till someone explains what's going on."

Morales turned to Hershel. "Are all your marshals this stubborn?"

Hershel hadn't taken his eyes off Andrew. "All my marshals have my back."

He put his hand on Morales's shoulder and again spoke to Andrew. "We're here to back up Jeff. He went undercover in order to infiltrate Garcia's camp. We had hoped to separate him from his men so we could mitigate the bloodshed. Things haven't quite worked out the way we hoped. Jeff just told us Garcia has managed to get to Rebecca. He has her there now. The guys were trying to keep me from rushing in to save her. They're right. I could have gotten her killed."

Andrew slowly replaced his gun in its holster. "I can explain some of that. Beth and I have been following Rebecca and the thug that was taking her to Garcia. We could never quite catch up."

At the mention of Beth's name, Bill's head shot up. "Beth? You mean the nurse from Hadbury? The one who helped rescue all of you six months ago on Clint Montgomery's Island? The one with the hypodermic needles? What has she got to do with this?" He stopped when he realized all the others were staring at him.

Andrew cleared his throat. "Well, she kind of tagged along when she found out I was going after Rebecca. It wasn't like she gave me any choice. I was well on the way before I discovered I had a stowaway. It was too late to take her back."

Before Andrew could continue, they heard Jeff's voice clearly through the earbuds. He was shouting loudly. They could have heard him even without the earbuds.

"Where the hell is my backup? Get in here now. All hell is breaking loose."

That was all the others needed to get them moving. They drew their guns and rushed the camp. Explanations would have to wait.

Back in the camp, Jeff had finally caught up with Beth. He tackled her and held on. He didn't know where Garcia had taken Rebecca but he wasn't going to let this one get away. He must have knocked the breath out of her, because she wasn't struggling.

Garcia's men were truly panicked now. They were running and firing in all directions. Many of their comrades were on the ground. Some were shot and others were the victims of Beth's syringes. The latter would only be out a couple of hours but that would be long enough to get them restrained.

Jeff raised his head just enough to get off a couple of shots. The ones still on their feet didn't seem to understand where the shots were coming from. The alcohol and sudden change from party atmosphere to attack had muddled their senses.

And then suddenly, all was quiet. All except the approaching footsteps. Jeff lay perfectly still. He knew he was at a disadvantage from his prone position. He couldn't roll and fire without exposing Beth.

The footsteps stopped when they reached his side. But Jeff's attention was now diverted to the muffled voice coming from under him. "If you don't get off me right now, I'm going to jab one of these needles in you!"

A voice above him responded, "You'd better do what she says. She almost cut off my—uh, almost cut me with a pair of scissors six months ago when she mistook me for a bad guy." It was Bill.

Jeff looked up to see General Morales and the other marshals standing around. He carefully eased off Beth and stood up. For the first time, he noticed Andrew. "I guess her being here is your doing?"

Andrew didn't hesitate. "I'm afraid so." He slapped Bill on the back. "But I'm going to let Bill take over now. He's going to need the practice."

Bill hadn't taken his eyes off Beth. He reached down and helped her to her feet. "You just can't seem to stay out of trouble, can you? It looks like you need a keeper."

Beth started to respond when they were all interrupted by Hershel. They hadn't even realized he wasn't with them any longer.

"Garcia is gone and he's taken Rebecca with him. They're nowhere in the compound."

In a flash, all the momentary light banner was gone. They had rescued Beth but Rebecca was still in danger. The trouble was, they had no idea where he would have taken her.

Beth reached for Bill's arm, and he didn't pull away. He was still mad at her for being here, but Rebecca was her friend and she had risked her life trying to save her. He placed his hand on top of hers. "We'll find her."

Hershel had been lost in thought. Suddenly, he looked up at Bill. "I think I know where he took her and they're waiting for me."

For a moment Bill looked blank, and then as if he and Hershel were on the same page, said, "Me too; he would go back to where his sister was killed and for some reason, he wants you there."

In a hurry, but needing to explain to the others what he had just now figured out, Hershel took a deep breath. "When we first got here, we raided a camp where we thought to find Garcia and his crew. They weren't there but his little sister, for some reason, was. Perez and his men jumped the gun and started firing. Garcia's sister was killed. Garcia must have been close by and saw the whole thing. He saw me reach his sister and take her in my arms, where she died. He must have thought I was the one who killed her. That's why he sent someone after Rebecca. He thought I had taken the most important thing in his life and he wanted me to suffer like he was and he knew just how to make that happen. He's taken Rebecca to the spot where his sister died and he's waiting for me."

Hershel started to back away from the others. "He wants me there. If all of you show up, he'll kill her before we can get close enough to stop him. He wants to watch me suffer; he wants to watch me beg. Well, I'm going to give him what he wants and then I'm going to kill him and take my wife home."

Morales stepped forward. "I agree, my friend, but you need me there with you. I represent the Mexican government. You are on our soil. You need a witness to swear, no matter what really goes down, you acted in self-defense. You'll be able to leave Mexico and take your wife home faster if you have me there to back you up and cut through all the red tape killing Garcia is going to create."

Hershel nodded and walked away. Morales fell in step beside him.

Bill spoke up, "I know where they're going. Cliff and I were there when all that went down. Hershel thinks he has to face Garcia alone but he's going to have backup whether he wants it or not."

"I agree," Jeff spoke up. "They have to get back to where they left the hummer. I wasn't there when all that went down, so I don't know where they're going. If one of you will ride with me on the Harley, we can get there before they do and be waiting. The rest of you can follow in one of these trucks."

Cliff spoke up, "Let me come with you, Jeff. I can take you to where Garcia's sister was killed. Bill was there too so he can follow in one of the trucks with Andrew and Beth. Let's finish this so we can all go home."

Bill nodded. He didn't much care for the junior marshal stepping up and taking charge but what he said made sense and this wasn't the time to discuss seniority.

Jeff and Cliff made good time on the Harley. They parked the bike well back and went the rest of the way on foot. They could see Garcia holding Rebecca with a gun to her head. No one else had arrived. They didn't speak but found a spot where they would be well hidden but close enough if they were needed.

Bill, Andrew and Beth hot-wired one of the trucks in Garcia's camp and weren't far behind Jeff and Cliff. When they were close, they pulled the truck into some bushes and covered it with more brush so that it was completely hidden.

Bill knew it would do no good to try to make Beth stay with the truck. He didn't have time to argue with her. Besides, she would follow them anyway. Best to keep her where he could see what she was doing.

The three made their way through the trees until Bill held up his hand for them to stop. Without speaking, he pointed up ahead. Keeping Garcia and Rebecca in their line of vision, they made their way around to the other side of where Garcia was holding Rebecca. They stayed hidden but with a clear view of the opening. All they could do now was wait for Hershel and Morales to arrive.

Hershel and Morales made it to the Hummer. As they got in, Hershel turned to Morales. "I understand what you're doing, General and I know you're putting your career on the line. I want you to know, I'll try to stay on the right side of the law. But I'm not leaving without Rebecca. If that means killing Garcia by any means possible, then that's what I'll do."

Morales looked straight ahead. "All I see is a United States Marshal going into a dangerous situation to try and save a civilian."

They drove on in silence. When they were close, General Morales eased open the door and disappeared into the forest. Hershel drove on, not even trying to hide his approach. After all, Garcia was waiting for him. He knew he'd come for his wife. Hershel pulled up well before reaching Garcia and got out. Garcia watched and waited. He was unsteady on his feet.

Hershel knew Garcia had been drinking and hoped to use that to his advantage. When he was within ten feet, he stopped. "Let her go, Garcia. This is between you and me."

Rebecca reached out her hand but Garcia yanked her back. "Not so fast. You'll both do as I say." He motioned to Hershel. "Get on your knees or I'll put a bullet in her head right now. Comply and I might let her live a little longer."

Not seeing another option, Hershel dropped to his knees. "She's not part of this, Garcia. She wasn't even here when your sister was killed. Let her go and do whatever you want with me."

Garcia just laughed. He had lost all touch with reality. He had finally slid all the way over into insanity and this time there was no coming back.

But Hershel had to try. "I didn't kill your sister, Garcia. Perez and his men were the only ones firing their weapons that day. I'm the one who stopped him."

Garcia only glared at Hershel. "I've already taken care of Perez. But if you had not come here looking for me, my sister would still be alive. She died in your arms. Just the way your wife is going to die in your arms now."

Garcia thrust Rebecca at Hershel and raised his gun to fire.

Jeff saw his chance and took it. He had crept closer to Garcia without the man realizing it. Launching himself at Garcia, they both tumbled to the ground. No one had a clear shot and before anyone could intervene, Garcia came up with his gun now pointed at Jeff.

"I always knew it would come to this. Something was off about you from the start. You made yourself too available for my men to find you and bring you into my camp. Even if you hadn't betrayed me, I had planned to kill you anyway."

Jeff realized two things right away. The first was that no one had a clear shot to take Garcia out. If they had, they would have done so already. The second was that Garcia didn't have his own gun. In the struggle, he had somehow come up with Jeff's. The one Garcia had himself rendered useless by tampering with the firing mechanism.

Jeff got to his feet. He knew what he was about to do was going to sign Garcia's death warrant. He didn't care. As long as Garcia was alive, this would never truly be over. He took a step toward Garcia. "Give it your best shot."

Garcia pulled the trigger. Nothing happened but Jeff fell to the ground anyway. Five shots rang out. Four to the head, one to the shoulder.

Well, Beth wasn't a marshal. Maybe she needed a little more practice at Mary Alice's firing range. But at least she hit her target.

Hershel made it to Jeff first. He knew Garcia was dead but he thought Jeff had been hit. By the time Hershel got to him, the others had made their way out of the forest and were right behind him. They all reached Jeff at the same time. Hershel fell to his knees beside his fallen marshal but before he could check for damage, Jeff sat up. "I'm not shot. I was just undercover."

Hershel got up, pulling Jeff up with him. "I think I've created a monster. Let's go home."

Chapter 28

Victoria was alone in the kitchen. She had chased everyone out. She needed a few minutes to herself. Everyone was finally home. It had taken a week for the marshals to file their reports and make their way through a mountain of paper work.

With the help of the other ladies, she had cooked a huge welcome home meal. They were all sitting in her large living room, at her bed and breakfast, waiting for Victoria to bring in the coffee. The last of her guests had left yesterday and more were not due for several days. It had been a perfect time to gather in all her friends. She looked up as Andrew walked in with a goofy grin on his face. He walked over and wrapped his arms around Victoria.

"Thanks for letting me get the kids settled for the night. Rosa was the last to give it up. She just wanted to hold on to me. She was afraid I'd leave her again. She's so young, only five. She doesn't understand what's happened to her world."

Victoria sighed. "Did she ask about her mother?" They had been notified several days before that Maria and Rosa's mother had died shortly after the girls had left Mexico.

"No, but Maria did. She's older and more aware of her circumstances. We're going to have to have a hard conversation with the girls. It's not going to be easy to tell them their mother is dead. They're going to want to know what's going to happen to them."

Victoria placed cups, along with sugar and cream on a tray. "I know. We can't put it off for long. I've been granted temporary custody, but who knows how long that'll last. The courts may not grant permanent custody to a widow with two small children."

"You're not alone in this, Victoria. I'm here to help. We'll do whatever it takes."

"Well, right now, you can help by taking this tray into the living room, while I bring the coffee."

When everything was set out on the sideboard, Victoria turned to the others in the room. "I'll let you each fix your own. I want to thank you for holding off the subject I know is upper most on everyone's mind. I didn't want the children upset by talk of something they couldn't possibly understand. We all have snippets of information but this is the first time we've been together as a group. I think it's important for each of us to understand what the others have been through. That's the only way we can help each other."

They all crowded around the coffee. As each lady fixed theirs and went back to their seats, the marshals waited for Cliff to finish. He was the only marshal not to drink their coffee black. Taking his time, he glanced over his shoulders. He knew they were watching him and going to rib him about the amount of cream and sugar he added to his coffee. It had become a ritual, well this time they were going to be disappointed. He carefully poured his coffee and turned around to take his seat without adding anything to it. As he rejoined the ladies, he heard one of the others say "killjoy." Smiling to himself, he was glad they couldn't see the packets of sugar and creamer in his pocket.

When they were all once again seated, Hershel stood up and faced the others. "I want to thank the ladies for this wonderful meal and the opportunity to get together. When I left on this last mission to Mexico, I never dreamed all of you would be dragged into it. I thought Jeff, Bill, Cliff, and I would go down to Mexico, arrest a drug lord and bring him back to face justice. Things didn't turn out to be quite that simple. We put Garcia out of business alright but he'll be facing a higher court than any we have on this earth. The rest of his gang scattered. Some were killed, some were arrested, and a few escaped and probably were able to hook up with other drug lords."

Hershel paused before he could continue. "When I realized he had sent thugs to kidnap Rebecca, I lost all objectivity. If the others hadn't stopped me, I would have probably gotten me and her both killed. Garcia thought I had killed his sister and wanted to punish me by killing Rebecca while I watched."

Jeff, seeing his boss flounder, got up and put his hand on Hershel's shoulder. "You're hogging the floor, let me take it from here."

Recognizing a lifeline when he saw one, Hershel took his seat and reached for Rebecca's hand.

Jeff continued, "I wasn't with the others when Garcia's sister was killed. I had been left behind at the police station so that my cover would remain intact. I didn't know at the time how huge that decision would become. I was able to infiltrate Garcia's camp. He seemed to accept my story of wanting to join up with him. I never felt like he really trusted me but was willing to play along at least for a while. I have no doubt he would have killed me at some point no matter what else happened. When first Rebecca and then Beth showed up in camp, I knew it was all coming to a head."

He stopped and smiled. "That group of thugs didn't know what had hit them when Beth showed up with her syringes. She took out at least five before I tackled her. I have no doubt she would have jabbed me with one of those things if I hadn't let her up when I did. I was glad when Bill showed up and I could hand her over to him."

Jeff glanced over at Beth. She and Bill were sitting mighty close together but he wasn't about to comment on that.

He continued, "When all the action in the camp died down, Garcia had disappeared with Rebecca. We followed. When I saw him holding Rebecca and Hershel at gun point, I had to do something. I was close enough to try to stop him. We fought but he came up with the gun. Only it wasn't his gun. It was mine. The one he had disabled by damaging the firing pin. I knew he couldn't shoot me so I forced his hand and got out of the way, to give the others a clear shot. They took it. All of them."

Jeff hesitated. "Being undercover for so long has had an effect on me. At times, I've felt like I was getting the undercover bad-boy I was pretending to be and the United States Marshal I really am confused with each other. When you pretend to be something you're not, sometimes those bad traits have a way of slipping over into your real life. It's lucky I have friends to turn to for help."

Jeff paused. It was hard for such a strong man to admit he needed help.

Bill and Beth went to stand beside him. Beth spoke up first, "As a nurse, I see this type of mental stress a lot. I knew Jeff needed a little help. This isn't my area of expertise. I'm more of a bind, stitch, fix, and poke kind of gal. Hence, my handy ability to weld a hypodermic syringe."

This last statement brought on some much-needed laughter to lighten things up.

Beth just smiled, then continued, "I talked to the head of that particular department in one of Richmond's most prestigious hospitals. They have agreed to work with Jeff on an outpatient basis. They assured us Jeff's problem is a common one among law enforcement. They'll have him back on track in no time."

Beth resumed her seat and this time Jeff claimed the seat beside her. Bill frowned and jerked his head to the side, in a signal for Jeff to move out of his place. Jeff complied, at the amusement of the others in the room.

Bill cleared his throat. "I have a few more updates while I'm still up here. Most of you know Andrew and Beth apprehended a border guard at the old school house where the children were found. He wasn't one of our finest law enforcement officers. He started taking bribes from the coyotes bringing immigrants across the border. At first, they would just slip him a little money and he would turn his head while they slipped across the border. Soon, his greed took over and he wanted a bigger share of the action. He became more involved in the smuggling process and began handling a lot of it on his own. He was familiar with the area and the abandoned school house soon became a rendezvous place for his illicit activities.

"Thankfully, he is now out of the smuggling business as well as the law enforcement business. He'll have a long time behind bars to consider the error of his ways. We thought it fitting, he does his time close to the area he used to patrol. I'm told he'll have lots of company since that's the same facility that holds most of the coyotes appended along the border. The very ones he took business from."

Victoria spoke up, "What about the old school building? Is it being torn down so no one else can use it for such a terrible purpose?"

Bill shook his head. "No indeed. We found a much better use for it. Thanks to Andrew's expertise, it's been equipped with cameras and sound equipment that can be monitored from the Richmond headquarters. Andrew has agreed to take on this extra responsibility and send the information on to the local authorities in that area. We hope to catch many more coyotes trying to hand off their human prey to other greedy hands in the human trafficking business."

Bill wrapped up by taking his seat beside Beth. The one recently vacated by Jeff.

For a few moments, no one spoke. This had been a lot of information to digest. The folks back in Hadbury knew their friends had a dangerous job. Heck, this wasn't the first time they had gotten tangled up in one of their investigations. United States Marshal's faced danger every day. Still, hearing all the details and being involved in some of it, put what the marshals do on a daily basis, in a whole new light.

When no one else spoke, Rebecca stood up. She had to prise her hand loose from Hershel's much larger one.

"I'm not a marshal. I'm not bound by rules and regulations and paper work and clearances to release information. I'm a woman and like most women I share almost every detail of my life with my girlfriends. This time has been no different. Beth, Nancy, Mary Alice and Victoria know every detail of what I've been through. The guys know the details too. Not through the channel of friendship but through the interrogation process at the marshal's office in Richmond. It wasn't pleasant but it was necessary. Every detail of my journey might prove useful information for future missions in that part of the country."

When it looked as if Hershel was about to speak, she held up her hand to stop him.

"Don't worry, I'm not fixing to give away any classified secrets. What I want to share now is a little bit about the quick trip you and I took a few days ago."

Rebecca took a seat in front of the others. She still hadn't fully recovered from her ordeal.

"All of you know me well. You know I've never stepped outside the law and if I ever did, I would be the first one to turn myself in. Because of my strong belief in right and wrong, there were some details that I had to set straight before I could put all this to rest. With Hershel's help, I believe I've done that."

Rebecca waited for a nod from Hershel, before she continued, "We paid a visit to Ida Grantham. It was her house I broke into. She had already had her window replaced and I doubt she even missed the small amount of food I took. Regardless, I had to make it right. I didn't count on her stubbornness. She absolutely refused to let me pay for any of it. She said I was running for my life and just trying to survive. She even thanked me for pointing out vulnerabilities in her security. She said she had always left all that to her husband and after he passed away, she hadn't given it a thought. She realized how foolish that had been.

"Since she wouldn't let me repay her for the damage I'd done, Hershel and I, with some help from Andrew, installed her a state-of-the-art security system. She no longer has to worry about anyone gaining access to her house."

Rebecca paused. "Miss Ida wasn't the only one I owed a debt to. I stole some clothes and a bike from the people down the road. I wasn't worried about the bike since I didn't get very far with it, but the clothes were another matter. I figured she might not take payment for them, so I bought several replacements in the same size and style. She was thrilled. We had a good time while she tried on each outfit and modeled it for her husband."

At the blank look on all the men's faces, she doubled over laughing. When she could catch her breath, she said, "It's a woman thing. Anyway, I can rest now, knowing I've done everything possible to right any wrongs that I did. No matter what the circumstances had been. My hands are once again clean and my conscience clear. I can face all the judges, attorneys and derelict parents in court and hold their feet to the fire."

Now, she turned to Andrew and Victoria. "I am also ready to help you go to court and fight for custody of Rosa and Maria. I have a lot of friends in the judicial system. I took the time to do a little research. I haven't been able to find any relatives in Mexico willing to take the girls. With both parents' dead, I don't think you'll have much trouble getting permanent custody. It won't happen overnight. The courts usually move slow in these cases but I don't see any roadblocks. If there are any, we'll deal with them as they come up."

At this welcome bit of news, everyone erupted in cheers and well wishes for the future of the two children tucked away safety in their beds upstairs. They had already become part of this family.

Assuming everything that needed to be said had been said, everyone headed back to refill their coffee cups. Everyone but Hershel. He sat watching the others as they settled back in their seats. Finally, he stood and held his hands up for silence.

"I was going to wait and make this announcement back at the office but in light of this latest development, I've decided all of you should hear this. I am very proud of what my marshals accomplished on this last mission and I would be the first to admit, we all deserve a break and a little down time. However, that is not to be. I was given our new assignment this morning. We only have a few days to prepare."

Having dropped that bombshell, he shook his finger at all the civilians in the room. "And don't any of you get the idea that we need help." To make sure they understood, he repeated his last sentence. When no one responded, he wasn't sure who had won that final round.